RUNAWAY WITNESS

S. J. Ritchey

• Canada • UK • Ireland • USA •

Note for Librarians: A cataloguing record for this book is available from Library and Archives Canada at www.collectionscanada.ca/amicus/index-e.html
ISBN 1-4120-7523-8

Printed in Victoria, BC, Canada. Printed on paper with minimum 30% recycled fibre. Trafford's print shop runs on "green energy" from solar, wind and other environmentally-friendly power sources.

PUBLISHING™

Offices in Canada, USA, Ireland and UK
This book was published *on-demand* in cooperation with Trafford Publishing. On-demand publishing is a unique process and service of making a book available for retail sale to the public taking advantage of on-demand manufacturing and Internet marketing. On-demand publishing includes promotions, retail sales, manufacturing, order fulfilment, accounting and collecting royalties on behalf of the author.

Book sales for North America and international:
Trafford Publishing, 6E–2333 Government St.,
Victoria, BC v8t 4p4 CANADA
phone 250 383 6864 (toll-free 1 888 232 4444)
fax 250 383 6804; email to orders@trafford.com
Book sales in Europe:
Trafford Publishing (uk) Limited, 9 Park End Street, 2nd Floor
Oxford, UK oxi 1hh UNITED KINGDOM
phone 44 (0)1865 722 113 (local rate 0845 230 9601)
facsimile 44 (0)1865 722 868; info.uk@trafford.com
Order online at:
trafford.com/05-2419

10 9 8 7 6 5 4 3

RUNAWAY WITNESS

ONE

Dave Randle knew he had a problem the instant the willowy brunette charged through his door. She locked onto his eyes with the vehemence of a challenge, saying, "The woman in the outer office said to see you."

She gestured toward Ellie, the paralegal in the firm of Jennifer Watson, Attorney-At-Law, and David Randle, Private Investigator. Ellie shrugged and smiled at Dave as she pulled the door closed.

"My sister's missing. Her bastard husband killed her and got rid of her body," she said, as she dropped into the visitor's chair, crossed her legs, straightened her black slacks. Her blue eyes never left Dave's face, analyzing his features, daring him to disagree.

Dave guessed she might be thirty-five. Her full red lips parted to reveal bright teeth as she brushed her black hair away from her face. Her mannerisms and her soft white blouse, sleeveless and unbuttoned enough to capture his attention, accentuated her sensuality.

"You've been to the police?" Dave asked, trying to focus on the problem that had brought her to the firm.

She nodded. "They won't do anything. Gerald told them she'd gone to visit a friend in San Diego and would be back in a few days. They believed him, but I know better."

"I assume Gerald is her husband and you don't accept his story?"

"Not in a thousand years. He's a lying jackass. Nicole and I are close. She wouldn't leave town without telling me." She stabbed the air with a finger, red nail flashing.

"Maybe this visit was different and for some reason she didn't want to confide in you."

Shaking her head, then raking long hair back into place, she said, "I refuse to believe that. She's been gone a week. Something bad has happened to her."

"That's not much to go on," Dave said, realizing why the police had not followed through. "Start from your first suspicion, including your name. I understand you have given this information to our assistant, but I'd like to hear it directly. Sometimes a potential lead jumps out that could be missed by reading the file."

She leaned back in the chair. "I'm Heather Farrell. Nicole is married to Gerald Dewberry, but uses her maiden name. I called her a week ago yesterday to arrange for our weekly lunch. It's something we've done for five years, our way of keeping in touch. Gerald said she'd gone to a friend's place in San Diego. I don't know of any friends out there. She's never talked about anyone in California. When I asked for a phone number, he got mad, yelled at me to stay out of their lives, and slammed the phone down. I called the next day, but he hung up as soon as I started talking. That's when I decided he'd murdered her."

"Who did you talk to at the police station?"

"Detective Rasmussen, a heavy-set, older man."

"I know him," Dave said.

"While I was in his office, he called Gerald, got the same story I did. He didn't seem interested in following up. Guess he believed the bastard."

"Have Nicole and Gerald had problems? Either of them threatening divorce or separation? Fights about money, anything?"

"She's been unhappy almost from the time they were married, four years ago this June. He's not what she expected. He's let himself go to pot, gained a lot of weight. He's loud, arrogant, avoids her family and friends. I've noticed a few bruises on her shoulders and arms, but she won't admit Gerald hit her."

"But you suspect he knocks her around?"

She nodded. "I haven't forced the issue. I'm scared of him."

"What line of work is he in?"

"He's a middle level executive with Black and Redfield Insurance." Dave knew about the organization. It was a successful company that had grown significantly over the past five years. Their coverage extended across the state and they aggressively sought new clients through television and newspaper ads. One of their reps had approached the partnership about liability coverage, but Jennifer had not liked some of the conditions the company insisted upon.

"Does Nicole work?"

"She's part-time with a local real estate group, Edwards and Sons. She's able to control her hours so she can participate in Gerald's social agenda. He gets mad when she can't make some event important to his business."

"Any children?"

"Gerald doesn't want kids. Interferes with his own life."

"Anything else you can tell me that might be useful in trying to get the situation resolved?"

She considered the question, twisting her hands together. "Nothing comes to mind."

"Tell you what," Dave said. "I'll ask around. Talk to Rasmussen and Gerald, then get back to you in a couple of days. Chances are she'll have returned by then."

"She won't ever be back. I know it."

Dave ignored her certainty. "I assume you left addresses and tele-phone numbers with Ellie?"

"Yes. You may find this useful," she said, dropping a photograph on the desk. "This is Nicole three years ago. She hasn't changed." The wallet size picture left no doubt she was related to Heather, same black hair, blue eyes, pouting lips and facial bone structure.

"I'll get back to you," Dave said, standing and coming around the desk to open the door. "Did Gerald say she flew to San Diego?"

"Her car is in the garage."

Heather stopped in the doorway, her perfume cutting through his allergies, the warmth of her closeness disconcerting. Almost as tall as his six feet, she studied his face as though recording each feature in her brain. "I read about you finding those old people missing from the retirement home and knew if you could figure out what happened to them, you could find out about Nicole. I'm counting on you."

Searching for missing residents in a local retirement community had led to uncovering a huge fraudulent operation by a prominent physician and an HMO. Publicity and the payoff from the settlement had put the struggling partnership of Watson and Randle on solid financial footing and had yielded a steady stream of clients.

Heather touched his arm and walked through the outer door. Dave stared at her retreating form until Ellie coughed, handed him the file labeled Farrell, saying "Sexy dame."

"That's for sure and probably mean as hell."

Back at his desk, Dave scanned the missing person report to confirm Heather's story matched her written information. Nothing jumped out to grab his attention. He gazed out the window for a moment, closed the folder, then reached for the phone.

On the phone with his cop friend, Rasmussen, Dave said, "Bill, Dave Randle. I'm calling about a Heather Farrell. She met with you about her missing sister. Remember?"

"Yeah. Her story seemed too shaky to warrant much time, especially after the husband confirmed his wife's visit to friends. Don't remember at the moment where she went."

"Heather Farrell thinks he's lying."

"I know. I chalked it up to family problems. There's no obvious evidence of foul play."

"She wants me to check it out. Any suggestions?"

"It's a waste of your time, but if she'll pay for your effort, good luck."

"You had any reports of abuse or reasons to visit the Dewberry residence?"

"Nope. I checked through the logs for the past two months after Farrell's visit. Nothing to change my thinking. Only thing we have is a minor incident six weeks ago in a local bar. Dewberry and some other guy got into a fracas. The man accused Dewberry of coming on to his girl friend. The bartender broke it up and called us. They had left by the time the patrol car got there. No charges or follow-up."

"I'll talk to the husband and go from there."

"My guess it's a dead end. The woman will return in a few days."

"Could be," Dave said. "Let's have a beer after your shift on Friday."

"I'll look forward to it."

"Meet you at Gibbon's at 5:30."

At 7:30 Dave drove through the upscale neighborhood of older houses that had been maintained in prime condition. Yards and hedges were trimmed, the streets and sidewalks recently covered with new layers of concrete, all shining in the fading rays of the warm mid-May sun. He was reminded of a Norman Rockwell scene.

Framed by four large oaks, the Dewberry home sat well back from the street. He eased up the drive and stopped near a walk leading to the front door. The lawn replicated others in the area. A lone dandelion challenged the ambiance of solid green. Red, white and purple azaleas brightened the borders around the house.

Gerald responded immediately to the doorbell as though he'd been waiting and observing Dave's approach. As the door came ajar, Dewberry blurted, "I consider this harassment."

When Dave had called to set up the appointment, Dewberry had initially refused, anger evident in his voice. He'd relented when Dave persisted, suggesting it was the only way to get Heather off his back.

Crowded in the foyer with Dewberry who towered four inches above him, Dave said, "Heather is worried. All I need is to confirm her sister's whereabouts and I'll not bother you further." He edged into the living room to gain space from Dewberry, a two-fifty pound, thirty-five year old headed for obesity. Dave pictured an ex-jock accustomed to blustering his way and who'd let himself get badly out of shape with excessive calories, alcohol, and no exercise.

Glaring into Dave's face, Gerald said, "I only know she went to see friends in San Diego. She didn't give me a phone number or an address."

"That's the crux of the problem," Dave said. "Most people don't leave for an extended time without a way to contact them."

"I've told you all I know." Dewberry's face reddened as he elevated his voice.

"Aren't you worried about her?"

"Nicole can take care of herself." His eyes shifted from Dave's face to scan the living room. Shadows of the trees and furnishings changed in the fading sunlight filtering through the open blinds.

"I promised Heather I'd try to locate Nicole. You have a list of possible acquaintances in the San Diego area?"

"I don't have any such information and if I did, I wouldn't give it out. I don't wish to have my friends subjected to cross exams by a rent-a-cop feeding off nosy relatives interfering in my life." He moved toward Dave as though to intimidate him by sheer size.

Suppressing the urge to crack the guy in the mouth, Dave said, "You know your refusal to help only increases the suspicion there's more here than the obvious."

"That's all I'm going to say," Dewberry said, turning toward the door and pointing the way out for Dave. "I want you to leave."

"I'll be back if Nicole doesn't show up soon."

"Don't bother me again," Dewberry threatened as Dave stepped onto the walk. The sun had disappeared and the crickets had emerged for their nightly chirping during the few minutes he'd wasted with an aggravated husband probably lying through his teeth. Dewberry remained in the door until Dave slid into his Blazer, then slammed the door to emphasize his irritation.

Dave backed into the street. His quick dismissal of Heather's charges had switched to an almost certain belief that something had gone awry in the Dewberry household.

TWO

The middle-aged woman in Jennifer Watson's office seemed irritated and frustrated, her tired round face creased in a deep frown highlighting the permanent wrinkles.

Jennifer said, "I'm sorry you had to wait, but this has been a busy day."

"It's okay. I should have called ahead. You were recommended by a friend of mine, but I don't know if you can help me." She twisted the handles of her green purse, her eyes shifting from Jennifer's face to the abstract paintings on the walls as though attempting to find some meaning in the shapes and colors.

"Tell me the problem and let's see," Jennifer said, encouraging her, but thinking she didn't need another complicated case at the moment.

"My life insurance policy has been canceled. No notice, no questions, nothing to suggest there'd been a problem had ever been mentioned. I've always paid my premium on time. Out of nowhere this letter." She pulled a folded and wrinkled sheet of paper from her purse and handed it to Jennifer.

Jennifer scanned a typical cancellation notice that could have been written by a clerk hidden away in the headquarters office randomly punching numbers into a computer. The opening line stated that policy number 596ART covering Maude C. Frame was hereby canceled. Methods of retrieving repayment of funds paid into the company were outlined. A second paragraph revealed bureaucratic details about the company's need to modernize to effectively participate with the growing competition in a rapidly changing business environment. Nothing specific had been divulged about Mrs. Frame's situation.

Recording the name and policy number on a legal pad before handing the letter back to Mrs. Frame, Jennifer asked, "How long have you had the policy?"

"Twenty-two years. My husband and I started it when our youngest son was born with mental retardation. Doctors told us he'd never be able to take care of himself and would never go beyond the abilities of a three year old. We intended to leave the money in a trust to take care of him after we're gone." She wiped her face with the sleeve of her brown jacket.

"Have you called the company. Perhaps there was a mistake. Errors occur frequently with all of the computer generated letters now."

"I called three days ago, the day after I received this letter." She waved it slightly. "Some woman said there'd not been a mistake and that they were canceling several others."

"Did you get her name?"

"No. I didn't think to do that." Her frown deepened even further at the thought she'd not been as vigilant as she might.

"Have you borrowed money using the policy as collateral or done anything that could have possibly nullified the conditions?"

"Nothing. I haven't borrowed money since my husband died five years ago. I don't owe anybody money, but I don't have much. It's been a struggle to pay the premiums on this policy with all the expenses of Robbie's medications and getting sitters for him when I'm working."

When Jennifer waited, she continued, "I work the day shift at the General Motors parts factory on West 45th street. It's the best pay I could find for my education but it's a hard job." The work explained her callused hands, the little finger on her left hand bent out of shape as a probable outcome of a job related accident.

When the intercom light blinked on the telephone, the office signal that others were waiting, Jennifer said, "We'll try to find out what has happened, Mrs. Frame. It could have been a mix up somewhere. If so, it will be easy enough to reconcile. If they have canceled for some reason, we'll have to determine the best course of action from there."

"How long will it take?"

Jennifer stood, saying, "We'll make some calls later today or by tomorrow at the latest. I'll let you know as soon as we can. I'd like to have Ellie copy your policy before you leave."

Maude Frame struggled to her feet and straightened her long brown skirt. Her frown lingered in its full intensity.

Jennifer watched her slow movements out of the office, thinking about her own grandmother who had toiled away on a small farm trying to keep body and soul together after her husband had died in a train crash. If they could resolve Mrs. Frame's claim, it would be a pro bono case at best. But the firm could tolerate some of those now. They'd become busier than she'd anticipated after eighteen months of struggling to make ends meet. She and Dave had discussed adding another lawyer and had interviewed a young man recently graduated from Missouri law school, but he'd rejected their offer to go with a larger firm. Nevertheless, her plan to establish her own practice after leaving a large corporate office in New York had been realized.

Dave had Nicole's picture reproduced at Bob's Camera Shop in the mall on his way to the airport. He showed Nicole's photo to the chief security officer at the Chester Municipal airport. "Marcus, I'm looking for this woman. I suspect she flew out of here about ten days ago. Any help you can give me will be appreciated."

Marcus Ralston, his burly features creased into concentration as he glanced at the picture, "Good looker." He returned the photo, saying, "Haven't seen you in a while. Doing okay?"

"Busy. Clients running out of our ears at the present time. How about you?"

"Same old stuff. More worries about security these days."

Dave said, "I realize the chances of someone recognizing this woman after ten days is remote, but I wonder if you could get me a look at the passenger lists for four or five days."

Marcus heaved his bulky frame out of the chair behind a cluttered oak desk. "Come on. Let's go up to the office."

Dave followed Marcus through the narrow hall of the basement level of the terminal. They took an elevator up three floors from where you could look down on the ticket counters and passengers lines. The terminal was crowded with long lines at the counters and others milling around, waiting for flights or the arrival of relatives or business representatives. Marcus paused a moment to survey the scene.

Ignoring the two women in the office, Marcus pulled a file from a green metal cabinet against the back wall. "These are the manifests for the last three weeks. You can sit at that vacant desk in the corner, but don't take anything away or get them out of order. I don't want to get in trouble with the airport manager. He'd raise hell if he knew I even let you see these, but he's away for the day."

Flights from Chester to destinations out of the state always connected with airlines in the larger cities in the region. Dave scanned through the flights to St. Louis and Kansas City for May 6 through 10, the dates around which Heather believed Nicole had departed. She was not listed. He expanded his search to include the week before and the week after, but without success. He closed the folder and left it on the desk.

Returning to Ralston's office, Dave said, "Thanks, but no luck. She might have used another name."

"That happens sometimes," Marcus said. "You want me to show the picture around?"

"It might jog someone's memory if you don't mind."

Marcus stood. "If you'll leave it with me, I'll circulate it to cover the shifts. Let ticket agents, security people, and baggage people take a look. It'll take twenty-four hours to cover everybody."

"I appreciate the trouble," Dave said, laying two copies of the photo of Nicole on the desk.

"No problem." Marcus turned the picture to look at it, then asked, "You ever hear from any of the guys we were with in 'Nam?"

"Haven't in four or five years. Lost track of them."

A year after he'd started as a private investigator, Dave had met Marcus in the airport. They had spent the thirty minutes before Dave's flight rehashing their experiences in the Marines, both young privates in a front line platoon. Most of their comrades had not made it back, but both still heard from a couple. Marcus had left the Corps after two stints, worked as a police officer in Chester for twenty years, retired and took the position of Chief of airport security. Dave had transferred to special forces, spent twenty-six years, retired, and moved to the Carolina coast. Bored with golf and fishing after four months, he'd returned to his home area, enrolled in criminal justice courses at the community college, and obtained a private investigator license. He and Jennifer Watson had moved into a downtown office building at the same time. After meeting at the community coffee room on the same floor of their offices, they'd shared interests and helped each other professionally for a few months, then decided to become partners. Dave acknowledged some spark between them other than professional conversations, but he'd never asked her for a formal date.

Heather Farrell phoned on the third morning after their initial meeting. "Any progress finding Nicole?"

"Not yet." Dave reported the conversation with Gerald and his tracking her departure from Chester then concluded, "Your story is more believable after meeting Gerald but it's all very fuzzy. I'll keep at it until we know something or reach a dead end."

"I'm worried crazy."

Dave asked, "Do you know if Nicole had insurance or an annuity of any kind? I'm looking for a reason if she's really disappeared. Some motive, a way for someone to gain."

"I don't know. We never talked about those things. But if she had anything, she'd have it through Gerald's company. He'd make her do that."

"I'll get back to you as soon as I know something."

Following a call from Ralston, Dave found Ernest Skinner in the baggage room at the airport terminal. Rows and stacks of luggage filled the rectangular space. Odors of diesel fuel permeated the air. Shaking the limp hand of the sallow-faced man, Dave said, "Marcus Ralston said you'd recognized the photo of the woman I'm looking for."

"I seen her early one morning. I was picking up bags at the outside check-in. She had a bunch of luggage—maybe five big bags. The reason I looked at her was she yelled at me to be careful of this one piece."

Dave handed Ernest the photo to remind him. "And you're sure about this."

"Pretty sure. I remember faces good, specially if the person gives me a hard time."

"And she gave you a hard time?"

"Not like some, but she raised her voice when I dropped the bag on the belt. Guess she thought I'd been too rough."

"You recall the flight?"

"It would have been the early morning run to St. Louis. Not another flight out for an hour."

"You remember the name on the identification tag?"

"No," shaking his head, "but it was an expensive piece. Maybe leather."

"Can you pinpoint the date?"

"That's hard." Ernest removed his cap, ruffled a hand through his greasy brown hair for several seconds. "I'm trying to think. It was a bright sunny day. My first day back from a shift break. Must have been Tuesday of week before last, but I can't be certain."

"Any chance you noticed how she arrived? By cab, someone drop her off."

Ernest shook his head. "Didn't see nothing until she yelled about the bag."

Dave shook Gibson's hand and called Ralston from a pay phone in the terminal to thank him for his efforts. If Skinner's recall had been correct, Nicole had traveled on May 7th. The date would jive with Heather's suspicion.

At five-thirty Dave jogged along the wooded trail bordering his property five miles from downtown Chester. Breathing easily after four miles, he thought about his conversation with Ernest Skinner, considering the credibility of the baggage handler. The fact that Skinner had recalled Nicole at all seemed astonishing with the number of people around when passengers were checking in. But the baggage clerk seemed certain, admitted he couldn't remember some details. Slowing to a walk as he neared his log house, Dave decided to accept Skinner's story and look for other things—how she got to the airport, insurance, the alias she'd used on the ticket.

He'd work hard on the Nicole case tomorrow. Now he had to do some cleaning around the place. Miriam was coming Friday night for the weekend. Their relationship had floundered after a few months of seeing each other as much as possible. Their future together could depend on how the forty-eight hours went.

THREE

At the end of the day and after the last client had disappeared, Ellie entered Jennifer's office, a page of notes in her hand. She dropped into the visitor's chair, saying, "I called about the Frame insurance. The policy had been sold to Black and Redfield by the original insurer. The local office of the company had issued the cancellation, but refused to tell me why. The clerk gave me the usual run-around, the same stuff in the letter. She recommended Mrs. Frame take her settlement and find another company."

"That could be difficult for a woman in her late fifties. The premiums could be astronomical."

"She may not have another choice." Ellie stood to end the conversation.

Jennifer said, "Set up a meeting with a manager at Black and Redfield in the next couple of days. Let them know we're interested in the Frame case and their rationale for their actions. We could have a situation as we did with Gaylord who started dropping coverage when clients became older and required more support."

"But that was health insurance."

"I know, but these companies always put profit above the welfare of the client. Greed is a powerful force. There's a reason for dropping the policy. We need to find it." Jennifer loaded three files into her briefcase, reading for the evening.

"I'll call first thing in the morning."

"Thanks, Ellie, for staying late."

Dave spent the morning dropping copies of Nicole's photo at the three cab companies in the city, requesting that they have drivers who worked early shifts on May 7th take a look. He attached a business card and asked that anyone identifying the passenger give him a call.

The offices of Black and Redfield were in a huge office building on the west side of the city, an area rapidly developing as professionals moved away from the crowded and deteriorating downtown to locate in office parks with ample parking. Wide streets with green spaces between the towering structures impressed visitors coming in for appointments. As Dave closed the Blazer door, he thought about spending the day on the creek near his secluded cottage. But looking for a motive for Nicole's disappearance seemed necessary if he were going to solve this riddle. And at the moment, somebody intending to collect on insurance represented his only lead.

After scanning the directory in the first floor lobby, he took the elevator to the sixth floor. Black and Redfield occupied the entire floor. Expensive paneling and carpeted floors confirmed insurance could be a lucrative business.

The receptionist, a middle-aged woman with graying auburn hair and a pleasant smile, asked, "May I help you?" Helen Thompson was on the name plate on the desk corner.

Handing her a business card, Dave said, "The family of a client has asked me to inquire about insurance coverage for her. I won't need much time if you can steer me to the right person."

"Is the client deceased?"

"I'm not sure. It may be irrelevant at the present time."

"It's unusual for someone other than immediate kin to inquire about such matters. We regard such information as confidential."

"I understand, but I'm acting on behalf of a close relative for whom travel to Chester is difficult."

Dave heard the elevator doors open, but didn't turn to observe until a voice boomed, "What the hell are you in here for? I warned you to stay out of my affairs."

Gerald Dewberry turned on the receptionist, "What does this idiot want?"

More calmly than Dave expected, she said, "He wished to know about coverage on a client."

"Which client?" Dewberry leaned toward Dave, his red face inches from Dave's.

Dave stepped back to get away from the foul breath and spewing fumes. "Your missing wife."

His face and neck turning purple with rage, Dewberry grabbed Dave's coat and jerked him closer. Dewberry didn't see Dave's short chop to the solar plexus coming until his breath exploded through his mouth. He staggered to retain his balance, his arms grasping for his mid-section. He wobbled to the couch, his head bent over his knees.

Dave turned to the receptionist, her eyes wide in disbelief. "I'll get the information another way."

Regaining his composure, Dewberry sputtered, "If you ever touch me again, I'll break your neck."

"Maybe that's what happened to your wife," Dave said, punching the elevator button. He looked back at the receptionist and winked. She smiled, then covered her face with her hand.

Dave and Jennifer were at lunch in Gibbons, a busy restaurant and bar four blocks from their office. Every table was occupied by workers from near-by offices.

"This Farrell case is bogged down. I could interview neighbors, but it likely won't go anywhere. None of the cab drivers recognized her. I suspect the baggage guy is wrong. He seemed confident, but nothing else fits."

"Maybe talk to people at her work and a couple of next door neighbors." She smiled over her coffee cup. "It's only time."

"I should pressure the husband. See if he cracks."

"From what you've said, he exhibits all the characteristics of guilt. He might get upset and spill something."

Jennifer watched Dave's face for reaction. She'd learned early in their relationship that Dave's quiet demeanor and slim physical build misled people, particularly males who used their bulk to intimidate others. Dave could not be pushed.

"How did it go with Miriam this weekend?"

Dave frowned. "It didn't. She backed out and didn't come. She can't get past the idea you and I have something going beyond business. She won't believe me. Keeps saying I couldn't avoid becoming involved with someone as attractive as you."

"Well, that makes me feel strange," Jennifer said, pushing aside her plate. "I need to move. I have a court case at two and need to look at my notes again."

Dave picked up the bill. "I'll add this to our expense tab."

He watched Jennifer wind her way through the crowd. A couple of males turned to follow her figure. Thinking about Miriam's concern, he concluded it was her method of breaking off their relationship. He'd been attracted to Jennifer, but after they'd formed the partnership, he'd vowed to avoid personal connections with her. He assumed she felt the same, but at times her signals were confusing.

From the restaurant, Dave returned to the Dewberry neighborhood, impressed again with the houses and grounds. He rang the door bell at the house next door to Dewberry's. The large house sat well back from the street and was seventy-five yards from the Dewberry residence.

An older woman answered, peering through thick glasses. "Yes, are you the real estate rep?"

Dave handed her a card. "No, but I'd like to talk with you for a few minutes about Mrs. Dewberry. I'm investigating a confidential matter concerning a possible promotion for her. This sounds fishy, but the organization I'm working for is adamant about the background checks they run on potential executives."

The woman examined his card. "I suppose it won't hurt anything."

"It's important you keep our conversation confidential. Rumors about these investigative checks can be disastrous for the candidate."

"I can keep a secret." She stepped aside and led Dave to a plush living room. Large sofas and dark drapes exuded money and sophistication. Table lamps provided scant light.

Waiting for her to take a seat on the couch, Dave said, "How long have you known the Dewberrys, Mrs....?"

"Our name is Kingsley. We've lived here for thirty-three years, but are putting the place on the market. We've gotten too old to maintain the property. The Dewberrys moved next door two years ago. We've not had much interaction with them. They both work and are gone most of the time."

"But you've met them?"

"Yes, we invited them for dinner when they first moved in. They never reciprocated, but I see them once in a while. Seem nice enough, but are in a different group than we, being younger and working." She removed her glasses and wiped the lenses with a tissue folded into her hand.

"Have there been any unusual happenings recently? The reason I ask, I've tried to telephone Nicole Dewberry without success. Wondered if they were out of town."

"I wouldn't know." Her face crinkled into a puzzled frown. "I've seen him coming and going, but not her. Didn't think much about it. But it's been a week or longer since I've seen Nicole."

"Do they entertain a lot?"

"Not much, but when they do, it's loud and long. Keeps us awake until the wee hours. The other night it went on and on, then there was a lot of noise early the next morning. A car drove away, spinning its wheels like it was going to a fire."

"Can you pinpoint the date?"

"Not precisely, but week before last, I'm certain."

"And have you seen Nicole since that time?"

Her eyes widened and she shifted in the cushions of the couch, "Don't think so. Now that you mention the event, I haven't."

Dave pushed out of the deep chair, saying, "Mrs. Kingsley, this has been helpful.

"I'll keep trying to catch up with Nicole. She must be very busy."

She said, "I'll keep it to myself, although I've not told you anything very revealing."

At the door, he asked, "Are the Dewberrys particularly friendly with other neighbors?

"I don't know for sure, but the Castles across the street are closer in age. I've seen them drive away together a couple of times, dressed for dinner or a social occasion. In fact, I believe Gerald and Norman Castle work together."

The Castle residence was dark and no one responded to the front door bell. Dave walked around the side. The garage was empty. He drove away, thinking he'd try the Castle household later.

Jennifer sat across the desk from Rogers Morton, the representative who had handled Mrs. Frame's policy at Black and Redfield. The gaunt man adjusted his glasses and without attempting to mask his intent leaned across the desk to look at her legs.

Jennifer asked, "We're inquiring about the reasons for cancellation of Mrs. Frame's policy. Our calls have proved unrewarding, thus my visit."

"I understand her frustration, but a clause in her policy allows us to cancel without notice. We've exercised that option."

"I've examined her policy, but find nothing that suggests you have such authority."

"Perhaps you don't have the amended document we issued when we purchased her contract. We sent her the updated version."

"Did an agent discuss the changes with her?"

"Someone should have, but it wouldn't matter. We told those clients they had to accept the new policy or drop coverage."

"I suggest you don't have the right to do so," Jennifer said, "unless the client agrees and certifies by signing off. Mrs. Frame has no memory of that happening nor does she have an amended policy." Jennifer trusted Maude Frame kept her records as meticulously as she guessed she did.

"I'm sorry. I can't do anything about it now. It's the clients responsibility to stay informed."

"How many others were victims of this scheme?" Jennifer asked, hoping to goad Morton into revealing something he hadn't intended.

He ignored her jibe. "I'm not at liberty to reveal information about other policy holders."

Jennifer stood. "You'll likely hear from us again under circumstances that could result in your admission of fraud against innocent people."

She felt his eyes following her through the door.

After his daily run, Dave grilled a small steak on the outside grill and made a salad. He relaxed in front of the television while he ate, a rerun of a sitcom on the local station providing background noise to his thinking about the Farrell case. A well known local news anchor broke in to announce, "We've just been notified of the death of Gerald Dewberry, a prominent insurance executive. His body was discovered in a motel on Route 78 south of Chester. Details will be released as soon as the police complete their preliminary investigation."

FOUR

Dave called Chester police at eight the next morning. He paced while he waited, hoping Rasmussen had made it in by now, watching the shadows projected by the morning sun on the wall of his office. The steady hum of traffic outside his window signaled commuters rushing to their work sites.

Sounding grumpy and sleepy, Rasmussen came on the line. "I guess you're calling about Dewberry."

"I know it's early, but I'd appreciate anything you can divulge."

"We don't know much yet. Dewberry had been stabbed in the neck and chest, apparently cut a major artery. We suspect he'd been knocked out by a heavy blow to the head. There'd been a hell of a battle in the room. The place was trashed, furniture busted up, a window broken. The motel owner is mad as hell."

"Any ideas of his assailant?"

"The motel clerk, a retired man working part-time to supplement social security, heard the noise and went to investigate figuring he had a couple of drunks to deal with. Two men knocked him down near the

26

door and sped away in a late model Cadillac. The clerk failed to get the tag number. He saw Dewberry on the floor and called 911."

"The clerk see anyone else around the place with Dewberry?"

"Dewberry checked in around seven, according to the records. Fifteen minutes later a car parked near his room, but no one paid attention to the visitor. A few minutes later, another car pulled in. Again no one bothered to look, figuring Dewberry was having a meeting in his room. Almost immediately, the ruckus broke out. No one saw anyone but the two males, Caucasian, heavy-set, bearded, hoods covering their heads."

"Sounds like a hired hit."

"Could be. That's becoming more common in Chester."

"Any suspects?"

"Not yet, but we received a report of Dewberry arguing with a woman in Arthur's two days ago. The description fits his sister-in-law, Heather Farrell. We're talking to her today." Rasmussen paused as though thinking about what to say, then, "I recall you're looking for her missing sister but I'd ask you not to tip her off."

Dave hung up the phone and paced his office, concerned Heather had gone over the edge and hired a couple of hit men to take care of Gerald. She'd likely not know who to contact for such an arrangement, but a few questions to the right people could put her in touch with people who could. He wanted to call her and ask about her knowledge of Dewberry's demise, but resisted. He intended to maintain good relationships with the Chester police, especially Rasmussen.

Dave showed his business card to the maitre-d at Arthur's, a posh restaurant on west Main Street, and said, "I'd like to talk about an altercation that occurred a couple of nights ago involving Gerald Dewberry. I hope you can help me."

His perpetual smile in place, Thomas straightened his bow tie, nodded to Dave and pointed to a coat room to the right of the front entrance. Two lunch guests interrupted their interaction as Thomas rushed to lead them to their seats.

His smile disappeared as he returned to the coat room and Dave said, "I know the police may have talked to you already about this, but I'd appreciate a minute of your time. It's important to a client of mine."

"The police came earlier this morning. I'll tell you what I told them." He waited until Dave nodded, his eyes flitting to the front entrance to be certain customers weren't waiting.

"I didn't hear how the argument started, but this woman being seated at the table next to Gerald suddenly confronted him and yelled something I didn't hear. At that moment I was occupied at a table in the rear of the dining room. I became aware of the spat when the entire room went quiet. She was standing over him and accused him of killing her sister. She tried to slap him, but he grabbed her arm and tried to lead her out of the room. Her companion intervened by shoving Dewberry. Dewberry swung at him. By then, the bartender stepped between them and stopped the fight. The woman and her date left the restaurant, without paying their bill."

"Do you know the woman?"

"Heather Farrell. She comes in here often at lunch. I didn't know her companion."

"Did Dewberry follow them out?"

"No. He returned to his table and acted as though he tolerated those minor inconveniences in life. His party stayed another hour or perhaps longer. I get busy and lose track of time."

Dave promised Thomas he'd come for dinner soon and left, acknowledging he'd not learned much except to confirm his suspicions that Dewberry's inconvenience had been Heather.

At 5:30 Dave went into Gibbons restaurant and grabbed a stool at the bar, ordered a Killian draft and watched Antonio Gibbons work the cash register. The old man had the reputation of a small town mobster, even rumors he had ties to a prominent New York family. Dave had come to know him in another case. Mutual respect had blossomed be-tween them, both regarded as characters who operated on the fringe of the mainline at times. Dave cultivated Gibbons as an ally who knew things about the city and some of its citizens that no one else could tell him. In his business Dave believed every reliable contact was a poten-tial asset to be cultivated. You never knew when they might be useful.

Gibbons came along the bar, wiping up drips with an ever present towel. Seeing Dave, he grinned and said, "How you doing? Haven't seen you in a while."

"Doing good. I've been in for lunch, but you've been too busy to notice."

Dave moved the mug around, creating circles of wetness. "When you have a free minute, I'd like to ask a question."

Gibbons yelled at a waitress to take care of the register and mo-tioned Dave to follow. The old man limped as he maneuvered his bulky frame through the tables to a back corner booth. Dave sat across from Gibbons, took a sip of beer and waited for the old man to settle in the creaking bench.

Dave explained the disappearance of Nicole Farrell and her sister's insistence she'd been murdered by the husband. Now the husband had been killed and Heather Farrell was somehow implicated, maybe even a suspect.

Dave said, "The deal is getting complicated. I'd about decided Heather was all wrong about Gerald and that Nicole had tired of the daily crap in her life and took off for a greener pasture. Dewberry's death has the markings of a hired gun or a shady deal gone sour. I won-dered if you'd heard anything around the streets about either of these two?"

Gibbons stared at Dave for several seconds, rubbed a thick hand across his thinning hair. "I knew Dewberry. Big wheel in an insurance company. Sort of a shit. You ever talk to him?"

"Twice. But I didn't get anywhere. He tried to throw me out of his office."

Gibbons grinned, crooked, yellowing teeth visible. "That could have been interesting."

"So you haven't heard anything?"

Shaking his head, Gibbons said, "Nope, but I could ask around if you'd like."

"Anything you learn is more than I know now. I'd appreciate it."

Gibbons struggled out of the booth, his face reddening with the effort. "Come back in a couple of days."

Dave finished his beer, dropped bills on the table, and left.

Jennifer watched Heather Farrell as she sat in a visitor's chair across from her desk. Dave stood near the door until Heather settled, arranging her short black skirt and crossing her legs, then sat in a chair next to her. Heather's eyes shifted from Jennifer to Dave, a brief smile.

Heather said, "I'm going to need a lawyer and since I've already hired Dave, I thought I'd approach you. Keep all my problems with one firm, so to speak."

Jennifer asked, "I assume this is connected with Gerald Dewberry's death?"

"Yes. The police have questioned me. For some reason they think I hired someone to kill the bastard. Honestly, I'd thought about it, but didn't follow through. Killing him would not have brought Nicole back. Only get me in more trouble."

Dave said, "Your threatening him in the restaurant brought attention to you. Otherwise, the cops wouldn't be interested. Likely would never have connected you with him."

Heather's face screwed up as though she'd been reprimanded. "I can't control myself when I see him. I know he did something to her."

"I'm still looking," Dave said, "but no solid leads yet."

Jennifer asked, "How much have you told the detectives?"

"Everything. I reminded them I'd asked them to find Nicole. I admitted getting into a ruckus with Gerald. But I didn't go beyond that. I wouldn't have a clue about hiring a killer."

"And you didn't go to Gerald's motel room on the night he was killed?"

"God no. I bet he was meeting some floozie and her husband caught on to them. Brought along a buddy and they knocked the bastard in the head."

"I assume you have no idea who his visitor was?" Dave asked. "The person who arrived ahead of the apparent killers and hasn't been seen since."

"No idea." She crossed her legs and rearranged her skirt over her knee.

Jennifer said, "We'll represent you, but I don't want you talking to the detectives again unless I'm present. If they approach you anywhere, insist on having your lawyer with you."

"I have nothing to hide. I didn't do anything."

"But you are a suspect. A throng of people can identify you as being involved in a yelling match with Gerald two nights before he died. The police are going to trace all your actions, probably obtain warrants to examine your telephone records, things you wouldn't think about. My advice is to talk to no one about this except Dave and me."

"I've told you what I know."

Jennifer stood, saying, "Ellie will have you sign a retainer and take a deposit. Let me know if the police come around again. You must understand this can become serious."

As Heather closed the door, Jennifer said, "You think she's told us everything?"

"Probably," Dave said. "Finding an assassin is out of her territory. The only possibility is she knows someone who could arrange such a deal. I'm asking around."

"Through your friend Gibbons?"

Dave grinned, remembering her opinion about dealing with a reputed mobster.

"He'll find out. We'll know before the police."

"Those kind of people scare me."

"I'll be careful."

Jennifer called Maude Frame at 6:30. "Mrs. Frame, I wanted to ask you a couple of questions regarding your insurance. I hope this is a good time."

"It's okay. I was just cleaning up after supper."

The mention of a meal exacerbated the hunger pangs in Jennifer's stomach. In the crush of a busy day, she'd missed lunch. Mid-afternoon she'd grabbed a candy bar from the machine next to the elevator in the basement and promising herself again to make time for a decent meal.

Jennifer asked, "Do you remember receiving any notice of a change in your insurance policy? The company insists they sent a letter changing the terms of your policy."

A long delay before Frame responded. "I never got anything until this letter I showed you. I'm careful about keeping records because of my son's condition. I have stacks of papers from the state about medical stuff."

"Have any of your co-workers complained about their insurance being altered?"

"Nobody else has the problem I have," Frame said, "but I heard this one woman say her health policy had been canceled. She was crying in the rest room to a friend of both of us."

"Does the company pay for health insurance and do they pay for part of the coverage you have for your son?"

"GM pays half of our health, but they don't help with the life insurance I had."

"Does GM have regularly scheduled physical exams for employees?"

"We went for years without nothing. Six months ago everybody had to have an exam. GM said it was because the insurance company wanted this and if our health was good, the premiums could be lowered. I never heard of anybody's going down though. We all thought it was another game being played by the insurance people."

"I don't know why your life insurance would have been affected," Jennifer said, thinking about recent news of insurance organizations using physical exam data to manage rates. If the employee followed prescribed health practices, the rate could be reduced with the lowered probability of a major illness.

Jennifer asked, "Could you get me a copy of the letter from the insurance company to the woman whose health policy was canceled?"

Frame thought about the question for a bit, then said, "Don't know, but I'll try."

"Can you tell me her name? Maybe I can find out if you're uncomfortable in asking."

"Ruth Fitzgerald. She lives in the country. I don't know an address."

"Let me know as soon as you talk to her," Jennifer said.

Her ideas about those policies being changed because of some finding in the physical exams mingled with thoughts of finding food.

FIVE

Dave knocked on the door frame of Antonio Gibbons' office in the rear of the restaurant. The square room, lighted by two halogen lamps, one on the desk, another on a table in the corner next to a visitor's chair, reminded Dave of a fortress. Two small windows provided scant light. Sunlight partially blocked by tall shrubs on the outside of the building created wavering shadows across the walls and floor. Odors of tobacco lingered.

From behind his desk Gibbons waved toward Dave. "Come in. I thought you'd be by today." Early in their relationship Dave had learned not to call Gibbons by telephone. Gibbons wouldn't reveal anything more than his opinion about the weather over a system he suspected of being tapped by the cops.

"Any word about Gerald Dewberry yet?" Dave asked.

"A source in which I have little faith let me know Dewberry had been knocked over on orders by some authority. He didn't know who or he was afraid to tell me who gave the signal."

"You don't trust the info?"

"Not completely. He's led me wrong in the past, but I don't know why he would on this deal. No one could trace the information back to him."

"You have any ideas about who'd like Dewberry removed?"

Gibbons shifted in the chair, causing it to creak in protest. He swiped his hand across his head, easing a couple of errant strands of hair into another position. "I've heard there's been a lot of shuffling of people at Black and Redfield during the last year. A couple of the big execs have been pushed out. It's been like a hostile takeover."

"There's been nothing in the papers or I haven't seen anything," Dave said. On a regular cycle, he promised himself to give more attention to the local papers, but after a determined effort for a few days, he lapsed into bored neglect.

"These guys have ways of squashing any news that draws attention. And it's easier to keep things under cover when it's not a public company. No board of directors questioning your motives. No investors looking over your shoulders and asking questions about stock performance."

"You think it's one of the mob families? Insurance seems out of their usual interests."

Gibbons grunted and shifted in the chair again. "Don't think so, but it's not impossible for one of the organizations to fan out beyond their usual haunts. Insurance has gotten their attention in the past few years. There's big money to be made when you no longer give a damn about your clients and you can influence the regulatory agencies to ignore shady practices."

Dave considered the ramifications of Gibbons' analysis. Jennifer's client, Maude Frame, had her policy cancelled. Rumors of others being dropped without any apparent reason would fit Gibbons' suspicions. He said, "Maybe Dewberry got caught in the middle and they took him out."

"That'd be the way they'd do it. But knowing something about Dewberry, he'd go along with any scams, especially if he believed he could make big bucks. More likely, he tried to bulldoze himself a larger share and threatened to go public. These guys wouldn't tolerate that."

"My job is to locate Dewberry's wife. Maybe he sent her away to protect her if he realized he was in trouble."

"Could be, but again I doubt it. He's too dumb to catch on until it's too late."

Dave stood. "Maybe I should nose around Black and Redfield. See if there are any rocks to turn over."

"Be careful. These people may be dangerous."

"I will. Thanks for your help."

In the city library Ellie browsed through back issues of the Chester *Register*, the local paper, in search of any item regarding Black and Redfield. After an hour of searching, she found a ten-line piece on an inside page of the business section announcing the retirement of James P. Redfield, one of the founders of the organization. He'd served for twenty-five years and had grown the company into a solid regional business with clients in several adjacent states. The last sentence of the article dated eight months ago reminded readers that the founding co-partner, Horatio Black, had died three years earlier. Ellie scanned editions for the two month period following that announcement for any other news, but found nothing. The absence of a big splash about the new CEO seemed unusual. Likely the position had been filled before Redfield's retirement or soon thereafter. Apparently the organization didn't want the free publicity inherent with a news release.

Feeding dimes into the photocopier available to library patrons, she copied the article about Redfield and returned the paper to the stack.

At 7:30 Dave rang the doorbell of the imposing residence of Norman and Stella Castle. The huge house, across the street from the Dewberry home, nestled among large oaks. A perfectly groomed lawn and flawlessly trimmed shrubs added to the aura of material abundance.

Norman responded to the bell. "Mr. Randall, right on time. Come in. I'm sorry my wife couldn't be here, but she never misses her bridge club." The enthusiastic voice of a salesman eased Dave's anxiety about confronting another Dewberry type.

Castle, a short, stocky man, balding on the back of his head, led Dave into a den featuring a leather couch, two leather recliners and a large-screen television in front of a floor-to-ceiling bookcase filled to capacity. Floor lamps illuminated the spaces near the chairs. Dave sat in the middle of the couch at Castle's invitation.

"What can I help you with?" Norman asked. "Would you like a drink?"

"No, thanks. I have a few questions about Nicole Dewberry. As I told you when I called, I'm investigating her disappearance and thought her neighbors might know something. Any help you can give me will be appreciated."

Norman leaned back in the recliner and crossed one ankle over the other. "We have no idea what happened to her. In fact, we didn't realize she'd left until Gerald mentioned there was a private investigator searching for her and we might get a call. That was the day before he was murdered. Everyone at the office was devastated and shocked by his death."

"You work at Black and Redfield?"

"I've been with the company for four years, but I've known Gerald since college. We were fraternity brothers. He helped me get a job at the company and made sure I got started in the right direction. We became good friends, both at work and as neighbors."

"So you know Nicole pretty well?"

"We've interacted socially many times. You know, parties at our homes, dinners together, country club events." His grin left no doubt the events had been pleasant.

"You have any feelings that Gerald sent her away to protect her? Rumors are his murder was directed by a mob representative."

Norman's face blanched. "I haven't heard that, but it's scary to think about the possibility. Gerald never told me about any problems with outsiders. To answer your question, I don't know except to suggest Nicole was pretty gutsy. She'd have to feel really threatened and insecure to leave. I doubt Gerald could have forced her to disappear."

"Could you tell me about changes in top management at Black and Redfield during the past year?"

The abrupt shift in questioning caused Norman to consider a moment, his eyes scanning Dave's face as though looking for clues about his interest. "I don't know much except Redfield retired without any warning after the company was purchased by an outside group located in the East. We were all surprised at the suddenness of his departure. We thought he'd be around for a while to ease the transition. Rumors were he'd been diagnosed with colon cancer and had only a few months to live, but he seemed full of energy and looked healthy for a man of his age. I've heard he moved to Oregon to be near a son."

"Who took his place?"

"Nicholas DeRosa. He came from Philadelphia. I met him at a reception when he was introduced to the staff, but beyond that, I've had little contact with him or with Bruce Hoyt, an assistant who came with DeRosa."

"Have the policies of the organization changed since DeRosa took over?"

Norman nodded his head, apparently thinking about where to begin or whether to respond at all. "I'm not comfortable in revealing details. But I can tell you a couple of things. One, DeRosa wants us to expand beyond the region and become a national player. He intends to challenge the larger firms for business. Two, he's sent memos about no longer selling insurance to buyers who are likely to cost the company money. As anyone might expect, he intends to maximize profits and avoid risks."

"Is DeRosa well known in the insurance business?"

"I'd not heard of him until he came here, but that wouldn't be unusual."

"Has he directed the cancellation of policies?"

Norman's face revealed his reluctance. "I'm not free to answer that."

Dave asked, "Do you remember any unusual activity around the Dewberry's home the day Nicole disappeared?"

Taking some time to reconstruct his memory and to adjust to another swing in the questioning, Norman said, "We don't know exactly when she left, but there were several cars around during the period. That was unusual. Gerald and Nicole led busy professional lives but tried to separate business from home. They were away a lot, but seldom had associates in during the week. He didn't like doing business from his house."

"I assume he was reasonably successful?"

Norman relaxed and settled back into the recliner. "Gerald had done well. He could be a bastard to staff working for him, but he was a good salesman and manager."

"Had he reached the point he might have been in line for Redfield's position?"

Norman shook his head. "I wouldn't think so. Several people had more experience than he, plus he had this quirky side that probably wouldn't sit well with big investors—too antagonistic when his opinion didn't immediately prevail. He couldn't objectively evaluate opinions to find compromise solutions to problems. We talked about it once after he was passed over for a promotion, but he couldn't control his urge to dominate."

"Had he gotten on the wrong side of the new management?"

Norman tilted the recliner forward to let his loafers rest on the carpet. "I hadn't heard if he had, but I wouldn't be surprised. He'd crossed swords with Redfield who was pretty laid back."

"Anything else you can share about Nicole's disappearance," Dave said, "might be useful in finding her."

"Nothing comes to mind now. As I said, we were not aware she'd left for several days."

Dave stood. "Mr. Castle, thanks. You've given me ideas to follow through on."

Norman stood to face Dave. "I'd prefer you don't tell anyone we met."

"I'll keep our conversation confidential." The moisture on Norman's hand suggested he'd been more nervous than his facial expressions had revealed. He'd be a good poker player.

Dave drove away from the Castle residence with the foreboding sense that somehow his search for Nicole was connected to Jennifer's client with the cancelled policy. He wanted to learn more about the new leaders at Black and Redfield. But he remembered Gibbons' advice and decided to move slowly, take logical steps, and focus on finding Nicole Farrell. Blundering into the middle of Black and Redfield's present environment could be counter productive and dangerous.

The morning mail stacked on one corner of Jennifer's desk included the usual array of advertisements, copies of depositions from the City Attorney's office related to a spousal abuse case, a reminder of the quarterly meeting of the local chapter of the Chester County Bar Association, and a hand-addressed letter from Ruth Fitzgerald. Jennifer scanned the depositions and tucked them into the case file, tossed the ads into the wastebasket, and stuck the reminder into the stack of upcoming events.

Fitzgerald's wrinkled envelope contained a note carefully written on lined yellow paper and a copy of the letter canceling her health insurance policy. The note revealed she'd been asked to have a physical exam prior to the termination. Obviously, Maude Frame had communicated the potential connection between the exam and the cancellation.

Taking a chance Fitzgerald was not working the day shift, Jennifer telephoned her home. A feeble voice responded after the fourth ring.

After identifying herself and acknowledging receipt of the letter, Jennifer asked, "Did you receive a report from the physical exam?"

"No, the only thing I got was the letter I sent you."

"And did anyone tell you the reason for the exam?"

"I got called into the office at work and was told I was one of the people who had to undergo this check-up because of insurance. We'd never had to do that before."

"Did you give a blood sample during the physical?"

"They took blood from my arm. Had a hard time. Stuck me three times before she got enough."

"Where did you have this exam?"

"At the little clinic in the administration building at the plant. It's the place where you can get help if you become ill while at work."

"Have you used the clinic before?"

"Once when I had a terrible headache. The nurse gave me aspirin and let me rest on a cot for a couple of hours."

"At the time of the exam did the regular nurse examine you and take blood?"

"No, it was some outside group—a doctor and two assistants. They had me weigh, took my blood pressure, listened to my heart, asked about any recent illnesses, then took blood."

Jennifer said, "Mrs. Fitzgerald, we'll find out about your policy, but it may take a while. I'll get back to you when I know something."

"I need that insurance. If I get real sick, I wouldn't be able to pay my rent and buy food. I can't lose my job now. I can retire in two years." Her creaky voice ended with a lengthy sigh of a person overwhelmed with the daily problems confronting her..

"I understand. We'll do our best to straighten it out."

"I can't afford to pay lawyers."

"We'll do some things for free. You take care of yourself, Mrs. Fitzgerald."

Jennifer leaned back in her chair and considered the conversation with Fitzgerald. Thinking the nurse in the GM clinic might know something, she found the telephone number for the plant and dialed the information desk. After a short explanation, she was routed to the clinic and to Gretchen Asbury, the nurse in charge.

"I'm calling on behalf of two of the employees who've had their insurance policies cancelled. Both had been given physical exams at the request of the insurance company. Soon after, they received cancellations notices. I was hoping you might help me understand what happened."

"Are you a relative of either?"

Jennifer said, "No, I'm an attorney at Watson and Randle. The women have retained me to look into the matter. Both need their insurance coverage to be reinstated."

"I was never told why certain workers were called in for exams. And I didn't know about their insurance being dropped."

"Who came in to do the exams?"

"A physician I didn't know, but the medical technicians are from a local private lab, Biological Assays Inc. They do routine blood and urine analyses for physicians on a fee basis. They have a reputation for doing reliable work."

"In normal practice, they'd send the results of any analyses to the physician, or in this case to the insurance company, rather than directly to the individual."

"That's correct," Gretchen said. "It'd be up to the doctor to share relevant information with his patient. He'd want to interpret the results and explain any need for treatment or to assure the patient everything was okay. But I don't know how the insurance people would communicate with the person."

"Ms. Asbury, thank you. This has been helpful," Jennifer said, her thoughts on potential implications as she replaced the receiver. It seemed time to bring Dave into this situation and have him visit Biological Assays Inc. Now she had to rush to the city administration building to meet with a building contractor and the city attorney about a zoning issue important to a client of Watson and Randle. Grabbing her briefcase, she walked out of the office, nodding to Ellie. But she continued to wonder what those blood tests had revealed to Black and Redfield to cause the dropping of two long-time clients. And the possibility of there being others entered her consideration.

SIX

Dave parked in one of the visitor's spaces on the north side of Biological Assays, a rambling one-story brick building. The steady whir of ·exhaust units cut through the quiet neighborhood of offices and small businesses. Inside a woman yielded her focus on a computer terminal when he rapped on the counter shielding her work station from the tiny vestibule. A white lab coat suggested she was not a typical secretary.

Twisting her chair to face him, she asked, "How may I help you?" Her brown eyes and calm demeanor conveyed professional competence. The name tag pinned to the pocket revealed her to be Rose Mitchell, Ph. D.

Dave handed her a business card. "I'd like to talk to someone who can tell me about the release of lab analyses results."

She glanced a the card and dropped it onto the desk. "Can you be more specific?"

Dave didn't wish to tip his real reason until he gained a feel for the operation. He said, "Suppose a physician requests analysis of a person's blood and urine. How do you handle that?"

She pushed out of her chair. "I'm Rose Mitchell. Maybe I can respond adequately. Come through the door over there." She pointed to a closed door on the side wall.

Dave entered a room obviously used for meetings—six desk-type chairs arranged around an oak table. A chalkboard filled with numbers covered the wall at one end. A pull-down screen mounted above the board made projecting slides a convenient operation. Neither artwork nor photos adorned the beige walls. The faint odor of solvents reminded him of high school chemistry lab.

Rose pointed him toward a chair and sat opposite him. "We do a wide range of analytical work for physicians, private clinics, small hospitals, and other clients in the area. Each analysis is based on a fee and depends on the actual cost of conducting the specific test. We give the results to the individual or organization who submitted the samples. Sometimes we will collect blood, urine, feces, or tissues, but usually we receive the samples from an outside organization and do the requested analyses."

She handed him a set of papers stapled together in the upper corner. "This is a list of analyses we're prepared to do. We don't take on jobs requiring research and development or refining of procedures because of the time and cost involved."

Dave scanned the list of assays, impressed by the scope of their offerings. Laying it aside, he said, "I'll come to the point of my visit. We have a client who had blood work done at the request of her insurance company. She's interested in knowing the outcome of those tests. Can she obtain that information from you?"

"That's unusual because we expect the physician to share appropriate information. Sometimes an explanation is required and we don't get into that. It's too close to giving medical advice. We're not licensed to do that and we'd get in big trouble if we did."

Dave said, "In the case of our client, her policy was cancelled after the physical. She wants to know if she has some unique problem. The insurance company hasn't told her."

Rose seemed to ponder the situation as she examined the table top. "We've never had such a request before. Perhaps I should confer with the director."

"Can you explain the type of analyses on this list and their significance? Maybe that would be useful."

Again she scrutinized the table before saying, "I suppose I could do that."

Rose came around the table to sit next to him and moved the list of assays so both could see.

She pointed to a heading. "This first group, hemoglobin, hematocrit, cholesterol, LDL, HDL, triglycerides, albumin, glucose, and creatinine, are typical of any physical exam." Her finger ran down the group, skipping across several items.

"The next group represents a set of enzyme tests often requested by a clinic." Dave read names like alkaline phosphatase and alcohol dehydrogenase that meant nothing to him.

He asked, "Are those used to define some health problem?"

Rose nodded. "Yes. There are a host of enzymatic parameters that tell you if metabolic functions are normal or if there is an abnormality. We do a lot of these for Chester General Hospital and private clinics." She smiled. "And they are always in a rush to obtain feedback."

Dave turned to the last page of the document. "What about these DNA tests?"

"Those are done when there's interest in forensic evidence or sometimes paternity suits. Often the city attorney and defense lawyers hire us to collect samples. Since we know the data will be used in court cases, we routinely do the analyses more than once to be certain of our numbers. "

"Would there be any other reason to do these DNA checks?" Dave asked, wishing he knew more about the potential implications.

"On rare occasions, we've done tests to identify specific genes that may be predictors of diseases. It's based on the probability that if a certain gene is present, the individual will be more likely to have a disease than if the gene is not there. Physicians use this approach more and more as we learn about the genetic basis of health problems. Our projections are that those assays will be requested with increasing frequency in the future."

Dave asked, "In a hypothetical sense, would an insurance company ask for genetic analyses as a means of predicting the life expectancy or future health risks of an individual?"

Rose returned to the chair across the table. "They might do that. Or an individual might if they're concerned about the potential onset of some disease. We've had a few cases in which a couple worry about passing some genetic defect to their offspring."

"You mean," Dave asked, "the presence of a gene that can prevent full development of the child?"

"Yes, or more likely increase the potential for the occurrence of diseases such as cancer, diabetes, and others early in life. Typically, those jobs come through their physician."

"In the GM workers, were you asked to look at any specific gene or health problem?"

Rose twisted in the chair. "I think I shouldn't reveal that. It's an issue between the requesting party and your client."

"How do I get these data released to my client?"

"In a strict sense, they belong to Black and Redfield. You could approach them."

Dave stood, folding the packet of analyses. "Thanks, you've been helpful." He shook Rose Mitchell's hand, but he left the facility wanting more information.

Dave waited for a client to leave Jennifer's office, then entered. Jennifer closed a folder and dropped it on a stack. "Well, did you discover anything?"

He handed her the list of analyses available at Biological Assays. "Not much. As you'd guess, the lab wouldn't reveal any specific information, but something perked my attention. Look on the last page. If genetic assays were conducted, the insurance company would know if the client is at greater risk for some health problem."

Jennifer scanned the list. "You think Black and Redfield used those analyses as a basis for dropping coverage?"

"Yeah. But it might be hard to prove unless we can get the actual data. And I'd doubt they'll give those to us."

"I'll get Mrs. Frame to request her results. She can say her personal physician would like to review the information and retain a copy for her file."

"It'd be the easy way if Black and Redfield will cooperate. But they'll refuse."

Jennifer said, "You're likely right, but let's try. If it doesn't work, I'll get a court order as part of a suit against the company for breaking their contract with Mrs. Frame."

"Let me know. I'm headed for the airport to check out a possible lead on the missing Nicole Farrell."

Following through on the possibility that the baggage handler, Ernest Skinner, had been correct about the date Nicole had flown out of Chester, Dave had arranged to meet with the two stewardesses who had been on the early flight to St. Louis on May 7th. Setting up a session with the two had been difficult because of their schedules which varied week-by-week.

He met Gwen and Faith in the crew's lounge located at one end of the main floor of the terminal. Airline crews, reading the newspaper or conversing quietly, occupied several of the soft chairs. The aroma of fresh coffee and freshly baked pastries permeated the room. Gwen, brown-haired and thirty-five or so, introduced herself and her colleague and led Dave to a corner with chairs arranged around a small table. Through the window, he could see the bustling activities of the airport. Planes taxied toward the runway. Food trucks eased against parked planes. Baggage handlers raced around on electric carts, but little of the noise penetrated the lounge.

Dave said, "I appreciate your meeting with me. As I told you over the phone, I've been hired to find this woman." He showed them a photo of Nicole.

"I suspect she took the early morning flight to St. Louis on May 7th, but I could be off a day or so. Do either of you remember her?"

Faith, brunette, short, slim, in her twenties, asked, "What's her name?"

"Nicole Farrell, but she used an alias. Her name was not on the passenger list for that date. My lead to Tuesday the 7th is a baggage handler who recalled her."

The two women looked at each other and shook their heads, discounting the probability. They continued to study the photo.

After fifteen seconds, Gwen said, "We see a lot of people. Faces become a blur, but this one looks familiar."

"She's been on our flights," Faith confirmed, "but I can't be sure of the precise date."

Dave asked, "Is that flight your regular assignment?"

"We are on it five days a week much of the time. When we have that assignment we continue to Kansas City then return here on the flight leaving late afternoon. But our schedules are altered at times and we're not always paired together."

Faith nodded in agreement, then added, "My best guess is your missing person was on the flight you suggest. I believe she sat alone in one of the front rows and ordered a Bloody Mary, an unusual request so early in the day. She also had difficulty storing her luggage in the overhead bin. I took one bag to a storage compartment in the rear."

Turning to Gwen, Dave asked, "You remember the same?"

"No, but I wouldn't have interacted with her. We split the cabin for drinks and snack service. If she were at the front, the only times I might have seen her were during boarding, then again as she departed the plane. We both try to be at the passageway to greet people and speak to them again as they leave. "

"Assuming you're correct about her being on that flight, would either of you know if she was terminating in St. Louis or connecting to another destination?"

Both smiling, Gwen said, "We wouldn't have a clue. We see the tickets only if the passenger has a problem and asks for help or if there's been a mix-up in seat assignments."

Dave handed each a business card. "If you have any other thoughts about Nicole, please give me a call. It looks like I've hit a dead end if she can't be found in St. Louis."

Gwen said, "You're right. Tracking her onto other flights under an assumed name would be almost impossible. And good luck in locating her in St. Louis. That could be equally difficult."

Dave rang the doorbell at Heather Farrell's house, a small bungalow in an older section of the city. Almost immediately, she opened the door and stepped aside to allow him to enter the living room. "I'm glad you called before you came. I'm planning to leave for several hours, but it will wait." Her hand on his arm was disconcerting for a moment.

"I wanted to report on what I've discovered about your sister and ask a couple of questions," Dave said, following her invitation to sit on the couch. She dropped into a wing chair. Her navy skirt revealed her knees when she crossed her legs.

"I've tracked Nicole onto a May 7th flight to St. Louis. But my leads are not as solid as I'd like. They're based on the memory of a baggage handler and the flight attendants."

Heather leaned forward. "They identified her by her picture?"

"Yes, but it's shaky in my judgment. People always try to help and if they think you want them to identify someone, they often will."

Dave related the conversation he'd had with neighbors, the unusual activities around the Dewberry house during the time Nicole disappeared, and the drastic changes that had occurred at Black and Redfield. He concluded, "I suspect Nicole's disappearance, Gerald's murder, and the late-night disturbances are all connected. I need your advice on the next steps in finding your sister."

"Okay, if I can help. I still think Gerald killed her, but apparently you disagree."

Dave ignored her deep-seated intent to place blame on Gerald. "One of my questions has to do with Nicole's potential contacts in St. Louis. Does she have friends there? Anyone she'd turn to for help?"

Heather shifted in the chair, then stood to pace across the room. "Nobody jumps into mind. She had a friend from her university days, maybe a sorority sister, who called on special occasions—birthdays, other dates meaningful to the two of them. But I've never met her and I can't recall her name."

"Could you go through Nicole's address file? Maybe a name would trigger something useful."

"I'd be willing to do that if the cops will let me in Nicole's house. I tried several days ago, but was told the premises were off-limits until the crime people had finished their work."

Dave said, "I'll contact Rasmussen. Perhaps he'd go in with you for the specific purpose of examining address books, files, maybe her computer."

"I'd like you to come with us." She stopped pacing and sat on the couch next to Dave. Her shoulder bumped his. Her closeness and the faint scent of perfume urged him to respond to her obvious come-on.

But he focused on the task at hand. "If I could use your phone," Dave said, "I'll call him now."

"Sure, and I hope he'll agree. If he can do it now, I'll cancel my other appointment."

Rasmussen was waiting at the Dewberry house when Dave and Heather arrived.

Dave said, "Thanks for helping with this. You remember Heather Farrell?"

His face a mask, Rasmussen nodded in her direction, then led the way into the house. "The crime scene crews have finished here, but there remains the question of who's responsible if we can't locate Nicole."

Inside, Heather led them up the stairs. "She kept her files in a second-floor bedroom she'd converted to an office. That's where to look first."

Heather hesitated as she entered the room. Rasmussen and Dave watched as she surveyed the furnishings, and as she sat in the desk chair. She shuffled through stacks of papers in the boxes, then examined contents of drawers. From the middle drawer she pulled out a small black book. Thumbing through the pages, she stopped at times to consider the information.

Dave asked, "Anything strike a chord?"

Heather shook her head. "I'm looking for St. Louis addresses, but it could be her friend lives in one of the suburban communities. All these cities are surrounded by smaller towns with different names."

Rasmussen said, "Let's look together. I've been around St. Louis enough to know the area."

He and Dave looked over Heather's shoulders as she slowly turned the pages. Into the D's, Rasmussen said, "That address is close to the city."

Heather puzzled over the name, shaking her head. "Doesn't seem familiar at all."

In the F's, Rasmussen stopped her again. "That's a community on the west side. Wouldn't be too far from the airport."

When Heather shook her head, Dave said, "Why don't I write down all the possible addresses and check them out, rather than ignoring some that might be the right place. If you're not certain of the friend, we could pass her by and waste time tracing false leads."

Following Dave's suggestion, they reexamined the pages. By the end of their perusal, they had a list of six possibilities, including a name in St. Louis Heather wanted to discard.

Heather returned the book to the drawer. "I'm sorry I couldn't pinpoint Nicole's friend, but I just don't know."

At the front door, Heather asked, "Is there any reason I can't have the keys? I'm the closest relative of either Nicole or Gerald. His parents are dead and he's an only child."

Rasmussen said, "I'll check with the Chief and get back to you."

SEVEN

After Maude Frame failed to get a positive response from Black and Redfield, Jennifer decided to give it one more try before undertaking a suit, a time consuming and in this situation a non-profit venture for the firm. She set up an appointment to visit again with Rogers Morton, the account executive who'd rejected her earlier request.

Morton stood as she entered, obviously inspecting her figure as she sat across the desk from him. He opened, "Ms. Watson, while I like your persistence, my answer remains the same. We will not release any information to you or Mrs. Frame."

Ignoring his tone and intent on ending the session quickly, Jennifer said, "I'm disappointed in your position. Mrs. Frame has every right to know why her policy was terminated. Apparently, her physical exam and the blood analyses were deciding factors. I'm convinced the court will favor her position, but I'd hoped we could avoid that step."

Morton leaned forward and placed his elbows on the desk. "We are sticking by our decision. Mrs. Frame will have to live with that and so will you. I'd suggest you let the matter drop." He seemed eager to add more, but stopped short.

Jennifer stood. "Then, Mr. Morton, you will hear from the court."

"Ms. Watson, it's in your best interest to let everything alone. We don't like to be placed in the public eye."

At the door, Jennifer said, "Perhaps you should rethink the stance you've taken with your clients. You could avoid the negative publicity associated with disgruntled people."

Leaving the Chester administration building the following morning, Jennifer passed a large man, dressed in wrinkled khaki pants, a black tee shirt, a brown windbreaker, and a Cardinals baseball cap, standing in the doorway of the Penney's store. She was aware of his stare, but dismissed it as a response of males who took pleasure in ogling attractive females. But when she turned the corner, she realized he was following ten paces behind. Without a conscious decision, she quickened her pace. He maintained the distance until she entered the office building. From the window in the second floor hall, she saw him leaning against the building across the street. In her mind, she dubbed him as "Stalker", but she wished Dave were here rather than chasing an elusive lead to Nicole Farrell in St. Louis. She recalled the veiled threat from Rogers Morton.

Turning toward their offices, her initial reaction was to report a stalker to the police, but Ellie met her at the door with a message to respond to an urgent call from a client. She forgot Stalker in the rush of the day.

Leaving the office at 5:45, Jennifer trudged toward her car in the lot behind the building, a heavy briefcase slowing her pace. The day had gone well. Clients had streamed in and out continuously, something she'd envisioned when she'd returned from New York to start a practice in her home town. She'd filed papers to obtain Maude Frame's records from Black and Redfield. She'd managed to bring two people to an amicable settlement rather than drag their divorce through the courts.

The appearance of Stalker, standing against a van parked three spaces from her car, snapped her out of her reverie. Her heart jumped. She looked around for other people, but the lot was empty. A quick study of his face catalogued his features—black hair jammed under a baseball cap, dark eyes, heavy lips creased into a sneer, a scar across his left cheek. He continued to stare until she closed her car door.

She had driven four blocks before she noticed the folded paper under her windshield wiper, but she didn't stop. The man hadn't followed her out of the lot, but she didn't take any chances one of his buddies had picked her up and was following. She sped as quickly as possible through the heavy traffic to her apartment building with security guards at the doors and an underground garage available only to residents with valid parking passes to open the gate.

Breathing a sigh of relief, she sat behind the steering wheel for several seconds, letting her nerves return to normal. She removed the paper from the wiper and spread it out on the hood of her Accord. The message—**Stay Out Of The Frame Matter. There Won't Be Another Warning**—was scribbled across the page. No signature or identifying .marks indicated the writer. But Jennifer was certain Stalker had been hired to place the warning and to intimidate her by his presence near the office.

In her apartment on the third floor, she decided to ignore the challenge unless he threatened her more directly. Within a couple of days, the court would respond to her request regarding Frame's records. That should signal Black and Redfield she was not backing down. Any threats from their hired intimidator would be reported to the courts.

But Gerald Dewberry's murder and Nicole Farrell's flight from danger wouldn't leave her thinking. She called Dave's cell phone at 7:30.

He responded on the second ring. "What's up? You okay?"

She told him about Stalker, trying to suppress her anxiety and not come across as a flighty female.

Dave asked, "Do you have to go in tomorrow? Maybe get Ellie to bring any files to your place. Work from your home computer."

"I have clients coming in for consultations."

"Reschedule them. I don't like this guy hanging around. He's probably trying to scare you, but don't take any chances."

"I could call Rasmussen."

"He'd only warn the clown to cease and desist. From what you've said, nothing happened to result in an arrest. And Black and Redfield's lawyers would have him out in ten minutes."

"How's it going? When are you coming back?"

"I struck out on one site today. I'm revisiting a second place tonight. If things go well, I'll get to the rest tomorrow. I'll be home on the late flight tomorrow."

She replaced the receiver. Her depression had been relieved, but the audacity of Black and Redfield irritated her. Dave would take care of the situation as he always did. He could be scary, but she felt safe when he was near.

Dave worried Jennifer wouldn't take his advice, but there was no way to get back to Chester tonight. He hated to waste the trip by not completing the check on all the potential leads. He'd call her early tomorrow and rush through the other addresses as fast as possible. Now he was returning to an house on Walnut Street for a second look. He checked the address again and pulled the motel door closed.

When he'd parked in front of the house around 4:00 this afternoon, he'd detected a movement of curtains in an upstairs room. But no one responded to the door bell. He waited, giving the occupant sufficient time to come down stairs and answer, but nothing happened. Going around to the side, he went through an open garage and rang the bell on the entry. Through the upper glass panel, he looked into the kitchen. Again, nothing.

He drove away, circled the block, stopped three houses down the street, walked toward the address, thinking Nicole was hiding out and refusing to answer while the owners were away. He took up a post across the street, scanning windows for any movement. Feeling vulnerable and silly and failing to observe any motion from within the residence, he gave up after thirty minutes.

At 8:15 Dave rang the front door bell at the Walnut street address. Within a few seconds, a man responded, his eyes honing in on Dave's face, prepared to reject any overture from a door-to-door salesman.

Dave said, "I'm sorry to bother you, but I'm looking for a missing person and your address was in her records. Her sister thought she might have come here."

Looking uncomfortable with Dave's tale, the man said, "I'm sorry. There's not a visitor here. My wife and I work downtown. My mother has a small apartment upstairs, but she's pretty well confined because of a broken hip."

Dave asked, "I assume you know Nicole Farrell?"

His scowl was replaced by a smile. "We do. She and my wife have worked on a real estate deal together and she stayed overnight with us last winter when she was in town for a professional meeting." His smile disappeared. "Has something happened to her?"

Dave said, "We think she's okay, but she disappeared several days ago. I appreciate your help and again, I'm sorry to have disrupted your evening." He retreated down the steps, mentally erasing another possibility.

The man called out, "Let us know if we can help."

Dave pulled away in the rental car. He was tired and concerned about Jennifer and the time he'd wasted on the trail of Nicole. He parked in the motel lot and walked a half-block to a lounge, its neon light flashing.

He sipped a Killian draft, his thoughts lingering on Jennifer's safety and the potential for locating Nicole at one of the remaining addresses.

Jennifer was at her apartment when he called at 6:30 the next morning. As soon as her drowsy voice answered, he said, "Just reminding you to do what I said. Don't try to be brave."

She said, "God, what time is it? I'm okay. I'll do what you suggest, but I feel stupid."

"Better stupid than dead or beaten by these idiots," he said. "I'll check back mid-morning."

"No, focus on the leads. I'll be fine."

Dave had struck out on two more of the addresses collected from Nicole's address book. One apartment stood vacant, the tenant having moved six months ago with no forwarding address. The potential of the occupant fleeing with Nicole crossed his thinking, but the timing was wrong to have involved Nicole's dash from Chester. The second one was a downtown office occupied by a professional acquaintances of Nicole's, but couldn't be described as a close friend. Her connections came through her real estate business and contact was limited to correspondence about clients relocating from the St. Louis area to Chester or vice-versa. At each place he left a card and asked them to call him if Nicole showed.

At an address in Pasadena Hills, a community west of St. Louis, he found the fifth address on his list after asking for directions at a local gas-food combination store. He drove past 216 Redwood, circled the block of mid-priced residences, and parked across the street. The response to the doorbell brought Nicole Farrell, standing behind a three-year old boy, into Dave's view.

She said, "Can I help you?"

Dave responded, "Your sister, Heather, hired me to find you. May I come in and explain?" He handed her a business card, opened his wallet to show his driver's permit and his license as a private investigator.

Nicole still hesitated, her hands on the shoulders of the toddler. She compared the photos to his face before stepping aside and allowing him to enter a small living area.

She called out, "Maureen, would you take Johnny for a few minutes while I talk to this visitor?" She led and directed the boy toward a hall.

Returning, she indicated a chair for Dave as she settled into a corner of the couch. "I thought about calling Heather, knowing she'd worry and make a fuss about my absence, but I was afraid the number would be traced. How did you ever locate me?"

Dave explained about the address book and his efforts to find how she'd departed Chester. "Heather was concerned. She believed your husband, Gerald, had done something to you."

Her calm features turned into a deep frown. Her voice quivered as she said, "I read about his death in the paper. I'm not surprised they did him in." She wiped the sleeve of her blouse across her face.

"Who?"

"Those hoodlums who've taken over Black and Redfield. I didn't understand everything that was going on, but Gerald had gotten in bad favor about the new policies. He'd had a couple of gangster types show up at our home and warn him about getting on board or he'd be sorry."

"Is that why you left?"

"I decided it wasn't safe. I'd heard them threaten Gerald his wife could be in danger if he failed to fall in line. I didn't tell anyone. The next morning I took a cab to the airport, bought a ticket under an assumed name, and came here. I called my company from a pay phone in the St. Louis airport to tell them, but no one knew my destination."

"Are you returning to Chester soon? The threat probably no longer exists since Gerald is out of the picture."

"I've been reluctant. Those people are so cruel and heartless, they'd kill me just for a lark."

"But you haven't personally threatened them."

"I'm concerned they'll believe I know more than I do and will blab to the police. But the truth is I know nothing. Gerald kept pretty close-mouthed about the arguments going on in the organization."

"May I tell Heather where you are?"

Without hesitation, Nicole shook her head. "I'd rather you didn't. She talks too much and is bound to let slip my location. I can't chance that for a while. But tell her you found me and I'm safe. In fact, I'm thinking about moving to Minneapolis. I have contacts there and could get started in real estate with little problem. I'll know what I'm going to do in the next ten days."

"Heather has told me you were close. She will miss you."

"I know and feel badly, but I can't risk returning to Chester. Those bastards may even harm Heather if they connect us. They're big on revenge and retribution."

Dave stood. "Be confident I won't reveal where you are. If you need assistance, give us a call at the number on the card. My partner is a lawyer who could handle any legal issues."

Nicole stood and moved closer. "I've heard good things about your firm. And I may need help before all this is resolved."

At the door they shook hands. Dave heard the door click closed as he descended the three front steps and headed for his Budget rental car. If the traffic wasn't too dense, he could make the six-fifteen flight to Chester.

Breaking his resolve to avoid phoning while driving, he called Jennifer from his cell phone on the way. She'd stayed in the apartment all day. To himself he admitted relief she'd not chanced going to the office. If something happened to her, he couldn't imagine how he would react, but it would be more than the loss of a professional colleague.

The plane, only half of the seats occupied, left fifteen minutes late. He'd not thought about seeing Faith and Gwen until they'd greeted him as he boarded.

After takeoff, Gwen stopped at his seat in the rear of the small jet. She perched on the arm of the aisle seat. "Any luck? Faith and I have a bet about whether you'd find your missing person."

Dave put aside the Sports Illustrated he'd taken from the rack. "Actually, I did. You helped me by confirming she had been on the flight." Her knees and legs captured his eye for a passing moment.

Gwen smiled. "Great. I won."

Dave said, "Then I should buy you both a drink after you've finished your chores."

"I'll be pleased to join you, but I suspect Faith is being met by her finance. I'll check to be sure."

Dave waited ten minutes after landing before the two stewardesses came off the gangway. He spotted them easily as the terminal had emptied rapidly, only a few people waiting for late-night flights. They moved quickly toward him, still looking neat in their blue uniforms after a long day. Both towed a small bag on wheels. He decided that was one of the identifying marks of the profession and wondered what they really carted around.

Faith said, "I'm sorry I can't accept your offer, but I'm meeting a friend outside the security checkpoint. Maybe another time? You should make Gwen buy with the money she won from me."

"It's my treat today." Dave was pleased he'd have Gwen to himself. Her healthy good looks and outgoing personality had attracted him from the first time they'd met. Observing her easy movements as she served passengers brought his attention to her trim figure and friendly, smiling demeanor. The absence of a wedding band whetted his interest.

In the lounge in the main terminal, they took a corner table. Only three other customers remained in the bar, each sitting alone and staring into space, waiting for their flights to be announced. Gwen ordered a gin and tonic from a scantily costumed waitress who acknowledged a greeting from a regular patron. Dave asked for a Killian draft.

"So you were successful in your search. I thought you would be." Gwen pulled a napkin from the holder and wiped away moisture left on the table by a previous user.

"It's always luck and persistence," Dave admitted. "I had a couple of leads beyond the knowledge she'd flown from Chester. One panned out."

"I read about your firm and the fraud involving a nursing home. I was impressed."

"That got our partnership enough recognition to last for a while. Business has really picked up," Dave said, sipping from the icy stein placed by the waitress.

They exchanged information about backgrounds, both having experienced failed marriages, and neither involved in a meaningful relationship at the present time. Careers seemed to play havoc with attempts to sustain long-term connections. They stayed until the bartender announced closing in fifteen minutes.

Leaving the terminal, Dave said, "I'll walk with you to your car."

"That's okay. It's in the crew lot. I can take a shuttle."

"How's your schedule for the weekend? Would you be interested in dinner Saturday or Sunday?"

"I'd like Saturday. I have to fly early on Monday and like to turn in early the night before. I live in an apartment in the building at 400 Jefferson Place."

"Seven okay?" Dave asked.

He waited with her until the crew shuttle arrived, then found his Blazer in the last row of the parking lot. The conversation with an attractive, intelligent woman had brightened his outlook. He looked forward to seeing her again.

Before getting into his vehicle he called Jennifer to tell her he'd follow her into work tomorrow morning.

EIGHT

Dave parked in front of Jennifer's apartment building and called. "I'm here. I'll drop in behind when you come out of the garage."

Five minutes later, she emerged and waved to him. He followed, watching for any other vehicles tracking them. Nothing suspicious appeared.

In the suite, she came immediately into his office, but remained standing, rather than dropping into the visitor's chair as she usually did during their almost daily morning discussions of cases and activities related to the firm. He recognized her edginess, along with the slight tremor in her voice, as clear signs of tension when she was worried about a case or frustrated by some event.

Dave told her about the relatively quick discovery of Nicole, her rationale for leaving, and her fear of returning. "I'll call or go see Heather later today and hope she can live with her sister's decision."

"She has no choice if Nicole decides it's too dangerous to come back. But I think you're right. With Gerald out of the mix, she shouldn't be bothered."

Dave said, "Now show me this goon."

Jennifer said, "Come to the hall window." She took him by the arm as though she wished him to hurry.

At the window, she pointed and said, "See that man standing under the overhang of the sports bar. He's been around for three days. He follows me if I walk out of the building and he's near my car every night when I leave. Plus, he or someone left a warning on my windshield to stay out of the Frame situation."

Dave eyed the man leaning casually against the wall, watching the pedestrians and glancing at cars on the busy street. His appearance seemed that of a mobster waiting for his prey to drop their guard or an out-of-work mechanic with nothing to do. "Has he said anything? Made any threatening moves?"

"No," Jennifer said, "but he's scary. I don't feel safe with him around. I thought about calling the police, but decided they couldn't do anything. He's within his rights to loll around the street as long as he doesn't interfere with anyone. After worrying about him for hours, I called you."

"Let me see the warning?" He led her back to their suite.

After examining the creased paper, Dave said, "You're right. Black and Redfield is trying to scare us off. They've hired this hood to intimidate us. If we go forward with the Frame case, they'll take a next step."

Jennifer's eyes widened, a hint of fear evident. "What do we do?"

"You do nothing," Dave said. "I'll think of something. But we won't drop our inquiry."

Jennifer said, "This is the kind of threat that caused Nicole to run, isn't it?"

Dave nodded. "But we'll react differently. Go about your business as usual. I'll worry about the thug."

"He parks a black Dodge van in a visitor's slot behind our building. It's there when I arrive. I assume he leaves as soon as I do. I don't think he follows my car."

As he turned away to leave, she said, "Dave, be careful."

With the worry about the threat from the stalker running through his mind, Dave called Heather Farrell. He reported finding Nicole without revealing her location, then added, "She's fine. But she doesn't want anyone from Chester calling or visiting her. She's afraid any contacts will lead Black and Redfield to her."

"I can't believe she's so scared. They won't care about her now."

"That's what I said, but she's not buying. And she's concerned any contact from you will put you in danger."

As though not hearing his warning, Heather said, "I'd really like to talk to her. Maybe she'll tell me things she wouldn't tell you."

"It's better not to for a while. If she needs something, she'll contact you. I promised I wouldn't reveal her location or even how to call her. My best advice is wait for her lead."

After a pause, Heather said, "If you'll send a bill, I'll reimburse you immediately, but I'd like to buy your lunch one day soon. Maybe we can talk more about what I should do in regard to Nicole."

Dave asked, "Have the police questioned you again about Gerald's death?"

"Yeah, that detective came by the day after we'd searched Nicole's house to drop off the keys. He asked again about my activities the week before the murder. I couldn't remember most of the things I'd done. They're trying to confuse me." Dave knew the scheme. Keep asking the same questions in slightly different ways until the suspect made an error. Then they'd hone in on the specific until the individual cracked.

"Don't talk to them again without Jennifer. If they come by, you insist your attorney be present. Okay?"

"Sure. And I'll call you about lunch soon."

From the back foyer of their office building Dave watched Jennifer leave for the day. Stalker had taken his usual position, glaring at her from the moment she left the building until she drove away. Dave caught up to him as the large man sauntered toward his van, one of two vehicles left. Dave's Blazer was the other.

As the man opened the door of his van, Dave said, "I've been watching you all day. I don't want to catch you again around this building or in this parking lot."

"Screw you. I do what I want." His dark eyes challenged Dave.

"Or what some jackass at Black and Redfield has ordered you to do. Spy on Jennifer Watson." Dave moved closer, now two steps away. He figured the guy had a weapon hidden under his windbreaker, an obvious ploy in the warm weather.

Taken aback for a moment, Stalker growled. "I don't ask questions. I do what I'm paid to do."

"You tell them today was your last on the job," Dave said. "If you're around tomorrow, you'll get a visit from the cops or worse."

"You're a smart-ass shit," Stalker answered, stepping away from his vehicle.

Suddenly, he lunged at Dave, who eluded the wild swing, but lashed a stiff backhand across his attacker's throat.

Stalker stumbled backward, collapsed to his knees, gasping for breath, his hands clawing at his throat. As his breathing became easier, he reached toward his back under his windbreaker. Dave kicked him in the nose, smashing the cartilage and sending blood spewing down his shirt and onto the asphalt. With a foot in his back, Dave pushed Stalker to a prone position on the asphalt. He reached under the windbreaker and pulled a semi-automatic Smith and Wesson .38 from his rear waistband. Dave checked the gun for ammunition. It was fully loaded.

Dave waited for the goon's recovery. After a few seconds, Stalker rolled from his stomach and got to a sitting position.

Dave said, "Take your van and get out while you're still breathing. If I find you here tomorrow or anywhere around Watson, you're a gone goose. And tell your employers I'll be on the watch for anyone else. They won't fare as easily as you."

The man stumbled into his van, fumbled to find his keys and get the motor started, and weaved out of the lot. When the van failed to stop at the exit from the lot, a car on the street squealed its brakes to avoid hitting it.

On the way to work the following morning, Dave stopped by the Chester police station. He found Rasmussen in the small lounge area, waiting for the coffee maker to finish its process. The apparatus emitted one last gurgle as the cloud of vapor dissipated. The pungent odor of the strong brew infiltrated their senses.

Rasmussen asked, "You want a shot of this stuff? Get your system going fast."

"I'll pass, but I want to give you a present."

"Sounds like more trouble." He filled a stained mug from the spigot of the twenty-cup reservoir. "Come to the office."

Dave handed Rasmussen the weapon he'd taken from the stalker. "You may be interested in running ballistics tests on this. The owner is employed by Black and Redfield."

.   "How'd you obtain his gun?"

"I talked him out of it after he'd been watching our office for three days and following Jennifer when she walked out of the building. He scared the wits out of her."

"Interesting. Why didn't she call us?"

"She knew you couldn't do anything except talk."

"So you convinced this goon it'd be in his best interest to turn in his weapon?"

"Something like that." He handed Rasmussen an index card. "And this is the license number of the black Dodge van he drives."

Rasmussen, who'd been helped by Dave on several occasions and who knew his methods would not be approved under the guidelines for interactions with potential criminals, said, "I'll send the gun to ballistics and run the number through our system. May turn up something."

Dave turned to the door, saying, "Let me know. I expect we'll hear more from this guy or his employer."

"Don't do anything I'll have to run you in for."

Dave grinned. "Go easy on that brew. It smells dangerous."

Jennifer came into Dave's office mid-afternoon. "I haven't seen my ever-present companion around today. What happened?"

"I talked to him in the parking lot yesterday. He agreed not to come around again, but we should be alert to his replacement. The next one may not be so obvious."

"I hope you haven't stirred up more problems."

Dave said, "It pays to be aggressive with those types. Who did you talk with at Black and Redfield?"

Jennifer hesitated, unsure of what he had in mind, but acknowledged he usually got results with his unorthodox methods. "Rogers Morton. He's an account executive who handled the GM clients. You think he put this stalker onto me?"

"Probably. That seems to be their mode of operation now. Intimidate people until they back off. If you go back to him for any reason, I'd like to go with you."

Jennifer looked at her watch. "Now, I have to meet Judge Young's clerk about the release of Maude Frame's records. There must be some glitch, but I can't imagine what."

"I may not see you again today. I'm scheduled for a session on the pistol range. Got to keep in practice." Dave had joined a gun club when he'd moved to Chester to gain access to their facilities. He tried to visit on a regular basis to maintain his skills.

"See you on Monday. Have a good weekend."

"If your buddy or anyone suspicious comes around your apartment building, let me know. Call anytime. Don't delay."

Jennifer had expected a positive response to her request about Frame's records, but recognized the call from Young's clerk signaled a delay. She considered the implications as she walked the four blocks to the administration building, relieved Stalker had not appeared today and wondering how Dave had convinced him to keep away. She was certain it had been more than a casual conversation.

In the cramped office of Andy Chaffin, the young lawyer who'd been with Young for only a few months, Jennifer sat in a hard chair and watched the clerk shuffle through a stack of papers. Law books and folders were stacked in seemingly random fashion on the desk, in a couple of oak chairs and along the wall under the single window.

Chaffin said, "I'm sorry to drag you over here on a Friday afternoon, but Judge Young has a question about the Frame records."

"It seems clear," Jennifer said, "that Mrs. Frame has the right to her records, especially when they have been used to terminate an insurance policy she's had for years. She deserves an explanation and an opportunity to know why."

Chaffin said, "He understands, but wonders why Mrs. Frame can't arrange for her own examination and then challenge the decision."

Jennifer leaned forward to glare into the clerk's face. "That's ridiculous. First, she shouldn't have to pay for an expensive set of assays. Second, she doesn't even know what data were gathered. She'd be shooting in the dark, trying to outguess Black and Redfield."

When Chaffin didn't respond immediately, she continued, "Has Black and Redfield stone-walled this release?"

Chaffin couldn't meet her stare. "Their attorney indicated the company would resist. He argued the files belong to the company and couldn't be given to anyone because of their policy on privacy. Judge Young wanted a stronger position from your client before ordering the release."

Jennifer tried to remain calm at the inaneness of the situation. She said, "He should know other employees have experienced the same problem. I know of another woman whose health insurance has been cancelled. She has no earthly idea why and the company won't tell her. She went through the same examination as Maude Frame. It's not a privacy matter. It's a fraud issue. If Judge Young refuses to order those records released, I'll be forced to sue Black and Redfield. He likely doesn't want to become involved in a lengthy court case and neither do I."

"If you get the records, will you agree not to sue?"

"No. I won't know Black and Redfield's rationale for dropping policies until I understand the background. They may have a legitimate reason, but why not just tell their clients rather than being secretive about it. If it's not reasonable, my only recourse is the courts to obtain justice for my client."

Chaffin said, "I'll relay this to Judge Young on Monday and let you know."

"If he can't agree," Jennifer said, "I need to know why because I will appeal to the Circuit Court if I think he's not followed the statutes appropriately."

Jennifer's return walk to the office turned out to be not as relaxing as she'd hoped. She couldn't believe Young's delaying tactics. The case was clear-cut. Had Black and Redfield somehow pressured the judge? Had some hired thug intimidated Young and his family? She'd heard of such occurrences in New York and other large cities, but couldn't believe it could happen in Chester.

Dave's reservations at Arthur's for Saturday evening dinner resulted in immediate attention by the hostess. Gwen's professional attire had been exchanged for a black dress that enhanced her figure and captured the glance of nearby males as they were led to a small table on one side of the large dining area. Linen and silver service proclaimed elegance. Dimmed lights and glowing candles added to the plush atmosphere.

After they were seated and had ordered drinks, Gwen said, "I'm surprised you know about this place."

"I've been in on business a few times. I thought you'd like it."

"Your job takes you to interesting places, but can't dealing with criminals be dangerous at times?"

"It could be, but I'm usually prepared. I don't walk into situations without knowing what's likely to happen. Then I can be ready to respond." He sipped his Scotch, thinking about the potential ramifications of his encounter with Jennifer's stalker. There would be some attempt to exact revenge. It was a given with those types.

Raising his glass, he said, "But let's focus on good food and pleasant companionship tonight."

Two hours later at her apartment door, Gwen said, "I enjoyed this evening. I'd invite you in, but I've had a change in my schedule and must be ready for the 7:00 a.m. flight tomorrow." She took a step toward him and quickly kissed him on the cheek before turning to the door.

Dave said, "I'll call you in the next few days."

"I'd like that. Or because my schedule is so erratic, I can call you, if you don't believe that'd be too presumptuous."

"I can handle that," Dave said, "and even look forward to it."

NINE

In the middle of the morning Rasmussen telephoned Dave. "You won't believe this, but the ballistics of the .38 you brought in match those of the gun involved in Gerald Dewberry's death. We' re on the lookout for the man driving the van. It's registered in the name of Carl Meade. We have nothing on him in our system."

"I should have brought him in the other day, but if I see him again, I'll give you a call," Dave responded. "I hadn't connected him with Dewberry, but I'm not surprised. This means Black and Redfield orchestrated the murder."

"You're guessing."

"Not completely. Meade began harassing Jennifer after she threatened a suit against the firm over a cancelled insurance policy. He didn't flinch when I accused him of being employed by Black and Redfield. But he could just be slow on the uptake."

"Maybe a completely different party contracted Meade to knock over Dewberry. There seems to be quite a number of people who didn't like him, including his sister-in-law."

"Rule her out. She has no clue about how to hire a hood."

"She gets around a lot. Probably knows someone who'd have the right connections to make a call on her behalf."

Dave respected Rasmussen's ability and tenacity, but his friend sometimes chased clues on a whim. He was reasonably certain Rasmussen's focus on Heather Farrell represented another dead end. Dave said, "Talk with Norman Castle. He worked with Gerald and lives across the street from the Dewberry residence."

Rasmussen considered the information for several seconds. "You've usually provided good leads, but why Castle?"

"He believes Gerald had rubbed the new management at Black and Redfield the wrong way. I had no reason to push him for details, but something is going on in the organization that's not altogether above board. I thought Castle knew more than he told me."

"I'll check him out."

"It'll cost you a beer if I'm right."

Jennifer received a call from Andy Chaffin on Tuesday morning. "I talked yesterday afternoon with Judge Young in reference to the Maude Frame claim. He's going to deny your request. You'll get a letter tomorrow."

"Frankly, Andy, I'm flabbergasted. There's not a legitimate reason to deny this woman the right to information about her physical condition."

"I'm only the messenger. I'm not privy to Judge Young's thinking."

"Then he may be forced to preside over a suit against Black and Redfield for wrongful acts against Mrs. Frame. I hope he can deal with that objectively or have the guts to remove himself without prejudice." She dropped the receiver into the cradle more forcefully than necessary. She couldn't believe Young had been compromised. He had the reputation of fairness and firmness in his court, but Black and Redfield had found some way to pressure him. He'd been forced to yield to their demands or had been paid off.

Jennifer retrieved from the Frame file the list of assays Dave had obtained from Biological Assays, Inc. She needed to learn more about these genetic tests. But first she had to find out if any of those sophisticated assays had been done for Frame. It seemed senseless to dig out a mass of background information if it didn't apply to her client. Maybe Young would issue an order for Biological Assays to release the data. He could deny knowing it related to Black and Redfield if the issue surfaced. But if Young caught on to her subterfuge or if the file became important in a court battle, she'd become the focus of his ire. She could ask for another judge if the suit went to a court hearing based on Young's rejection of her first request. She'd argue Young was too biased to render a fair judgment. But she'd probably lose anyway and irritate the judge so all her future cases would be more difficult.

Responding to Heather Farrell's invitation, Dave met her at Arthur's for lunch. He arrived five minutes early and waited in the foyer. A steady stream of patrons soon filled the place, but Heather's reservation had assured them of a corner table. He followed the hostess and Heather, her clinging white dress, high heels and sheer nylons, contrasted with her dark hair and eyes and highlighted every sensuous curve of her body.

Immediately after being seated, she dug into her purse and handed him a check. "Here's your payment. I'm grateful for the way you stuck with the search for my sister, especially when the cops wouldn't budge." She touched his arm, allowing her fingers to linger. Her perfume cut into his senses. Suppressing his desire to hold her hand, he put the check into his wallet and opened the menu, as the waitress approached.

"Finding her turned out to be easier than I expected," Dave said.

Heather ordered a Chef's salad and Dave requested a club sandwich.

As they waited for their orders, Heather said, "I caught up with Nicole last night."

"What do you mean? Has she come back here?" He swallowed an urge to curse, knowing Nicole would believe he'd revealed her hideaway to her sister.

"No. I went through the list of addresses you'd checked out around St. Louis and started calling the numbers. I got through to her on the third try."

Dave drank water from the icy glass. "Was she upset you called?"

"At first, then we talked about her next move. She's afraid to return to Chester as you said."

"Did she tell you where she might go?"

"She mentioned Boston or Hartford. Her company has offices in those cities, so she could start in easily. Actually, those large cities would be good for her since she's focused more on commercial sales in the past couple of years."

Dave recalled Nicole's plan to move to Minneapolis, but he didn't argue with Heather. Nicole was still worried about being tracked by Black and Redfield and had deliberately fed disinformation to her sister. He said, "I hope your call doesn't lead Dewberry's murder squad to her. Calling her was not in her best interest. Plus, it could put you in their sights if they know Nicole has talked to you."

Her face crinkled into a frown. "I don't accept she's in danger. Gerald did something stupid and got killed, but it's got nothing to do with Nicole. They don't even know I'm her kin."

"Let's hope you're right," Dave said, "but if they're really interested, they would have made the connection based on the news article after your spat with Gerald." The waitress placed their orders on the table, refilled their water glasses, and brought coffee.

His mind still on Nicole's safety, Dave said, "You should get your phones checked to be sure there're not bugged. If they are, calling Nicole puts her at risk."

Heather took a bite of her Chef's salad, sipped coffee, then said, "I'd like you to come back with me and do that." Under the table she crossed her legs, allowing her ankle to rest against Dave's calf.

"I can, but if it's some sophisticated device, I might not find it. I'll look, then maybe we should get an expert. I can recommend a couple."

They ate in silence for a few minutes. Dave finished the club sandwich, drained the coffee cup, and when Heather shoved aside her plate, signaled the waitress for the check.

Heather took the check from him. "Remember, it's my treat."

She took his arm as they threaded their way to the cashier.

Dave parked behind Heather's Cadillac coupe, retrieved his tool kit from the rear compartment, and followed her into the house. Her soft curves and long legs aroused his primitive urges again. He resolved to stick to the task of checking telephones.

Inside, she showed him the downstairs phone and stood near while he removed the bottom plate of the phone. A listening device, obvious even to an unskilled technician, grabbed his attention.

He looked at her, pointed to the bug. "There. I can either take it out or leave it in place. You'd know to be careful of what you say or who you call if I leave it. No one would suspect you've discovered it. Use your cell phone if you don't want your conversation to be overheard."

"Bastards. Take it out. Can they track Nicole?"

"Yes, but it will take some time. Whoever is interested will be able to trace the number to the address."

"Should I warn her?"

"Tell you what, let me do it."

Dave carefully detached the wiring, lifted out the small device, then checked for a dial tone. "It's okay."

Her hand on his shoulder, she asked, "What about the extension upstairs?"

"I can check, but I doubt they'd touch that. One is enough for a line."

"I'd like to be sure," Heather said, leading him up a flight of carpeted stairs into a bedroom. She pointed to the phone on the night table.

Dave went through the process of checking, then stood. "Nothing here."

"That's a relief," she said, stepping closer to him. Her perfume, the touch of her hand on his arm, the image of her swaying hips, and her parted lips turned up to his face were more than he could resist.

He slipped his arm around her waist and pulled her against him. Her arms circled his neck and pressed his head toward hers. Their lips met as he caressed her hips. Their mouths explored as they kissed deeply. He unzipped her dress and pushed it off her shoulders. The silken fabric dropped to her waist. She stepped out of it and tossed it onto a chair. She unsnapped her bra and dropped it on the dress. She came against him as he caressed her back and kissed her breasts. She pulled him toward the bed.

Later, they came alert after a respite following their love-making. Heather said, "I knew we'd do this the first time I met you."

Dave sat on the edge of the bed, recalling his shattered resolve to avoid such situations. "I don't like getting involved with clients. I could lose focus on the real problem."

"But you're willing to take a chance sometimes."

"I have in your case." A mixture of guilt and satisfaction swirled through his thinking. Sex with Heather had been great. He'd find out later if she made outlandish demands of him. Then it might be a serious problem and he'd have to deal with it. He pulled on his pants, socks and shoes and walked to the window overlooking the street, absent-mindedly scanning the outside through a space between the drapes.

Carl Meade's green van was parked across the street, three houses down the block. From the driver's side, the beefy features of Meade jumped out at Dave. Shadows across the windshield obscured the face of the second occupant. Meade was scanning Heather's house through field glasses, waiting for movement, or a signal from someone to move in or follow her when she left.

Dave said, "Don't get excited, but we have an observer of your place parked across the street. I'm going to call the cops."

Heather tightened the belt of her robe and came to stand next to him as he dialed and asked for Rasmussen. After a few seconds, she turned away.

"Bill, Dave Randle. You'll find Carl Meade and a buddy parked in the block across from Heather Farrell's house."

"You certain? We've been on the lookout for a couple of days without success."

"I'm sure. He's in the same van he had behind our office."

"Don't do anything. Give us ten minutes. I'll alert a couple of patrols and get them in place."

"Avoid the sirens. He won't rush away." He heard Rasmussen ordering someone to alert cars 22 and 36. Heather was pulling clothes from her closet.

Back on the line, Rasmussen asked, "Was he following you or on a stakeout at Farrell's?"

"You'll have to ask him, but I haven't seen anyone tailing me. This guy isn't smart enough to follow me without being seen."

"Patrols are on the way," Rasmussen said, ending the conversation and hanging up the phone.

Heather, who had donned slacks and a cotton sweater, came to the window. She peeked through the slight space between the drapes.

When she reached to open them farther, Dave said, "Don't move the curtains. If he thinks we've seen him, he might take off." Dave put on his shirt while they waited.

Five minutes later, police cruisers approached from both ends of the street, moving toward the parked van. Meade and his partner leaped from the Dodge and ran in different directions. Meade crossed the street and cut through a yard. His buddy took off around a large brick house. Shouting for the suspects to halt, a uniformed cop from each car followed them.

Dave asked, "What's behind this neighborhood?"

Heather hesitated, obviously unsure, then said, "I believe nothing but woods until you reach Route 19. I've never been into the area."

"I'm going to help them grab Meade. I'll come back here." He rushed down the stairs and out the back door, letting the screen close quietly. He'd reached the edge of the woods before Heather got to the door.

Dave hustled along what had once been a well defined trail, now grown over in places with brush and thick weeds. Large limbs had fallen across the path in places. He stopped at intervals to listen. Hearing nothing, he left the trail and scrambled through dense woods and around clumps of undergrowth toward the direction he guessed Meade had taken after clearing the residential area.

The crackling of a radio followed by the voice of the cop made Dave stop. The cop was receiving directions or orders from someone. Through the trees, Dave saw the blue uniform turn and head back toward Farrell's street. They'd given up on the chase. They'd wait for Meade or his buddy to return to the van rather than risk his eluding them in the woods and returning to the vehicle.

Knowing Meade would have heard the racket also, Dave waited for several seconds, then crept forward, looking for signs Meade had made as he ran pell-mell. Recalling his training and experience in tracking enemy agents into wooded areas, Dave searched for broken limbs of low bushes and crushed grass. If Heather was correct about Route 19 and if Meade knew the area, he'd head for the road and count on hitching a ride. Dave doubted the overweight and out of shape Meade could sustain a vigorous pace for very long. He'd be forced to stop at intervals and regain his breath and energy.

After passing a small bush that Meade or someone had recently mashed flat, Dave headed for Route 19 as rapidly as possible hoping to spot Meade when he emerged from the woods. He wished he'd retrieved his weapon from the Blazer, but in his dash from Heather's, he hadn't. But, if he'd gone to his car, the cops would have stopped and questioned him, wasting time and interfering with his pursuit of Meade.

Fifteen minutes of jogging, slowed by efforts to dampen any noise and by detours around the thicker brush, brought Dave to the asphalt road. Scanning the shoulders of the highway in both directions, he settled into the middle of a cluster of small oaks, apparently a second growth after the mature trees had been cut during construction. He could see the straight road for five hundred yards in either direction and he was reasonably well concealed. Meade would be intent on reaching the highway and would no longer be concerned about a cop on his heels.

Dave eased into a sitting position. The slight breeze felt refreshing after his dash through the woods. He wiped sweat from his eyes. The western sun cast mid-afternoon shadows of trees across the road. Birds chirped from the tree tops and a couple of swallows lighted on the power line running adjacent to the two-lane secondary road. Five minutes apart, two pickup trucks sped past, their noise erasing for several moments the tranquility of the afternoon.

Ten minutes into his wait, Dave heard a thrashing noise and heavy breathing. Peering through the brush, he saw movement as the bulky Meade pushed limbs away and stomped through high grass. He was twenty yards away from Dave's hideout.

Dave remained still as Meade lumbered up the terraced shoulder. Meade looked both ways, wiped his face on his shirt sleeve, took a dozen uncertain steps in Dave's direction, before dropping to the grassy slope. His hope for a quick ride frustrated by the lack of traffic along the little-used highway, Meade sat for a minute, then stood and shuffled slowly to a shady spot near a large tree. He was now ten yards from Dave's secluded position.

Dave waited until Meade, now feeling safer, settled into boredom. When he saw Meade's head jerk to stay awake, Dave edged away from his spot, careful not to break a twig beneath his feet. Staying low in the cover of trees and brush, Dave moved to be directly behind Meade. He hoped an approaching vehicle didn't destroy his plan.

When Meade's head dropped and remained lowered onto his chest, Dave jumped him. Knocking him sprawling sideways with a kick across a shoulder, Dave twisted Meade's arm behind his back. Surprised by the assault from out of nowhere, Meade flailed his free arm and uttered curses. Dave jerked the thug's gun from his waistband, ignoring Meade's feeble grasp of his arm. Dave stepped back saying, "We meet again. But this time, I'm not letting you go."

Meade eyed Dave for several seconds, apparently considering resistance. He muttered, "You know that gun ain't loaded."

"I'll chance it," Dave said. "But if necessary, we can go through the parking lot routine again."

A woman in a Chevrolet sedan passed, ignoring Dave's signal to stop. He settled in for a prolonged wait, alert to a quick move by Meade.

An hour later, Dave pushed and prodded Meade through the front door of the Chester police station. To the dispatcher at the front desk, Dave said, "Tell Rasmussen I have his escapee."

Rasmussen came from his office. He directed a uniformed cop to put Meade in a holding cell then asked Dave, "Where'd you nab him?"

"I chased him through those woods after your guys gave up. Got him as he came to Route 19. A farmer in a pickup brought us here. Haven't ridden in the back of a pickup in a long time."

"Did you question him about Dewberry's death?"

Dave said, "No, but I found out he's been watching Heather Farrell for several days. And he knew her phone had been bugged but won't admit who was responsible. Could be he doesn't know."

"Why her?"

"Black and Redfield believes her sister knows something through Gerald that's potentially damaging to the organization. That's why Nicole ran."

Rasmussen grinned. "You've learned a lot. I could use you on the force."

Dave shook his head. "Pay is poor and the hours are bad. Did you catch up with Meade's partner?"

Shaking his head, Rasmussen said, "No, the patrolman lost him when he ran out of the neighborhood and into the shopping district. Too many people around. But we brought the van in. Maybe we'll garner something from it."

"Let me know," Dave said, "and could one of your patrols drop me off at Farrell's? Save me cab fare to get back to my car." He didn't mention his sports coat and tie he'd left in the upstairs bedroom.

TEN

Heather met Dave at the door as the black and white sedan backed out of the driveway. "I was worried after you took so long." She grasped his hand.

"I caught up with your spy and turned him in to the cops. He'll likely be charged with Gerald's murder. But now, I need to retrieve my coat and get to the office."

"Can you stay long enough for a drink?" The pressure of her hand on his promised more.

"I really must get going."

"Am I safe here?"

Dave considered the situation. He'd been surprised the goons had honed in on her, but the phone call to Nicole or her argument with Gerald Dewberry might have triggered their interest. He couldn't be sure Meade's partner or a replacement wouldn't take up the vigil. They could become more assertive after they discovered her telephone bug had been removed and Meade was in custody. They'd know their plans had been exposed.

"It'd be better if you could move in with a friend until we get a clearer picture of what's going on."

Heather edged closer to him, brushing against his shoulder. "Could I come to your place?"

"It'd be better to go somewhere else," Dave said, thinking about the implications.

Disappointment swept across her face momentarily, then she said, "I'll move into a downtown hotel for a few days. I've done that before when I had problems with an old boyfriend."

"Call me at the office if you need help or if you're being followed."

Jennifer arranged for lunch with Anita Chandler, a former classmate from law school who was now a judge in the county. After stewing about dealing with Young for a day, she recalled a news item about her colleague's promotion. She and Anita had been thrown together in law classes when most of the class were men, many of whom regarded the small percentage of females as inferior until the first year rankings were posted. The top four were women. When Jennifer took a position with a prestigious firm in New York, Anita accepted a clerkship with a judge on the state supreme court. She'd worked as a prosecutor on the county staff for a while and made a reputation as a steady, reliable attorney. The local bar had recommended her for the judicial post.

Jennifer suggested Gibbons' as they'd be less likely to be seen by court personnel who would avoid the suspected mobster's establishment for fear of becoming associated with Antonio. Anita balked at the site until Jennifer assured her they wouldn't be tainted since the restaurant was used by many other professionals working in the downtown area.

Jennifer hardly recognized Anita whom she hadn't seen in a year. Anita had lost weight and her pale facial coloring suggested a serious illness or extreme tension. Her thick black hair had thinned and grayed. They hugged without saying a word among the crowd waiting to be seated. After a two minute wait the hostess approached and led them to a booth in the back of the restaurant. From behind the cash register, Antonio Gibbons exchanged nods with Jennifer.

Settled into the booth, Jennifer asked, "Have you been ill?"

Anita fingered the menu, a one-page sheet with items listed on both sides. "I'm recovering from breast cancer. I went through a double mastectomy and chemotherapy. I'm cleared now, but it was a difficult time for me."

"I'm sorry. I didn't know," Jennifer said. "I wish I could have helped." She reached across the table to touch Anita's hand.

"I didn't tell many people, but I missed a lot of work and avoided public events. My husband was great. He did everything around the house and went with me to every treatment session. We became a lot closer."

After they'd ordered beef noodle soup and a pastrami half-sandwich, Jennifer said, "I appreciate your willingness to hear my problem." She explained the issue with Maude Frame and Judge Young's refusal to order release of the records.

"Did Young provide any reason for his rejection?"

"Some lame excuse that Frame should get her own exam, even after I told him she didn't know which tests had been ordered by the insurance company."

Anita asked, "Are you certain the physical exam was the reason for the cancellation?"

"Not absolutely, but it's a reasonable assumption. Only after the results came in was her policy terminated. Then the company's refusal to provide her copies of the results adds to my suspicion. I'm planning to sue Black and Redfield for reinstatement of her coverage. I want to be certain those assays were the trigger for dropping Frame's policy. It could be something else, but it's not obvious. And I suspect the same thing happened to several others. Only one has come forward, but I'd bet others were impacted."

Anita started eating her soup as soon as the cup was placed in front of her. "I'm always starved now. My physician tells me that's a positive sign I'm recovering. Before I had to force myself to eat and could keep down only small bits at a time."

Anita nibbled a cracker, then asked, "How'd you find this place? I figured you'd take a sandwich from home and work at your desk as you did through school."

Jennifer said, "Dave Randle, my partner, and I come here often. The climate is far from elegant but the food is good and the service is fast." She smiled, remembering their debates about taking lunch breaks during the hectic days of law school. "And I still eat lunch at my desk most days."

"And you never feel out of place here?"

"The first time, but Dave and Antonio Gibbons have become friends. They've helped each other at times."

"You're okay with that?"

"It's a concern sometimes, but I've accepted the fact Gibbons gets information Dave could not obtain from any other source. It's benefited our practice by being able to solve crimes the cops failed to crack. That makes the police more cooperative with some of our investigations. He and Dave operate behind the scenes. No one ever knows Dave's source of information."

"It sounds like your partnership is flourishing. I've seen both your names in the papers."

"We struggled to make ends meet for a year, then we got a big break with those scams in the retirement facilities. We obtained a nice settlement for both our clients and the firm. The good publicity brought us business."

Anita pushed aside the empty cup and reached for the sandwich. "I take it you'd like me to issue an order releasing your client's records?"

Jennifer leaned away from her sandwich plate, pleased Anita had raised the critical issue. "My only other option is to appeal to the Circuit Court. I'm reluctant to get on Young's bad side by doing that, although I believe he was wrong to deny my request."

"I'm reluctant to go around Young," Anita said. "As the presiding judge, he has more influence in the local court system than anyone else. I don't want to be relegated to routine cases. Life becomes too boring."

Anita glanced around the room, almost every table and booth occupied. "Is there some way you don't have to get the information from Black and Redfield? If the scuttlebutt I hear has any merit, they'd inform Young immediately."

Surprised by the revelation, Jennifer said, "With a court order I could get the test results from Biological Assays, the company that did the lab work, but what's this about the connection between Young and the insurance company?" Maybe her guess Black and Redfield had gotten to Young wasn't so far-fetched after all.

Anita wiped her lips on the paper napkin and checked the table of four men closest to them. Lowering her voice, she said, "There are rumors that Young is on the take from Black and Redfield. Your rejection adds credence to the hall talk."

"Has this relationship been going on for a long time?"

Anita examined her fingers for food residue. "I'm not sure, but I began hearing the rumors three or four months ago."

"Maybe about the time Black and Redfield changed its top management?"

"I don't keep up with those things, but it could be."

Jennifer said, "Soon after the change, policies of several long-time clients were dropped. There may have been other things, but I wouldn't have heard about those."

"I'll try to help," Anita continued, glancing at her watch. "Submit a formal request to my secretary. I'll call Biological Assays and have Frame's data released to you. I'd like to keep the issue out of the papers. That'd be better for both of us and remember, Young has a long reach."

Jennifer touched Anita's hand. "And these people worry about Antonio Gibbons contaminating them."

She picked up the check, but Anita said, "Let's split the bill. I don't want a meal to be held over my head as a bribe."

On the sidewalk outside the restaurant, Jennifer said, "I appreciate this and trust it won't come back to haunt either of us."

"It'll be okay," Anita said. "Let's get together for dinner before the bar association meeting next month. It's time I started attending again."

"I'd like that." Jennifer watched her friend walk slowly toward her car in the lot across the street. She remembered trotting to keep up with Anita's rapid pace during law school. The cancer had exacted a toll and reduced Anita's rush through life to that of normal humans. Almost automatically, she scanned the crowd near the restaurant for anyone loitering and watching her before heading toward the office.

At 9:30 Dave's telephone rang. Thinking it was Gwen, he cut the television and grabbed the instrument. It was Nicole Farrell.

Dave asked, "Where are you?"

Nicole hesitated for a few seconds. "Where I told you I was going before my nosy sister found me. Please don't tell her."

"Did something happen after she called?"

"It was frightening. Two days after her call, a man came to the door. Fortunately, my friend's husband answered and told him I wasn't there any longer. But the next day, I saw two guys sitting in a car across the street. I realized it was too dangerous to stay. I stayed out of sight throughout the day, but the next morning I left by the back door and caught a cab from a neighbor's house to the airport. My friends called the cops."

"Are your friends safe?"

"I hope so. They took a big risk sheltering me."

Dave asked, "Can I do anything for you? I'm afraid your sister didn't understand the danger until I found a listening device in her phone. That's how they tracked you."

"I suspected such. I'm working under an assumed name and living in a hotel until I find a suitable apartment. But I don't need anything from Chester. I just wanted to let you know. I'll send you a card or call again with my address and phone number when I'm settled. I may want your partner's help when I'm ready to dispose of the property in Chester."

"Take care of yourself," Dave said.

As soon as he replaced the receiver, the phone rang again. This time it was Gwen. "I just got in. Tough trip today. Every seat was occupied and we had a couple of small babies. Heating formula and helping young mothers take care of diapers adds to our work. But I'm free next weekend if you'd like to get together."

"Would you consider coming to my place? We could hike through the woods on my land, do steaks on the grill, whatever you'd like."

After a pause in the flow, Gwen said, "This could be a big leap in our relationship."

"I understand if you're not ready. We could have dinner instead."

"No, I'd like to come there. Maybe you could meet me at the airport on Friday evening. I should be free by nine but you could call the airport to be sure the flight is on time."

Dave said, "I'll see you at the front entrance. Bring a change of outdoor clothes."

Thinking about his previous times with Gwen and his growing feelings for her, Dave switched on the television in time for 10:00 p.m. local news. Midway through the news segment, the announcer reported the finding of a badly deteriorated body by two hikers. The body appeared to be that of an elderly male, but identification had not been completed yet. No one had been reported missing in the past months. Police suspected the remains were those of a hiker who'd become lost in a heavy storm last winter and was not those of a local resident. But the absence of a wallet and watch hinted at foul play. Additional details were promised as they became available.

Dave heard the late scores of the Cardinal-Braves game. Disappointed the Cards were trailing by five runs in the eighth, he turned in for the night.

ELEVEN

Dave had been elated, but surprised when Gwen accepted so quickly his obvious scheme for more intimate relations. He thought there had been a mutual attraction between Gwen and himself as they'd talked in the airport lounge and during their dinner date, but he could never be certain of his reading of the female mind. Since he'd last seen her, he'd reviewed images and sensations—her friendly personality, the touch of her hand, the quick peck on his cheek, and her enticing facial features and figure. An image of Jennifer strolled through his thinking, but he shoved it aside as he focused on the weekend.

Gwen was waiting at the front entrance to the terminal when he arrived. They held hands for a brief moment as they spoke. She wheeled a bag to the curb and tossed her purse and a smaller case into the back seat while he loaded the larger one into the storage compartment. She touched his arm after they'd fastened the seat belts.

During the twenty-minute drive they talked about her flight, one of the easier trips she'd had this week with the plane filled with tired business types prepared for naps after a quick drink. He told her about his house located in a wooded area five miles from Chester, how he'd purchased the property from a man he'd met during a previous case, and the enjoyment he'd experienced exploring the ten-acre property.

Gwen seemed comfortable immediately in his isolated log home. He showed her through the place, telling her about the modifications he'd made since purchasing it a year ago and plans for future refurbishing.

She removed her uniform jacket and draped it across a chair, then tucked her white blouse neatly into the waist band of her skirt. She slipped off her heels, saying, "The worst part of this job is being on your feet in shoes that cramp your toes."

"You look nice in the uniform," Dave said. "But I guess you get tired of the same outfit every day."

Gwen laughed, "It makes for easy choices. No worries about matching blouses with skirts or slacks every morning."

Dave said, "Let's have a drink on the porch. It's a nice evening."

"I'd like that," she said.

While he made gin and tonics, Gwen explored his living area, the masculine furnishings, a few paintings on the walls, the huge stone fireplace dominating the room.

She asked, "Did you select the paintings? They're nice. Add color to the space."

Dave brought her drink. "Jennifer Watson, my partner, advised me."

Gwen asked, "I'd like to meet her. She has good taste."

In the warm June night, they sipped drinks on the porch swing, listening to the chirping of crickets and the croaking of a frog. Dave pushed the swing with his feet so it rocked gently.

She asked, "You like this, don't you? Away from the noise and bustle of the city."

"Yeah, but sometimes it's too quiet. You feel like you're the only person in the world. It's hard to believe that only three minutes from here you're confronted with traffic jams and impatient drivers."

"I've always lived in big cities, but wondered often how it'd be in an environment like this." She swung her arm toward the sky and surrounding trees.

As the swing swayed gently, they leaned against each other. She curled her legs under her, her feet resting against his leg. He massaged one foot then the other. She smiled at his effort to ease the tightness, saying, "That feels good."

He put his arm around her shoulders. They kissed and remained silent for a time. They kissed again, more deeply. He ran his fingers across her face and neck. She didn't object when he caressed her ankles and legs, then moved across her knee, raising her skirt. She uncoiled and stood, taking him by the hand. He led her inside, up the stairs, and into the bedroom. Their love-making became more passionate then either thought likely.

The next morning, after a prolonged breakfast of pancakes, sausage, juice and coffee, they strolled through his woods and along the small stream. They stopped for a picnic lunch under a huge oak by the bubbling water where the creek coursed over a set of rocks. Back at the house Gwen napped on the couch while Dave worked on flooring in one of the outbuildings. They grilled steaks for dinner and went to bed early.

He drove her to her apartment after lunch on Sunday to give her time to prepare for the coming week's schedule, beginning with an early flight on Monday morning. Back at home Dave jogged along the trails on his property, his mind on Gwen. Maybe he'd found the right person to fill the loneliness he often experienced. Memories reminded him that another time he'd believed he'd married the right person while in his early twenties, but his career involving long absences and perhaps personality differences had intervened. She'd filed for divorce two years after their marriage. Trying to ease the bitterness and frustrations, he'd focused his energies on his job. He'd excelled in the Marines and later in the special forces and had been promoted to the highest non-commissioned rank. He'd made numerous friends, but nothing filled the void of a life partner. Twice he'd failed in relationships since coming to Chester. He intended the one with Gwen to develop without hitches. But the running debate with Miriam, his last failed try, about his feelings for Jennifer wouldn't go away.

On Wednesday morning Jennifer received a call from Anita Chandler's office. The secretary said, "Judge Chandler issued an order today for Biological Assays, Inc. to release to you the records of Maude Frame. She intended the order to include the records of others who might request your representation in the specific case against Black and Redfield. If there is any confusion, please send those names to our office. A copy of her order is in the mail to you."

"Thanks and tell Judge Chandler I appreciate her swift response."

The afternoon mail included the communication from Chandler. With the notice in hand, Jennifer drove to Biological Assays. Without any resistance or questions, the woman at the front, Rose Mitchell, gave her a folder. "These are Mrs. Frame's records. Since the Judge's order didn't list others specifically, I've not tried to guess who they might be."

"I understand," Jennifer said. "I may call you if it becomes necessary to review others."

Back in her office, Jennifer scanned the list of assays and the results for Frame. Most of the names and numbers had little meaning. She'd seen several of the tests, including hemoglobin, hematocrit, albumin, and glucose, on her own physical exam reports, but her physician had included notations showing normal ranges. Once her hemoglobin had been low and he'd prescribed an iron supplement and vitamin C to treat the anemia.

But the data for the DNA type analyses were incomprehensible. She needed assistance in deciphering the strange information. Law school had not included courses in genetics or whatever stuff she was looking at.

She set up an appointment to revisit Rose Mitchell.

Each day the *Register* carried on the inside pages short blurbs about the body found in the woods on the outskirts of the city. Speculation about its identity ranged from a lost hiker to a victim of a gang-related killing. Dental records and DNA were being explored with definitive information promised by the end of the week. No one claimed a relationship to the victim nor had anyone been reported missing.

On Thursday morning Rasmussen called Dave and asked that they meet for lunch at a small family-type restaurant on the outskirts of town. Between bites of chili and cornbread and sips of iced tea, they discussed weather, baseball and crimes prominent in the news. Dave knew his friend intended to talk about something bothering him, but didn't press.

As they completed the chili, Rasmussen said, "Carl Meade confessed to being involved with the murder of Gerald Dewberry, but refuses to name his accomplice. The District Attorney is charging Meade with first degree murder and will push for the death penalty."

"Did ballistics from the second gun I brought in match anything?"

"Nothing in our records."

"Does Meade have an attorney?"

"Some guy from out of town who charges around acting important and high-powered. He's been in to see Meade and tell him the usual stuff—don't talk to anyone without his being present. We don't know who's paying the lawyer, but if we're on the right course, it's probably Black and Redfield."

Rasmussen fingered his tea glass. "I assume you've read or heard about a hiker's body found a few days ago."

"I have, but haven't given it much attention. It didn't seem related to any of our cases."

"The body was too decomposed for a visual identification. But based on the dental records, we're pretty sure the body is that of James Redfield, the former CEO at Black and Redfield. DNA comparisons have been impossible to get because there's not a reliable sample from Redfield and no relative has been found for comparison purposes. I'm telling you this because you've been looking at Gerald Dewberry and people associated with him. You might see a connection between Gerald and Redfield we've missed."

"That's a shocker," Dave said. "Everyone believed Redfield had moved west."

"That was the line put out by the company when he retired. We've checked out some aspects of the story."

"You think he came back and got knocked over in a random hit while roaming around the national forest?"

"Doesn't fit. Redfield wasn't an outdoors type. He was involved with a couple of charitable organizations that supported the arts, but he never did anything like hiking or hunting. We suspect he was killed, the body dumped in the woods where it wouldn't likely be found, and his personal things taken to avoid easy identification."

"Any idea of how he was killed?"

"The Medical Examiner reports he was whacked across the head with a heavy instrument, like a tire iron or metal rod. The cranium had been fractured. The M.E. speculates severe trauma to the brain tissues and internal bleeding caused death."

Dave said, "Maybe this is the link between Black and Redfield and Nicole Farrell's running for her life."

Rasmussen finished his tea and said, "Could be. If the brains behind the murder suspected Gerald knew something about Redfield's death, they'd not hesitate to do him in and anyone he might have confided in. His wife would be a prime suspect."

"You guys running background checks on the new team in the company, DeRosa and his cronies?"

"We've had no reason to until now," Rasmussen said, "but if this body proves to be Redfield, we would initiate checks on DeRosa and his buddy, Hoyt. They're the only new guys in the organization."

Thinking how to help Rasmussen get on track, Dave asked, "What happened to Redfield's home? You might find something there with

DNA—hair on his clothing, toothbrush, something he'd used and not cleaned well."

"He sold his home a couple of weeks before he disappeared. The house was emptied and the new owner has been in for some time now. After selling the property, Redfield lived in the Marriott downtown for ten days. Based on his conversations with bellmen and the front desk, everybody there believed he'd gone west." Rasmussen signaled the waitress for coffee. "We're stuck with no family. His wife died three years ago. For a while we believed there was a son in Seattle, but his close friends confirm he had no children."

"This is really strange," Dave said. "To the public, Redfield sold the company, separated himself from the insurance business, and intended to relocate across the country. Yet he turns up dead in a remote wooded area."

Rasmussen said, "It's true he planned to settle in Seattle, but someone intervened before he tied up loose ends here. He'd put down a month's rent on a condo but never showed."

Dave tried the coffee. "Have you searched Meade's van? If he was the hired gun for Dewberry, maybe he was involved with Redfield. And if Redfield was killed somewhere else and the body moved, could be the van was the vehicle. There might be traces of blood, hair, something left in the van that could contain DNA. I'd bet Meade never cleans the thing."

Rasmussen smiled. "That's why I like talking with you. We've never considered that. It's a long reach, but worth a try." He cut into the slice of lemon pie.

"Maybe you have enough. Dental records are reliable."

"We'll have the forensic boys check out the van though. We'd like to tie this up pretty tight."

Dave shoved aside the pie plate and drained the coffee cup. "I'll keep my eyes open. For now, I'll assume the body is Redfield."

"That's a safe bet and the one we're basing our investigation on," Rasmussen said. He picked up the check. "I'll let the city buy your lunch this time."

Dave slipped out of the booth. "That'll probably cost me in the future, but I enjoyed our discussion."

Jennifer met with Rose Mitchell in the conference room of Biological Assays, Inc. She laid out the results of Maude Frame's blood analyses. "I don't believe these routine things are important to my inquiry, but I'd like you to explain in lay terms some of these genetic tests."

Sitting next to Jennifer, Mitchell pointed to a series of codes, all composed of the letters A, C, G, and T, but in different orders. "These letters represent nucleotides, the base components of DNA. Segments, but not every piece, of the DNA molecule are genes. The groupings recorded on the page represent genes within the DNA of the individual we tested. We were asked to check for the presence of several genes for those workers at GM. Those genes are signals to a physician or geneticist that the probability of certain diseases are more likely to occur in that individual than in the population generally."

Jennifer asked, "Can you be more specific?"

Placing the tip of her pen on a group of letters, Rose said, "Sure. This gene is prevalent in women who will likely have breast cancer. It's not an absolute, but predicts the chances as being high. Based on our limited knowledge, these are regarded as reliable indicators and tells the person to adopt life styles that reduce the probability and alerts the physician to conduct routine checks to catch the actual cancer appearance as early as possible."

Rose continued, pointing to a gene containing a dozen letters. "This gene is being used by health professionals as a predictor of Type 2 diabetes, but several other factors come into play making its reliability less certain than for some others diseases."

Jennifer said, "Mrs. Frame had several of these present. Does that mean she's in poor health or has a greater risk for a major disease in the future?"

"Maybe both. But in her case an insurance company would be interested in life expectancy. If the person dies younger than normal, the pay out becomes less profitable for them. I've heard of organizations running these genetic checks on applicants for positions. They screen out the individuals with increased risk of contracting major illnesses during their careers. Saves health costs, reduces turnover, and keeps the premiums lower if they have a healthy work force. Also, the employees will be more productive if they are healthy."

Jennifer said, "I've had no reason to research the cases, but there are court challenges to this practice. Attorneys are arguing these tests invade the privacy of an individual to an unacceptable degree."

Rose returned her pen to the pocket of her lab coat. "I've heard. We've discussed the potential for our professional staff spending time as expert witnesses in such trials. It'd be costly to us because of lost time, but it would enhance our visibility."

"You'd be reimbursed as a witness."

"I know, but it's a different hassle than we're used to."

Jennifer had gained immediate respect for this professional woman and took advantage of the open conversation mode they'd adopted to ask, "Would you speculate that Black and Redfield used the results of Maude Frame's exam as a basis for dropping her policy?"

Rose smiled. "It'd be a good probability, but difficult to prove. I'd be unable to testify with certainty that's the case."

Jennifer said, "Why do it, if you're not planning to use the results for your own gain? Their unwillingness to release the data to Mrs. Frame tells me they had no interest in assisting her with her health."

"True, but if I were you, I'd look for comparisons. Find some of Frame's coworkers who underwent the medical screening, but whose policies were not cancelled."

Rose ran her hand across her forehead. "I'm going to reveal something I probably shouldn't, but I don't like companies who do this kind of stuff. My brother was dropped from a good job because he had the predictive gene for prostate cancer. My father and one of our brothers died from the disease, so the probability would be even greater for him. If you wish to make those comparisons I suggested, I'll give you the names of the workers from the GM plant who were tested by Black and Redfield. How you use the information is your call, but I trust you won't divulge how you obtained the information."

Jennifer said, "I'll charge you a dollar and we'll call it client-lawyer privilege. A court will not force me to tell."

Rose stood and straightened her lab coat where it had crinkled in the back. "Give me a minute."

She returned with a brown envelope. "Here is the list of the people from GM."

Rose handed her a dollar bill and a blank receipt form. Jennifer filled in the information and signed it.

"Let's hope I never need to call you for actual representation," Rose said, smiling.

Jennifer shook her hand. "You've been more helpful than I dreamed. I hope you won't hear from us again. But after this case is closed, I'd like to meet for lunch."

Jennifer left, rewarded with critical information and knowing she'd made a new friend. Jennifer hoped any follow up of Rose's suggestion didn't place Rose or her associates in physical danger or make them the target of some law firm determined to discredit Biological Assays and Rose personally.

TWELVE

Ellie and Jennifer set out to contact the forty-two names on the list given to her by Rose Mitchell. Following a consistent strategy of inquiry, they explained that Watson and Randle was representing a client who worked at GM and were checking to determine if other workers had experienced the same fate regarding insurance coverage. Neither the name of the client nor the source of their information was revealed.

The first name on Jennifer's part of the list, John Bannister, had worked as a machinist in the GM plant for eighteen years. He'd undergone the tests at the clinic and recalled giving a blood sample.

Jennifer asked, "Has your insurance policy been altered since then?"

"It got cancelled," Bannister said. "No good reason given. I called Black and Redfield at the number on the letter, but the woman was useless. Just said the company was dropping the policies of a lot of people because of the poor economy."

"Have you received reimbursement from them?"

"Not yet, but she said I'd get a check in a month to six weeks. It's a return of part of the money I paid in, but that's not any consolation. Now I have no life insurance and at my age, it's too costly to go with another company. I worry what'll happen to my wife if I die first."

Jennifer said, "Mr. Bannister, this may seem overly personal, but it's important. Is there a history of any major disease in your family, such as heart problems, diabetes, cancer?"

After a moment of reflection, Bannister said, "My dad died from colon cancer when he was fifty-four."

"What about other relatives?"

Again, a pause while Bannister remembered. "His brother passed away in his fifties, but I'm not certain it was cancer. He lived in California and we seldom heard from him. We got a note from his daughter telling us he'd died after a long illness. We all figured it was exposure to something in their childhood that caused their early deaths from the disease or just plain bad luck."

Jennifer said, "I'd like to check out the reason for the cancellation of your policy. To do that, I need to review the results of those blood tests. If you don't object, I'll obtain the records and try to determine if there's a defensible basis for the actions of Black and Redfield."

"Yeah, go ahead. I never got the results myself, but that didn't matter. I can't decipher most of those things anyway."

"I'll call you back in a few days," Jennifer said, "and let you know what I've found."

"Will I get money?"

"It's too early to know, but if Black and Redfield cancelled a worker's insurance without just cause, we can file a suit to reinstate policies. There could be payment for damages and reimbursement of any expenses clients had as an outcome of their actions. But first I must assess the rationale for the cancellations. Then I can tell you if going forward poses a reasonable chance of success."

Bannister said, "I hope you can make the bastards pay."

"I can't make any promises, but will get back to you."

She'd progressed through four names before she had to meet with a woman accusing her supervisor of sexual harassment. When the woman had called to set up an appointment, Jennifer's initial reaction had been skeptical. But she agreed to hear her story and discuss potential actions.

By mid-afternoon on the second day of calling and recalling because of missed connections, Ellie and Jennifer had contacted each person on the Mitchell list. Fourteen had their policies cancelled by Black and Redfield. Each one had received a letter from the company. None believed they'd received an adequate explanation.

Jennifer submitted the names of those to Judge Chandler's office with a note she'd appreciate having those records released by Biological Assays.

Rasmussen called Dave. "I wanted to let you know we checked out Meade's van, but came up empty. Apparently, he'd cleaned it thoroughly the day before you brought him in."

"For a character like Meade, that's suspicious in itself," Dave said. When Meade had scrambled into his van after the altercation in the parking lot, Dave had seen an abundance of papers, drink cups, rags and unidentifiable items on the floor and seats.

"I know, but we can't do anything on such reasoning. We'd never make it stick."

"The dental records for Redfield should be sufficient."

"They are, but the D.A. is pushing us to find more corroborating evidence. The real problem is we don't have a viable suspect."

"What about Meade?"

"He maintains he didn't whack Redfield. Meade claims he was in New Jersey until six weeks ago. We're checking the places he said he was employed. If his story can't be confirmed, we'll pressure him. My gut feeling is he's telling the truth."

Dave asked, "Back to evidence on Redfield personally, does the hotel have anything he used? I don't understand a lot about DNA, but you're able to get samples from some unusual places."

"Our forensics team has checked it out pretty well. We're trying to gain access to a safety deposit box he had at the Farmers' and Merchant's Bank. There could be envelopes he'd licked, or skin cells lost as he sorted through the contents."

"Good luck."

Jennifer sat across the conference table from Rose Mitchell at Biological Assays. Rose handed her a stack of papers. "Here are the records of those people on Judge Chandler's order. I took the liberty of noting in the margins what the genes represent."

"That will help us," Jennifer said. "Were you surprised at the number?"

"Yes," Rose said, nodding. "One-third seems a high proportion, but we don't have much experience with genetic assays yet. I don't know what would be expected in the population."

Jennifer said, "Your recommendation about doing comparisons turned out to be valuable. These fourteen had policies dropped. I assumed none of the others had a genetic marker predictive of a life-shortening disease appear in their assay."

"I checked out of my own curiosity. None of the markers appears on any record except those fourteen."

Jennifer said, "Then only those with the incriminating genes have their policies dropped. Based on these comparisons, Black and Redfield used these markers as a screening tool to drop clients."

"That'd be my conclusion," Rose said, then smiled. "In fact, that's about the only logical deduction you can make of those data."

Jennifer stood. "Now I have to convince the court the practice is illegal and there's not solid precedents to guide me or the judges. Nevertheless, you've been a great help."

Rose shifted in her chair. "I know I sound like a broken record, but I hope we can avoid court appearances."

"We'll do our best to keep you out of the system, but I may want to call you as an expert witness."

Rose frowned. "I'll do that, but it's not something I look forward to doing."

Following the session with Mitchell, Jennifer arranged a meeting of all the GM workers who'd had policies dropped. They crowded into her office, three standing in the doorway to Ellie's space, at 7:30 p.m., the only time she could get them all together because of work schedules. Dave stood behind those in the door.

Jennifer began by telling them the approach she'd taken to determine their situation, reminding them she'd called to obtain their permission to move forward. She said, "It's highly likely Black and Redfield used your genetic make-up as a basis for canceling your policies. So you better understand what I'm telling you, the presence of certain genes increase the probability you will have a serious disease earlier in life than the general population. This is not certain, but is a reasonable predictor." A hum of muttered concern swept across the group. They looked at each other as though seeking consolation and support.

Bannister asked, "Should we tell our family doctors?"

"By all means. I'll give you a copy of your records to take with you."

Jennifer continued, "I've agreed to sue Black and Redfield on behalf of Mrs. Frame and Mrs. Fitzgerald for the reinstatement of their policies. If any of you wish to be included, I can do that, but it's your option."

A burly, red-faced man in the doorway asked, "What's the cost?"

"I've agreed to submit the suit for no charge to you. If we're successful in court, I'll ask for Black and Redfield to cover court costs and to pay punitive damages for the way you've been treated. If damages are awarded, the firm will receive one-third of those monies. If nothing is given, the firm will treat the case as a pro bono situation and will not receive anything. And neither will you."

The same man, his tone tinged with insolence, asked, "You must think there's a good chance of success."

Jennifer ignored the suggestion she wouldn't attempt the suit if she couldn't predict success. "Frankly, I don't know. You must understand, we're in an area where there is little case law or previous court decisions to guide us. I can't predict how judges will react or how they might rule on evidence. In many ways, we're plowing new ground and can't know where the rocks will be."

From a seat near Jennifer's desk, Bannister said, "I suggest we all join. The more of us, the stronger will be the case."

In her frail voice from the corner, Maude Frame said, "I agree with that. I hope you all will allow Ms. Watson to represent you."

From the side, a man asked, "What if I wanted to use my own lawyer?"

Jennifer said, "You could do that if you're more comfortable. I could work with other attorneys or you could file separate suits. But I believe we have a stronger case if you stick together rather than going it alone. But, it's your decision. You may want to discuss the issue with your family and with your attorney before you decide." Involving another attorney who might know more about genetic issues than she could be beneficial. But not many were willing to take on contingency cases when the odds were unknown.

Bannister asked, "How soon do you need to know?"

Jennifer said, "I'd like to move as quickly as possible, but I will need time to search for other court rulings and to prepare documents for filing the suit. It would help if you would let me know your wishes within ten days. But if for some reason you need more time, I can work with you. I only ask that you not delay until we're in court. Adding clients at that point could be regarded as suspicious and might damage the entire case."

The crowd began to stir and rise. Over the bustle of chairs being moved and conversation starting, Jennifer said, "If we don't hear from you within ten days, we'll call you to confirm your decisions."

Bannister came forward to stand in front of her desk. "You can sign me on now. I don't need to think about it any longer."

Standing near, three others nodded and signed the agreements Jennifer had prepared.

After the last person had departed, Jennifer went into Dave's office. She said, "Thanks for staying. I had no idea how this would go."

"It went well. Most will join with Frame. The guy in the back asking all the questions likely won't. He was muttering about it being another ploy for some lawyer to make money."

Jennifer smiled. "Let's hope that happens, but it's a long shot in this situation."

"Can I buy you a drink? We can walk to Gibbons. It's a nice night."

"I'd like that," she said. "I'll drop my things in the car so I won't have to come back up here."

The usual dinner crowd in Gibbons had thinned by the time they arrived. But several tables were filled with diners. Around one table six men had their heads together as though conferring about some important deal. Dave and Jennifer found a booth along the side near the back. Both ordered draft beer.

While they waited, Jennifer asked, "How's your social life? You've been pretty close-mouthed lately." A mischievous gleam lighted her eyes.

"Actually, things are looking up. I met this stewardess while tracking Nicole Farrell. We've spent some time together and seem to mesh well. What about you?"

"Went with George to dinner on Saturday. It's okay."

George had been in her life for two years, but Dave suspected she was looking for someone else. At one time she'd confessed George was comfortable, but they'd not discovered any real chemistry. Dave had been surprised more males hadn't focused on her. She was bright, attractive, even sexy when she wore nice dresses and gave up the boxy pantsuits she seemed to prefer at work. Before they'd become partners, he'd considered asking her out. After they united professionally, he decided it was a bad idea to be involved with such a close associate. Several acquaintances assumed their relationship was more than professional, nodding and winking when either disclaimed a personal interest.

The beer steins were placed and they drank, quiet for a while. Jennifer's eyes swept the room, then stopped at the group of men, now noisier than earlier. They laughed and clinked drink glasses, then shoved away their chairs.

Lowering her voice to the point Dave had to lean across the table to hear, she said, "Rogers Morton, the account exec from Black and Redfield, is in that group that's breaking up. He's the guy with glasses and brown thinning hair. I bet it's a bunch from the company, probably celebrating the screwing of clients."

Dave twisted slightly to see the group. "Has he recognized you?"

"I think so."

After a few seconds, she said, "In fact, he's coming over."

Morton stopped at the booth. "Ms. Watson, nice to see you." He scanned her face and upper torso, avoiding any recognition of Dave. Jennifer said, "Mr. Morton, I'm surprised to see you in here. But I'd like you to meet my partner, Dave Randle."

Morton said, "I've heard of you." He kept his hands clasped in front of his waist.

Dave said, "Jennifer has told me about meeting with you about a client."

Morton stepped back a couple of feet. "I hope, Ms. Watson, our last discussion ended any further probe of our practices at Black and Redfield."

"I'm afraid that's not over," Jennifer said, "but I can't reveal anything more."

"You do recall my suggestion?"

Jennifer glanced at Dave. "I didn't appreciate your sending that goon around to try to intimidate me."

"Not my doing," Morton said.

Dave said, "Your man didn't deny who hired him, but I'm certain it won't happen again."

"And if it does," Morton said, his focus now on Dave's face.

"We're going to charge Black and Redfield with harassment," Dave said.

Morton glared at the two for a moment, then turned away to join a couple of friends waiting at the door for him.

Dave said, "Maybe I shouldn't have said anything but I hate to be threatened."

Jennifer smiled. "I was afraid you'd do more."

THIRTEEN

The dirty Ford pickup idled behind Dave when he stopped for the traffic light at Main and 24th. He gave it little attention, other than to confirm the presence of two males in the cab. But when the truck followed him until he turned into the parking lot behind the building, his instincts warned him he was being tailed.

Jennifer was waiting for him when he entered the office. "I'd like to discuss the Maude Frame case with you and Ellie. We must decide the direction we'll take."

After filling coffee mugs, they assembled around the small conference table in the corner of Jennifer's office. She said, "Black and Redfield dropped those clients because they'd identified a genetic trait predicting a high probability of a disease. I need to decide the approach to take. I'd like Ellie to search for precedents. There won't be many, but you may find something that could improve our chances."

Ellie said, "I'll do a search on Westlaw this afternoon."

"Focus on genetic diseases, insurance coverage, hiring and retention practices of large companies. Big organizations are the ones who'd be in a position to use genetic data to screen out applicants. Small organizations won't have the capability to pay for the expensive testing."

Dave asked, "Can I do anything? I'm chasing a lead on a disgruntled husband who thinks his wife is having an affair, but that can wait."

"A friend of mine told me there are rumors around the city administration building that Judge Young has been compromised by Black and Redfield. If he has, I'd like to avoid his ruling on the case. Even if I know he's in their pocket, I may get stuck with him, but I'd be prepared for an appeal."

"Where should I start?"

Jennifer pondered for a moment, brushing her hair away from her face, a habit she employed when considering options. "Start with Andy Chafin, Young's clerk. I'm not sure he'd know about the relationship between Young and Black and Redfield, and he may not tell you if he did. But a reading of his reactions might be useful. Maybe talk with a couple of defense attorneys who've had cases with Young recently. If possible, find out if Young has made any rulings involving Black and Redfield in the past few months."

Ellie said, "I can check the court records easily enough."

"Discovering the ethical lapses of a judge sounds tricky," Dave said.

"It will be. The rumors about Young may be wrong, but I doubt it. He had no apparent reason to deny Maude Frame's access to her records. That makes me suspicious." Jennifer paused, looking at the two of them, then added, "I'll talk with my friend again. She may be able to fill in some details about her suspicsions."

Dave had settled into his chair, thinking about how best to get Chafin to open up about Young, and booted up his computer when Rasmussen phoned. "I wanted to let you know your suggestion about Redfield's safety deposit box paid off. The forensic crew found a saliva sample. We're checking the DNA match."

"I bet it's Redfield, but why did he get killed?"

"Good question. Could be a random hit. Some punk saw an affluent-looking man, set out to take his money, Redfield resisted, and got banged across the head. Hauled him to the woods and dumped the body."

"Maybe," Dave said. "A lot of murders happen that way, but in Redfield's case, I'd guess it's something different. I'd look at those hoods hired by Black and Redfield."

Rasmussen said, "Meade's alibi checked out. He wasn't here when Redfield got bumped. Plus, it doesn't make sense for Black and Redfield to go after the old guy. He was leaving the area. They could ignore any arguments he might have had with the new management."

"Unless he threatened to turn them in to the regulatory agency for malpractice of some sort. Or drop hints to the press."

"You don't like those people, do you?"

"They're suspicious."

At 12:15 Dave walked to Gibbons for lunch. Working on a brief at her desk while she ate a sandwich, Jennifer had declined when he'd invited her to join him. On the sidewalk he automatically scanned the area. He didn't see the truck or anyone lolling around. Everyone seemed to be rushing to some destination, their eyes shifting from one person to another, nodding to acquaintances, dodging around slower walkers, as they scurried along in the bright noonday sunshine.

The restaurant was filled. A couple had taken his favorite corner booth. He eased onto a stool between two men at the bar and ordered a pastrami on rye and a draft beer.

By the time he'd finished the sandwich, the crowd had thinned. He'd drained the last of the beer and reached for his wallet, when Gibbons came along, the ever-present towel draped across an arm.

Gibbons said, "How you doing? Staying out of trouble?" A mischievous grin split the old man's face and showed his crooked yellowing teeth. He swiped the towel through a wet spot on the counter.

"No problems lately," Dave said. "How about you?" He dropped a tip by the plate and turned on the stool.

Gibbons placed his hand on Dave's arm. "Before you go, I need to tell you something." He glanced around the room, now almost empty of the lunch crowd.

Gibbons leaned onto the bar. His voice became little more than a gruff whisper. "Yesterday I heard there was a contract out on you. Last night I checked around with a couple of sources. They say it's true. So be careful."

"Anybody know who?"

Gibbons shook his head. "If they do, they won't say. My guess is they don't know."

"Thanks. I'll stay alert."

He paid the cashier, paused at the door for a moment, then headed toward the office. After two blocks, he ducked into a pharmacy, circled the stacks of merchandise, and returned to the front entrance. No one had followed or was visible nearby. Maybe Gibbons' sources were wrong. Then he remembered the truck. He recalled Rogers Morton's conversation with Jennifer. He felt exposed and pissed.

Dave fretted about the information from Gibbons through the afternoon, unable to concentrate on reading a background file related to genetic data and privacy issues. He had always been the hunter during his service career and never the target unless he or one of his team inadvertently exposed the operation. After mentally berating himself for wasting time, he resolved to be alert and ready, but now he had to get on with his assignment in helping Jennifer succeed against the insurance company.

Deciding the truck would follow his Blazer, he walked the ten blocks to keep his 5:15 appointment with Andy Chafin at the lounge in the downtown Marriott. Alert to any unusual activity around him, he dodged through the crowd of afternoon shoppers and professionals leaving work for the day.

Based on Jennifer's description, Dave located Chafin at a back table, partially hidden behind a plant, and out of the view of anyone passing through the lobby. In his dark suit and conservative tie, Chafin had already learned the uniform of his profession.

Dave introduced himself, shook Chafin's hand and sat adjacent to him. They ordered draft beers when the waitress appeared.

Dave said, "I appreciate your meeting me."

Chafin viewed the gathering throng. "I hope this won't take long. My wife doesn't like me to be late for dinner."

"Then I'll start," Dave said, " by asking how long you've been with Judge Young?"

"Since July. I finished law school in May, passed the bar in June, and was offered this clerkship."

"It's worked out well?" Dave asked, shifting to allow the waitress to place the mugs.

"So far. I'm learning a lot. Young takes time to explain things that might not be obvious to a neophyte. I've appreciated his efforts."

"He has a fine reputation around the city and I expect that carries beyond."

Chafin sipped his beer. "It does. One of my law professors recommended I seek the clerkship position with Young. Everybody knows who he is and thinks I'm lucky to have him as a mentor."

Dave said, "As I told you over the phone, I'm following up on the Maude Frame issue between Young and Jennifer Watson." When he'd called, Chafin had been reluctant to meet with him, but Dave persuaded him it could be important and promised their conversation would be confidential.

Chafin squirmed around in his chair, turned his head away from two men taking an adjacent table. "I told Ms. Watson I didn't know why he denied her request. I thought he'd explain his rationale, but he seemed withdrawn and close-minded when I asked. I didn't press because he's been different the past few weeks."

"How do you mean?"

"Worried, disorganized, walks around in a daze. I've found him a couple of times staring out the window in the middle of a busy day. He wasn't like that when I first came."

Dave drank from his mug, watching Chafin who shifted in his chair to view the crowd, lowering his head almost to the table top.

Dave asked, "Has anything happened in Young's life to cause him to be distracted? Sometimes problems beyond work overwhelm you and it's impossible to focus on your job."

Chafin's face screwed into a deep frown. "I'm reluctant to tell you, but there have been rumors of payoff and rigging of a case. I don't believe it."

"Can you think of any other reason for Young's erratic behavior in the last few weeks?"

"He doesn't share much of his private life with me, but his secretary, Janice Wiley, told me Young's son had gotten into some scrape. Young intervened to keep him out of prison and the case was settled with the son being placed on a long probation."

"What's the son's name?"

"Same as his father. He's known as Junior."

"Why did she confide in you?"

Chafin said, "I asked her if Young was ill. I was trying to pin his aloofness on his being diagnosed with some major disease. That's when she told me he was worried about his son. The boy is twenty-two, flunked out of college, and has become entangled with a group of shady characters who are into drugs and other illegal activities."

Dave finished his beer. "Anything else about his behavior seem unusual?"

"My concern has been elevated because lawyers representing Black and Redfield have been in to see him a half-dozen times in the last month. They've just barged in and demanded an audience. He's allowed them to screw up his schedule pretty badly at times, even delayed a court hearing by thirty minutes one day."

"But you don't know the specific case?"

"No. I've suspected it has something to do with the son, but Young has never talked about those meetings."

"Have you been personally involved with the Black and Redfield attorneys?"

Shaking his head, Chafin said, "No, it's been off the record as far as Judge Young is concerned. He updates me on most things going on in the office, but not the Black and Redfield issue." Chafin twisted his beer mug, his face lined with concern. "Now I'm worried about getting associated with some scandal. I've considered resigning, but that would look bad, like I couldn't perform satisfactorily and Young had chased me."

Dave wanted to advise the young man who had inadvertently been caught in a web of intrigue and could be damaged professionally, but he didn't have the experience with such matters to be helpful. Talking with Jennifer might be a first step. She'd know the rules of the game by which lawyers operated.

Dave said, "Stick it out, but don't get involved with those people from Black and Redfield. If they pressure you to do something wrong, call me."

Chafin's eyes widened. "I'm not important to them. And there's nothing I could do for them."

"Keep it in mind," Dave said, "and thanks for talking with me. You've been helpful." He dropped bills on the table to cover the check and tip.

Chafin stood and said, "I'm going to the men's room before I leave."

"See you around," Dave said.

On the street, Dave stood against the hotel's brick facade and eyed the street in both directions. Nothing out of the ordinary caught his eye. He left the hotel in the direction opposite to the office and turned right at the corner. A block later, he veered right again.

He strode, almost jogging, along the street parallel to Main, cut along a side street of older homes, then approached the parking lot behind the office building from still another side street.

He eased the Blazer onto Main Street, after waiting for the traffic signal to interrupt the flow of traffic long enough to make a left turn. Two blocks along Main, he passed the truck parked in front of an apartment building. The truck pulled out and followed, two cars behind him.

The truck maintained its position for five blocks. As traffic gained momentum after being stopped for a red light, Dave jerked his Blazer into a parking slot without signaling or noticeable slowing. He braked hard to avoid plowing into the rear of a parked Volvo. Drivers behind honked, irritated by his maneuver, and sped past. The truck driver hesitated, caught off-guard, but had no option other than to keep moving.

As it passed, Dave focused on the license plate. He wrote the number on a pad from his pocket. He pulled back into the flow of traffic, turned right at the next intersection, did a U-turn and parked so he could see the movement on the major street, suspecting his pursuer would backtrack and try to regain his position. After fifteen minutes, Dave gave up and continued toward his house, alert to any other tailing vehicle. He accepted he had to become more aggressive or these guys would wait for the perfect opportunity.

FOURTEEN

As soon as he reached home Dave called the Chester police station and asked for Rasmussen. To his surprise Rasmussen came on the line, growling, "What's up? I was on the way out."

"I took a chance you'd still be in and could help with something." He told about Gibbons' warning and the truck following him.

Rasmussen sighed. "You'd like me to trace the license for you?"

"It'd help. I can wait around until the idiots try something and hope they screw up the first time, but I'd rather gain an edge." He read the number, then repeated it for Rasmussen.

"I'll set the search in motion. It'll be Monday before I know. I'd rather not have a weekend fill-in call you and figure out I've obtained the information for someone outside the system."

"Thanks." Dave would've liked to have the trace sooner, but he didn't want to push Rasmussen.

The partners and Ellie met on Monday morning around Jennifer's conference table. Dave relayed the information he'd discovered with Chafin. Jennifer had learned nothing new from her friend.

Ellie's internet search had been productive. "There's quite a lot of information about genetic background checks and employment, although most employers rely on applicants revealing family histories of problems rather than going to the expense of actual testing for suspected genes. Because of a Presidential Executive Order, Federal agencies are not allowed to ask about those issues, but private employers continue to use the practice.

"One important development was a suit filed by the Equal Employment Opportunity Commission against the Burlington Northern Santa Fe Railway for genetic tests to determine if job injury claims were predisposed to symptoms associated with carpal tunnel syndrome. Those employees weren't told why they were required to give blood samples. The company stopped the practice as a result of the suit."

Ellie referred to pages of notes and printouts. "If Black and Redfield has done what we suspect them of, they've gone against the trend by focusing on low-wage workers. Most companies doing genetic testing are those who are hiring highly paid employees requiring investments in their training and development. They don't want to do that if the worker, usually a salaried professional, doesn't stick around because of some early onset disease."

"Has that been challenged?" Jennifer asked, twisting her coffee cup.

"There have been arguments that it's unlawful because the employer might be classifying the applicant as disabled before there is any sign of the disease. That goes against the Americans with Disabilities Act."

Jennifer asked, "Anything about using genetic backgrounds to deny or cancel insurance coverage?"

"I didn't find anything. But I saw one article suggesting insurance companies would be inclined to deny coverage if a serious disease appeared likely. I didn't have time to explore for denials of coverage by insurers for individuals outside the work place, but you know it happens based on revelations by an applicant. If you have breast cancer or diabetes or a family history of those diseases, an insurance company is less likely to sell you a policy."

"Or, they jack up the premiums so most people can't afford the policy," Jennifer said.

"True."

"I've read that many states have laws prohibiting so-called genetic discrimination. Did you run across that?"

"You're correct, but laws are not comprehensive. Legal scholars have described the statutes as piecemeal and full of loopholes. And most of the laws on the books have not been tested in court cases. Even the edict from the Employment Commission has not been challenged. It's an evolving situation and will gain momentum as science finds out more about the genetic code and can tie specific genes to potential health problem."

Jennifer smiled and said, "You found a lot. Good job."

"There's more speculation and editorializing than fact," Ellie said, "and it's changing rapidly."

Jennifer concluded, "So Black and Redfield went the extra step of testing rather than depending on questions about personal or family history. And they never revealed their reasons. Maybe the best approach would be to charge them with unlawful invasion of privacy or failure to obey the Disabilities Act."

Ellie said, "The act has enough support to hold up in a court."

Dave said, "I'm going to follow through on the possibility that Black and Redfield is coercing Judge Young because of something his son did. That seems the most likely spot he could be vulnerable."

"What about your errant wife case?"

"I'll follow her this afternoon. Her pattern has been to leave home after lunch on Mondays and Thursdays and return around 5:00 or 5:30. Last week, I lost her in the crowd downtown. I think she went into the Marriott from the mall entrance, but I'll be more vigilant today."

Jennifer chuckled, "If she leaves home at all."

"If she doesn't, I'll waste another half-day of the husband's money."

Jennifer stood. "Let's get together again Wednesday morning."

Dave refilled his coffee mug and phoned Rasmussen at 9:30 to ask about the license check on the truck.

Rasmussen said, "I was getting ready to call you. The vehicle is registered to Jasper Hicks at an address in East St. Louis."

Dave asked, "Anything locally?"

"Nothing. He's probably a hired gun who moves around."

Dave said, "Thanks. I'll work out a strategy."

"Be careful. Some of these guys are pros. They're not just some bum who'll try anything for a few bucks."

Dave asked, "About another subject, can you tell me about the problem of Judge Young's son?"

Rasmussen hesitated, coughed a couple of times, then said, "He represents one of the most frustrating incidents I've experienced. The kid got caught dealing drugs by our undercover squad. They had followed him for weeks, put together solid evidence, and were pushing for a heavy sentence. Then the case got squashed without a plausible explanation. We suspect the prosecutor caved in to some pressure to protect Young but I didn't try to find out the real reason. The kid's on probation, but it's a matter of time before he's arrested again."

"I take it this was not his first offense?"

"He's had several problems, mostly minor, but escalating in severity. Now that he's into the drug business, he's headed for major trouble. They won't rescue him again."

"Who were his lawyers?"

"A couple of out-of-town attorneys. I assumed Young had lined them up to keep the flak down in the local legal community."

"Thanks again. You're always helpful."

"Someday my tips will land us both in hot water."

Dave replaced the receiver, thinking about the pickup drivers with the contract. He'd not seen them on the way in this morning but they were around. Now he needed to know where they had positioned themselves and work out a plan to gain an advantage.

He left the building through the back door into the parking lot. He cut through a hedge of lilac bushes between their office complex and a strip of small shops, a laundromat, and a used bookstore. He hurried for four blocks and returned to Main. Edging along in the shadow of buildings, he progressed two blocks before he spied the truck parked under an elm and facing the entrance to the entrance of their parking lot. Vehicles could be seen regardless of the direction they departed the office. His Blazer was an easy target.

At 1:00 he parked across the street from the home of Edgar and Grace Smithson. He'd taken a cab from the office to the Avis rental car agency, leased a Toyota Corolla, and now waited for Grace to make her usual move.

Promptly at 1:15, she emerged from the side door of the house, looked up and down the street and climbed into her white Pontiac. After she'd turned the corner, he followed.

Guessing she'd follow the same plan as before, Dave passed her on the heavily-used four-lane Maple Avenue when she slowed for a traffic signal. He parked in the four-story garage between the downtown mall and the hotel and took up a station at the news stand inside the Marriott a few feet from the mall entrance.

Five minutes later Grace walked by him without a glance in his direction. Dressed in a pink summer dress, her heels clicking on the marble floor, she attracted the attention of those in the lobby as she made her way to the bank of elevators. Along with four others, Dave followed her into the car.

Two men left at the sixth floor. At the tenth floor, Grace exited. Dave got off at eleven and walked down the stairs to the tenth. By then Grace had disappeared. He assumed a vigil at a three-chair waiting area at the end of the hall. Boredom set in soon. He skimmed a magazine some-one had left on the table. A housekeeper eyed him curiously, returned his smile, and entered a suite along the hall. Not wishing to chance the woman would notify security if he was still there when she finished the suite, he waited in the stairwell until she emerged and pushed a cart of cleaning supplies and dirty linens onto the service elevator. He returned to the comfort of the soft chair.

After two hours, he'd begun to suspect Grace had pulled the same ruse he'd employed by getting off at a different floor and walking up or down to her rendezvous. He paced along the hall for a while, viewed the downtown scene from the window for a few minutes, stood by the elevators as though waiting for a car, his mind reviewing his strategy with the guys chasing him, and remembering his time with Gwen on Saturday. They'd enjoyed dinner at a nice place, gone into a lounge for an drink, danced to the music of a trio, and spent the night at her place. He believed their relationship had taken another positive step.

Three hours after she'd entered the hotel, Grace emerged from room 1024, only three doors down from Dave's station. He delayed until she disappeared on the elevator, checked the room number to be certain, and returned to his chair. Fifteen minutes later a tall, black-haired man, dressed in a dark business suit, left the room and boarded the elevator.

Dave gave him sufficient time to depart the hotel before he went downstairs and approached the front desk. To the young female clerk, he said, "I happened to be on the tenth floor when this gentleman left. He dropped a set of papers near the stairwell. I'd been to the ice ma-chine and wasn't dressed enough to chase him here, but if you'd give me his address, I'd be glad to deliver the package to him. He checked out of room 1024." He lifted a stack of papers he'd grabbed from a reading table in the lobby.

She said, "Maybe it'd be better if we held the item. He'll come back."

"Maybe, but he may not remember where he lost it. It might be important or it could be nothing, but in either case he'd like to retrieve it as soon as possible."

"Do you know him personally?"

"No, but I've seen him around the city. I know he's local."

She hesitated, looked around for someone to ask about the request, then smiled and said, "We usually don't give out names of guests, but in this case, I guess it'd be okay."

She fingered her computer for several seconds, then said, "The person who paid for the room is Thomas Guidry. I don't have a home address."

"Thanks, I'll find him in the telephone directory and get the package to him." He hurried away before she caught on to his ruse and called hotel security.

He drove the Corolla past their office building on a back street, circled onto Main and approached the building so he'd pass the truck if it were still there.

In heavy traffic, he passed the truck, the two men slouched in the cab. The vehicle had not moved since morning. Dave went around an eight block area and parked three cars behind the truck. They had to move soon. If he was guessing correctly, they wouldn't wait until dark and chance missing the Blazer. They'd acknowledge he'd given them the slip, give up the chase for today, and try again tomorrow.

At 6:30, the passenger door opened and a man, dressed in jeans and a blue sports shirt, trotted to the driveway into the parking lot. He disappeared for thirty seconds then appeared again, running back to the truck. He opened his hands and said something to the driver. Dave grinned at their confusion. They'd maintained their lookout all day and something had gone awry. The Blazer was in the lot, but the building was dark.

After a couple of minutes, the truck pulled into the line of traffic, now thinning as the downtown emptied for the night. Dave waited for a car to pass, then followed.

Several turns and three miles later, the truck parked in front of an old residence now used as a rooming house for low-wage workers or older men who had no home or family. Dave stopped a half-block away in front of a seedy looking bar and grill. His pursuers entered the house, rifle cases held beside their body to partially obscure the weapons. Dave eased past the house, 210 Blount, and circled the neighborhood once to gain a feel for the territory. Once a middle-class area, the homes had eroded as the owners moved away and the new landlords failed to maintain the structures.

He drove home with a sense of accomplishment while reviewing his plan for the night.

FIFTEEN

At 9:15 Dave parked the Corolla across the street from 210 Blount. Hicks' truck was still in front of the house. Dave delayed a minute as he surveyed the surroundings. A brown-and-white mongrel lapping at a liquid spilled on the sidewalk raised his head when Dave stopped, but returned to his interest. Two older men meandered toward the corner bar, attracted by the flickering neon sign with two letters dark. When they entered, Dave stepped out of the car and to the side of the truck, shielding himself from anyone looking out the windows of 210. He checked his gun in the holster and adjusted his beret. He'd put on his special forces fatigues and boots, thinking he'd gain some psychological advantage if he were dressed like a trained killer, but now he felt a bit foolish.

He passed the edge of the porch and crept along the side of the structure. He avoided a rusting sheet of tin and an eavestrough that had dropped from the roof. The blare of a television drew him to a window through which he saw two men, slouched in upholstered chairs that had seen better days. The rifles leaned against the wall. An empty pizza carton had been dropped on the floor. Each had a beer bottle in his hand. They were talking, but he couldn't hear them over the announcer for the baseball game.

Dave walked to the front door, confident the men would not hear a creaking board over the television. He entered through a screen door, pulled it and the wooden door closed to deter unexpected visitors, and eased along a narrow hall cluttered with paper and other debris. Their backs to the open hall door, Hicks and his buddy were clapping about a home run for their favorite team, not aware Dave had stepped into the room.

Dave waited until they saw him, both scrambling to rise from the recliners and turned to face him. He pointed the .38 and stepped closer. "Don't move again."

The larger of the two continued, taking a step before Dave kicked him in the knee. He screamed and buckled, grasping at his battered joint. The second man, wide-eyed with surprise, slumped back into the chair.

Dave asked, "Which of you is Jasper Hicks?"

"None of your damn business," the one on the floor muttered. "What the fuck you doing?"

"You have a contract on me. You've been following me. Now you're going to tell me who hired you. Then you're leaving Chester."

"You crazy, man. We ain't telling you shit." This from the one on the floor. Regaining some courage, the one in the chair edged forward until Dave pointed the gun at him.

"You will," Dave said, "if you wish to live through the night."

"You must be Hicks," Dave said, pointing the gun at his other knee. "You seem to be the big talker here."

Dave kicked Hicks in the face, breaking his nose and knocking him backward. Blood spurted down his shirt and onto the floor. The second man gasped and cringed deeper into the chair as though he wanted to push through the back and disappear.

Hicks moaned and grasped his face. After a minute of muttering, he sat up and wiped his bloody hand across his pants.

Dave pulled a small recording device from his side pocket, placed it on a table among empty beer bottles, and switched it on. "Now let's talk. And I want straight answers to just a few questions."

Ten minutes later, Dave prodded both men out the front door and into the truck. "I'll follow you to the interstate and make certain you drive west past the next three exits. After that, I'd suggest you keep going but you may want to visit a hospital before that knee gets worse. If I ever see you around here again, I'll kill you. And thanks for the information."

Dave stood behind the truck until they started. He jumped into his rental car, made a U-turn and followed as the truck turned off Blount onto 36th street, a direct route to the interstate.

When they passed the third exit, Dave left the interstate, circled around the ramps, and returned to Chester. He stopped at the Blount street address, entered the house and retrieved the rifles. He searched for other weapons and items potentially evidence. But other than changes of shirts, socks and underwear, nothing remained.

From the Avis dealer, he took a cab to the office, and drove home in his Blazer. He'd learned a lot. Now he had to decide how to use what he knew. He wanted to talk with Jennifer before his next move.

At 7:45 the next morning Jennifer came into his office, a mug of coffee in her hand. "I saw your note about seeing you. What's up?"

He told her about his tip from Gibbons, being followed by the truck, and meeting with his stalkers, leaving out the details of their confrontation. "Rogers Morton hired these idiots to do me in. He gave them two thousand in advance and promised two more when they'd completed the job. I'm ready to confront him with the evidence or maybe go to the cops. I need your advice."

Jennifer guessed he'd knocked the stalkers around and scared them badly. She said, "You won't have much to give the police. They may not accept what's on the tape. Then it'll be your version against Morton's. He won't admit he's involved."

"Will my confronting him jeopardize your case against Black and Redfield?"

She sipped from the mug, her eyes on his face. "Actually, it might help. It'd show they're worried about our investigation. But, maybe the more important question is will he react by hiring another killer to carry out his mission?"

Dave said, "That depends. If I don't challenge him with the evidence, he'll believe they took his money and left town. He could hire another shooter when he figures out the first pair weren't successful. But he needs to be stopped. I don't want to go through the same thing again."

Jennifer said, "Neither do I. The next one might succeed."

"I'll talk to Morton."

"It shouldn't make any real difference with the employee insurance case." She stood and moved to the door. Turning back, she asked, "You want me to go with you to Morton's?"

"I'd rather talk to him alone."

"Don't do anything you'll regret."

"You sound like my mother," Dave said, "when I was a teenager."

She ignored his attempt at banter. "What else is on your agenda?"

"I'm setting up a meeting with Edgar Smithson to turn in my report about his wayward wife and give him the bill." He told her about the wife's meeting with Guidry.

"What will he do?"

"He was so irate when he contacted us, I'd bet he files for divorce. You want to represent him?"

"Not particularly. With this suit coming and a couple of other things, my plate is full."

He watched her walk out of his office, realizing she usually responded to situations with good sense and obtained the desired results. She'd suggested she become involved because she didn't like his roughhouse tactics. Maybe it'd be better to meet Morton with her rather than knock him around as his instincts dictated. If their talk with Morton didn't succeed, he could resort to a more physical approach later.

He went to her office.

Dave parked behind the Chester police station in a visitor's space and carried the two rifles inside. He waited until Rasmussen completed a phone call, then knocked on his door frame.

"I brought you a couple of presents from my would-be killers. They might be worth an examination to see if they fit some other crime. At least, it'll get them off the street."

Rasmussen came around his desk. "I'll get ballistics to check them out. Never know what'll turn up. I assume they left town after you convinced them to give up their weapons?"

Dave grinned. "That's about how it went. I never learned the second guy's name. He kept pretty quiet."

"I'll let you know how this works out."

At 11:00 the following morning Jennifer and Dave appeared at the offices of Black and Redfield for their appointment with Morton. When she'd called, Jennifer had asked for a time to visit with Morton, letting him guess it was about the Frame case. She'd not mentioned Dave.

Morton almost jumped out of his chair when Dave followed Jennifer in. Without waiting for his greeting or signal, they took visitor chairs near his desk. Morton's eyes shifted from one to the other, unsure of what was coming.

Jennifer said, "Mr. Morton, there's been a series of misunderstandings between our firm and you. We've come to clear the air."

Without pause for his acknowledgement, she continued, "First, there was the little problem of you sending a stalker around to intimidate me. Hardly had that been resolved when two men began trailing my partner and we learned through a reliable source they'd been employed to murder him. Dave met your hired guns night before last and convinced them they should abandon their contract. Now, we're here to ask that you cease this harassment."

Morton finally spoke, "You're both crazy. I had nothing to do with either of those incidents."

Jennifer smiled. "We have solid evidence you did. Both of your hired parties admitted you employed them for the specific purpose of intimidation or worse. We know you intended for us to back away from our disagreement about the Maude Frame case. If you persist with these antics, we will file criminal charges. In fact, we might do so anyway."

"You can't prove anything." Morton had gained confidence and leaned forward on the desk.

"We can. Conversations on tapes are fairly convincing. Two different admissions of your direct involvement are almost fool-proof. You have the choice— leave our firm alone or face the consequences."

"Why did you bring your body guard? Afraid I'd have you thrown out?"

Jennifer remained calm, still looking pleasant. "I shouldn't have to remind you he's my partner. Sometimes when the situation demands, he employs force to get results. You'd be better served to cease and desist as I can't always direct his actions."

"Don't threaten me, young lady. I'll call security and have you thrown out."

Dave broke in. "It's no threat, Morton. You and your hired goons stay the hell out of our business." He wanted to jerk Morton from behind his desk and kick his butt, but he didn't want to disappoint Jennifer.

Jennifer stood. "We thank you for your time. It'd be well to give serious attention to our request. We won't be back to ask again."

Dave followed her out of Morton's office.

In the elevator, Dave asked, "Did he get the message?"

"I think so. He didn't want to cave in and admit any wrong doing, but he knows we won't tolerate further harassment."

"I hope you're right. But if not, next time, I'll do it differently."

"I know," she said, tucking her arm through his as they left the elevator and departed through the front door. As always, her touch and closeness quickened his senses. He wondered what she might do if he made an advance but he didn't want to wreck their relationship.

"You interested in lunch?" Dave asked.

"Sure, but let's go somewhere other than Gibbons."

Without a reservation they waited ten minutes to be seated at Arthur's. They passed Heather Farrell and a male companion on route to a back table. Heather nodded and smiled at both of them.

While scanning the menu, Jennifer asked, "How's your relationship with Gwen progressing?"

"Good. I like her a lot. She's sensible, practical, and willing to put up with my bad habits."

"Not to mention sexy and beautiful," Jennifer added.

"That too. But it's been great between the two of us. How're things with George?"

Jennifer flipped a page of the menu. "Okay. He surprised me on Saturday by asking me to marry him."

A feeling of pending loss oozed through Dave. "What'd you say?"

"I put him off."

"You know him inside and out by now. He seems like a nice guy."

"He has a lot of good characteristics—dependable, reliable, good salary and bright future in banking, courteous to everyone, not bad looking." She bored in on the menu for a while, then looked at Dave. "But I'm not sure I love him or ever will. Somehow our relationship doesn't measure up to what I've always imagined it'd be like in finding the right person to spend the rest of your life with. You understand?"

Dave nodded. "Maybe. But I'm not the one to give advice about matters of the heart." The consternation that had swept through him when she had mentioned George's proposal had both surprised and confused him.

SIXTEEN

Ten days after meeting with the potential participants in the proceedings against Black and Redfield, Jennifer had documents ready to submit to court. Twelve of the fourteen workers identified with genetic defects had joined the suit. Dave's prediction about the man complaining about greedy lawyers had proved correct. He'd called the next morning to say he wouldn't be a party to beating money out of firms so lawyers could get rich. Another person who'd come to the orientation session, a fifty-eight-year- old woman, had been killed in an automobile accident.

Jennifer's approach to secure reinstatement of the policies had come down to a two-pronged attack. First, she argued Black and Redfield had invaded the privacy of those workers for monetary gain and without informing them of the potential consequences or giving them the option of participating in the physical examinations. Secondly, she charged that Black and Redfield had violated the Americans With Disabilities Act by declaring those workers disabled and thus not eligible for continuing insurance coverage under their present policies. After debating with herself, she had added a section demanding punitive damages of $10,000 per person, arguing that each worker had undergone serious mental anguish because of their inability to adequately plan for the care of loved ones. The deciding factor had been the treatment by Black and Redfield of the workers when they'd tried to find out about their dropped policies and the arrogance of executives like Rogers Morton. Although she didn't like to admit it, she wanted retribution from a group of high-handed executives.

After deliberating the problem for a week and talking with a couple of other attorneys who had had some experience with the Chester courts and for whom she had respect, Jennifer requested a jury trial. A panel of peers would be more sympathetic to the plight of these workers than would some judge who'd never known life on a low-wage salary.

But her primary concern was the potential actions of Young. As the presiding judge of the court, he assigned cases to maintain an even work load or to take advantage of unique experiences of certain judges to handle specific cases. After his previous ruling on her request, she'd thought Young would recuse himself, but she couldn't predict with any satisfaction.

Based on Jennifer's gnawing worry that Young would intervene in spite of his obvious conflict, she and Dave concluded they should push ahead with finding out if and how Young had been compromised.

With Rasmussen's help, Dave arranged to meet with one of the undercover detectives who'd been involved with the case of William A. Young, Jr., the Judge's son. Dave met Kent Adams in a small bar on Cedar Street.

Adams had taken a corner table and had consumed half of a draft beer when Dave arrived mid-afternoon. Dave introduced himself, confirming he'd met the right person, and got a draft Killian from the bartender before sitting. They were the only ones using a table in the dimly-lighted space. At most tables the chairs were still stacked on top from the previous night's cleaning. Two elderly men, mugs in their hands, perched on high stools and leaned onto the bar itself.

After they'd talked some about weather and sketched their backgrounds, Adams said, "Rasmussen told me you were interested in this Junior Young situation. How are you connected?" Adams' jeans and sports shirt, black running shoes, tousled black hair and three-days growth of beard coincided with Dave's image of an undercover operator trying to divert attention from his real mission.

Dave explained his partnership with Jennifer Watson and the type of cases they typically handled. He told about the request for the Frame records and the actions of Judge Young. Then he said, "Maybe you've heard, but during her follow-up of the Judge's ruling, my partner heard rumors that Young had become obligated to Black and Redfield. When I discovered his son had been in trouble and his case had been whitewashed, I thought there might be some connection. Our concern comes down to how Young might rule on a suit being filed against the insurance company."

Adams finished his beer and waved at the bartender for another. "We'd tailed this kid for months. He'd gotten into drugs and had become a small-time dealer in the region, but his territory was expanding. We aimed to stop him and find out who was backing the operation. One of our undercover guys actually made a purchase from Junior. Based on that and other evidence, we arrested him. Through the whole thing, we'd worked closely with the prosecutor who kept encouraging us. He thought we had solid stuff and charged the son with possession and distributing.

"Sometimes the first arrest jars open the door to the entire scheme. We were working hard to bring others in and crack the organization, but four days after Junior was charged, everything was dropped. I was pissed, even considered resigning, but I have too many years in." The low growl permeating his discourse revealed his feelings as well as his words.

Dave asked, "Did you learn who brought pressure?"

His fist clenched on the table top, Adams said, "No, but Judge Young intervened. And somehow a bunch of out-of-town lawyers got involved and muddled the situation even more."

"Do you know if money was involved or some trade off?"

"Don't know, but something must have happened."

Dave said, "You have any suspicions the prosecutor has become tainted by Black and Redfield as well as Young?"

For a moment, Adams considered the question, his eyes on Dave's face. He crossed one foot across his knee and tugged at his sagging white sock. He sipped from the beer bottle, then said, "Don't think so. He was mad as hell when the case against Junior was dropped. I've known him a long time and it was not an act. His frustration was real."

"Did you ever learn the rationale given for dropping the case?"

"The Judge ruled there was insufficient evidence. That's not uncommon, but we had it locked up pretty tight against Junior. I would've bet six-months pay we could put him away for years."

"I'm surprised Judge Young didn't remove himself from the case. He has no business dealing with charges against his son."

"By all rights, he should have. A couple of us tried to persuade the prosecutor to do something—appeal to the Circuit Court, take it to the bar association, whatever it took to get Young out of the picture—but he wouldn't, arguing Young would hold it against the prosecutor's office for the rest of his career."

"I take it," Dave said, "that Young uses all the power available to him as the presiding judge. From what I've seen, that's what happens with the appointments for life with these damn judges accountable to no one. The longer they stick around, the more power they accumulate, and the more they learn about how to manipulate the system."

Adams drained the beer. "More than most people understand. For years, Young had the reputation of going overboard to be fair and impartial, but he's slipped badly in the past months. I wouldn't at all be surprised if he's being used by outsiders, but I don't know who."

"Any idea how I can find Junior?"

"He's often around Roscoe's Bar and Grill, meeting people and making deals. It's four blocks from here at the corner of 36th and Cedar. So you know, we have a detective posing as a bartender in the place. We're still collecting evidence against Junior and his cronies. Ask for Angela. She'll point out Junior for you. But don't do anything that'd give her up. It could be dangerous for her and destroy our operation."

"Is she there most of the time?"

"She works from four to midnight. She'll be the only woman behind the bar. So you don't screw up, I'll let her know you're coming by. And don't talk to the owner, an overweight bald guy who's usually at the cash register. We suspect he's part of the organization. He must know what's going on and doesn't discourage it. Probably gets a cut."

Dave left bills on the table to cover his drink. "Thanks for your insights. If our suit gets treated inappropriately, we're going to dig into Young's connections until we can get him off the case."

Adams looked skeptical. "Could be tricky, but if I can help nail the bastard, get in touch. Rasmussen usually knows where I am."

In their continuing discussion about the Young situation, Jennifer decided to discover who the lawyers were who represented Junior. She asked the Clerk of Court to provide the files for Junior's hearing. Sitting at a cubicle within the clerk's office, she soon found the transcript of a preliminary hearing presided over by Judge Young.

The prosecutor outlined the evidence which appeared conclusive in Jennifer's thinking. An undercover policeman enumerated the steps they'd taken to obtain the incriminating material, including a taped record of the exchange of money and drugs between Junior and the officer.

Neil Frawley, the attorney for Junior, had argued briefly that the evidence was tainted. He charged the police with setting up a young man while he was under the influence of alcohol. His request that the tape be ruled inadmissible on the grounds it was obtained under coercion was taken under advisement by the judge.

Two days later Judge Young had ruled the prosecutor had failed to present sufficient evidence to hold the accused over for trial. Charges were dismissed.

From a public phone in the lobby of the administration building, Jennifer called the Chester Bar Association office and asked if Frawley was licensed to practice in the state. After checking through records, the woman who attended the office, said, "Mr. Frawley was granted a license in May of this year. His primary practice is in Delaware. He is a partner in the firm of Benedict, Morse, Frawley and others."

Returning the file to the desk, Jennifer asked the attendant for the log of court cases since May. Frawley had appeared on behalf of Black and Redfield in a contested settlement of a man who'd been killed in a home accident. She vaguely remembered the case—the insurance company had argued the man had been murdered by his wife who was the only beneficiary of a $200,000 policy. Judge Anita Chandler had ruled in favor of the woman, but the company was appealing. A final decision could be months away.

A week after submitting the suit against Black and Redfield, Andy Chafin called Jennifer.

Her fears were realized when he said, "Judge Young asked me to call you. He intends to throw out your case. You haven't sufficient evidence to go forward. Frankly, he regards the suit as frivolous with little merit."

Although expecting the message, Jennifer's frustration boiled over. "Andy, you know damn well the actions of Black and Redfield against those workers is illegal and my documents show clearly Black and Redfield violated the Disabilities Act."

"He doesn't think so," Chafin replied.

Rather than continuing the argument with the messenger, Jennifer hung up and went to Dave's office to tell him.

At 9:30 Dave dropped onto a stool at the bar in Roscoe's. His jeans and wrinkled tee shirt, a baseball cap angled on his head, fit the dress code of the patrons. A large-screen television blared forth from a shelf above and behind the bar. He waited two minutes before the woman bartender approached. He ordered a draft beer.

When she placed the mug, the foam oozing over the sides, he asked, "Are you Angela?"

She eyed him cautiously, wiping the bar with a towel. "Yes. Do I know you?" Her round face, with little or no makeup and a scar across one cheek, framed by dark hair loosely pinned into a ponytail made her appear rather unattractive..

"Not before now," Dave said, "but I've talked with one of your buddies. He asked me to say hello and ask how you were."

Glancing at the nearby customers for a moment, she said, "I'm good."

Dave said, "Our mutual friend said you could point out Junior Young."

"You have business with him?"

"Yeah, but different than his other clients."

Her eyes glued to his face, Angela said, "He's the younger man with that group of four at the corner table. It'd be better if you wait until they leave to speak to him. They usually are gone by 10:00." She moved away to wait on an older man who'd struggled onto a stool two seats away.

Dave focused on the television for a while. The Braves were leading the Astros in the middle of the seventh. As he watched, Chipper Jones knocked a homer, increasing the lead.

Movement of chairs and loud voices caused him to turn toward the corner. Junior was smiling and shaking hands with each of the others. A man dressed in a suit said something to Junior before joining the others headed for the door. One waved toward Angela who nodded in response.

When no one approached Junior's table during the next five minutes, Dave ventured over. Standing across from the young man, Dave said, "I understand you might be able to help me with a problem."

Junior was wary. "Do I know you?"

"Nope," Dave said, "but I'd like to introduce myself and discuss a possible business venture. May I sit down?"

Junior nodded. "Yeah, but I don't have long." His dark eyes circled the room as he spoke.

Dave pulled out a chair and put his beer mug on the table. "If you are who I think you are, I've had dealings with your father. Rather unpleasant ones, in fact."

"Is that your business?"

Dave grinned at the kid's discomfort. "Just my way of breaking the ice, so to speak."

Shifting in his chair, Junior said, "The less I hear about the old bastard, the better my life is."

"I assume you don't get along too well. Then, you might understand my feelings toward him. He put the screws to me. Sent me up for seven years for a first-time offense."

"He can be hard on people." Junior sipped from a Budweiser bottle and bit into a pretzel. He shoved the bowl toward Dave.

Dave snapped off a chunk of pretzel. "Not to belabor the issue of your father, but I've heard he's doing some work for Black and Redfield lately."

"He has, but I don't know much. Their lawyers have become close to him."

"Since I got out, I've been checking up on the judge. People tell me he's different."

"I avoid my old man when I can," Junior said, his face frowning. "But he got me out of a bad jam recently. Trying to make up for the lousy way he treated me and my sister as kids."

"Parents can be hard on children," Dave said, hoping to open the floodgate for more revelation.

"My father can be a bastard," Junior said. "But if he hadn't helped me, I could be serving time now."

"Did those lawyers from Black and Redfield represent you?"

"Not in the typical way." A wave of uncertainty swept across his face. "Why the hell you want to know that for? I thought you wanted to do some business."

Dave stood. "I might in the future. Tonight was just a get acquainted session. I may get back to you."

He passed two men in suits as he returned to the bar. They took up stations at Junior's table. Junior said something and they all looked at Dave.

When Angela approached him, he asked, "Could I talk to you after work? You tell me where and when." He placed bills on the counter for the beer.

She mumbled, "Call Rasmussen tomorrow." She moved away.

SEVENTEEN

When Dave called Rasmussen about meeting with Angela, the detective said, "She'll meet you at the second-floor cafeteria in Johnson's Department Store tomorrow at 12:30. She's worried any contact with you will put her under suspicion around Roscoe's. It'd be smart for you not to go back there. And, if she thinks she's being tailed, she won't show for lunch."

"Did someone comment after my visit the other night?"

"One of the regulars asked who you were. Not many strangers venture into Roscoe's."

Dave said, "I'll avoid the place and will see her tomorrow, but I'm curious. Have you become the contact for all the undercover operators?"

Rasmussen laughed, "Yeah, a change of responsibility. Gets me off the street and behind the desk more. The department is calling it a promotion, but I'm not so sure other than a few more dollars every month. It's a recognition of my age and associated limitations. There are no great perks related, such as a better office. "

"And the coffee's no better."

Rasmussen laughed, his deep chuckle reverberating across the line. "I meant to call you earlier, but got busy and forgot. Anyway, the DNA sample from those envelopes in Redfield's safety deposit box matched those of the corpse."

"Any leads on a culprit?"

"Nothing. Nobody remembers seeing Redfield after he checked out of the Marriott. He must have been killed the same day. There's no record of his flying west. He'd purchased a ticket to Seattle several days earlier, but never used it."

Dave asked, "Can you pinpoint the date?"

"He paid his bill at the Marriott on the morning of May 3rd. No one recalls his taking a cab, but he and his luggage disappeared. A bellman remembered Redfield standing around the lobby for a few minutes, but when a group checked in from the airport, he doesn't recall anymore. He thinks Redfield just walked out."

"Someone had arranged to pick him up, but rather than take him to the airport, knocked him off and dropped his body in the woods."

. "That looks like the scenario," Rasmussen said.

"That's four days before Nicole Farrell ran. Somehow Gerald Dewberry was connected or knew about Redfield and the killer suspected he'd told Nicole."

Rasmussen asked, "Can you get in touch with Nicole? Maybe she remembers something that would be useful to us."

Dave said, "I'll call her, but she swears she knows nothing. But I never pushed her, thinking it didn't matter much after I'd found her for her sister."

"Quiz her about impressions, bits of conversation she may have overheard, anything to get us started."

"I'll get back to you," Dave said. "And watch out for holes in your pants. Those desk jobs can be hazardous."

Rasmussen snickered, "You always have good advice."

* * *

Dave hadn't been in Johnson's for over a year. Since his last visit, the main floor had been renovated with new sections for merchandise. New lights, wider aisles, and brighter carpeting had been installed giving the old establishment a more sophisticated look. He wandered by an upscale counter for perfumes, a young woman spraying samples of exotic scents for a customer. The escalator near the sporting goods displays led him directly into the cafeteria on the second floor.

Angela was waiting on a bench near the entrance to the serving line. She looked different than she had in the bar. Her hair floated neatly to shoulder length. Makeup masked the scar and added color to her lips and cheeks. A navy blazer over a white blouse contrasted with tan slacks adding to her professional aura. She could pass for an office manager or teacher.

Dave said, "Sorry, have you waited long?"

She stood to shake his hand, her eyes scanning the area near the escalator. "Actually, I came in to shop a bit and got here early. Let's get our food."

They chose soup and sandwiches from the line servers and found a small booth on one side of the large dining area. Bus boys scurried around as they cleared tables for waiting customers. Women piled purchases on empty chairs. Business professionals hurried through their meal, constantly glancing at their watches.

As they ate, Angela said, "Rasmussen said I could trust you. Otherwise, I couldn't risk this meeting."

"I understand," Dave said. He explained the suit against Black and Redfield, the problems they'd encountered with Judge Young, and his reason for checking out Junior.

She ate her clam chowder for a while, then said, "We're reasonably sure Junior is making arrangements for selling drugs in the bar, but the actual exchanges take place somewhere else. We're trying to record conversations between him and those who visit him. He always uses the same table and regular patrons avoid his little domain so it's been easier to place a listening device near the table. But often the conversations are garbled or drowned out because of the shuffling of ash trays and tumblers, not to mention general background noise."

"Is he there every night?"

"Only Tuesday and Friday. Nobody ever asks for him on other nights, so he's established a regular schedule and his contacts know it. He comes in around 8:30 and begins to have visitors immediately. Those continue until 11:00 when he leaves. There's never any trouble or excessive demands on the bartenders or waiters. Everything works smoothly, like it's an office."

"How'd you trace him to Roscoe's?"

"Another undercover operator had been following Junior since his release. He figured out Junior was using the bar as a routine hang-out and meeting place. At that juncture Rasmussen decided we should switch people."

"Any idea about who schedules the visitors? It seems too organized for random drop- bys."

Peeling off the wrapper from a cracker, Angela said, "No idea, but it's likely from some office. We've checked out his apartment and monitored his phone calls without success."

"Is Roscoe, or whoever the owner is, associated with Junior's operation?"

"I don't think so, but he likes the arrangement because they buy drinks and leave good tips. It's steady business for him."

"Then why there?"

Angela shrugged, shoved aside the soup bowl and wiped her fingers on the paper napkin. "We suspect it's because of the openness. No one would usually guess a drug operation was being run in the middle of a rather seedy but busy bar. We find the small dealers more often in warehouses, street corners, or residences. The big operators are more sophisticated with sales going on in upscale offices or a business establishment."

Dave nibbled at his club sandwich for a minute. "Do you know the people who meet with Junior?"

"Sometimes I overhear a name or another customer speaks to a person as they pass. Or a name shows up on the tape. We're slowly collecting a roster of visitors with the hope they somehow connect in a sensible way. We don't want to jump in too early and miss the key supplier."

"What about those two guys in suits who were there when I was?"

"I'm reasonably certain they are lawyers. One is named Frawly or Farley. I overheard Roscoe talking to him about a problem with the lease on the place."

"Who's the owner?"

"Black and Redfield Insurance. They received the property through a settlement several years ago. I haven't tried to learn any details." Her eyes widened as she considered the implications. "You think Junior is connected to the insurance company and they're involved with the drug running deal? Maybe the visits to Junior are coordinated through an office there."

"Could be," Dave said. "It might explain why Judge Young protected his son and why lawyers from Black and Redfield were involved."

Angela looked at her watch. "I wish I had more time to discuss the various possibilities with you, but I'm scheduled to meet with my daughter's teacher in a few minutes. It's one of those regularly scheduled parent-teacher conferences, but I can't make it during the evenings she sets aside like most parents. "

"Maybe we can get together again," Dave said.

"Call Rasmussen, but don't contact me directly," Angela said, as she slipped out of the booth.

Dave hailed a cruising waitress for a coffee refill, thinking about the information he'd gained and giving Angela several minutes to exit the store before he moved.

Dave called Nicole Farrell, alias Betty Jane Johnson, at 9:30 p.m. using the number she'd sent him by a note.

When he identified himself, she asked, "Anything wrong with Heather?"

"Not to my knowledge, but I'm calling about another matter." He told her about Redfield's death, the date he disappeared, and the possibility the insurance company had been involved.

Nicole said, "I can't believe anyone would kill Mr. Redfield, but I realized quickly those people were dangerous."

Dave said, "You've told me you knew nothing about the events that occurred before Gerald's death, but you'd heard enough to become scared. We're trying to piece the puzzle together. I'm wondering if you've thought more about the conversations Gerald had with representatives of Black and Redfield."

"I've tried not to," Nicole said, "but fragments linger. Gerald got mad over something that had happened and called three or four people from home. For him to do that was unusual enough, but the tone of the conversations became more tense as he talked. Gerald could be difficult to deal with, but this seemed more strident than the typical business deal gone sour or a disagreement over a company policy."

"Once you said you'd heard someone threaten Gerald's wife. You remember anything else, other than deciding it was too dangerous to stay there?"

She hesitated as though trying to recall or taking time to organize her thoughts. "A man came to our home around 10:30 one night. He was dressed in a suit and seemed like a professional. But he acted like a hoodlum, pushed by me when I cracked the door, and demanded to see Gerald. He and Gerald went into the den and closed the door, but soon they were yelling at each other. I could hear snippets of their exchange although I had gone upstairs."

"Anything about Redfield?"

"Not by name. But when Gerald accused them of killing someone, the man screamed his threat about Gerald's wife not being safe if he didn't fall into line. That's when I decided to leave. At the time I planned to disappear for several days, let matters settle and return home. Then Gerald was killed."

"What day was the confrontation?"

"Two days before I left Chester."

"That would be May 5th. You flew on May 7th."

"Sounds right," she said. "I needed one day to finish a couple of deals at the office, arrange for a leave of absence, withdraw money from the bank, get my essential stuff together. And I didn't want Gerald or Heather to know my plans."

"Did you ever learn the name of the man who came to your home?"

"Not really, but he was one of the new people at the company. It wasn't DeRosa. I'd met him at a reception."

"Maybe Rogers Morton?"

"No, I know him. He's been around several years."

Dave was stabbing in the dark. "How about Bruce Hoyt? Does that name strike a bell?"

Reluctantly and without confidence, Nicole murmured, "Maybe, but it's a guess."

"Can you describe him?"

Again, a measured response as she said, "Big person, thick across the shoulders, maybe six feet, dark hair and coarse facial features." She stopped, audibly breathed.. "I remember big hands like those of a construction worker."

"Anything else about him?"

"No, but he terrified me."

"How do you mean?"

Nicole thought about the question for a couple of beats. "His demanding tone, maybe his sheer bulk, coarseness about his personality."

Dave said, "You've been helpful. I'm sorry I didn't ask these questions when I saw you, but it didn't seem important then."

"I hope you can put them in prison if they really killed James Redfield. He was a dear man who treated everyone with dignity and respect."

"I'll let you know," Dave said. "Then it'll be safe for you to return to Chester."

"I've settled in here. My work is going well and I've made several friends, so I'm not so sure I'd want to come back. Tell Heather I'm okay, but not where I am."

Dave replayed the conversation with Nicole while he put away dishes from the washer. Maybe Rasmussen's team could find out about Hoyt who'd been invisible up to now. If he was the man Nicole remembered, he seemed like the typical enforcer who made sure players didn't stray from the company line.

EIGHTEEN

Rasmussen returned Dave's call mid-morning. "Sorry I missed you, but I was in a meeting about Junior and his friends. Angela has some interesting pieces of conversation. We'd like more, but we're concerned about dragging too long."

Dave shoved aside a file regarding a husband-wife battle, a case he had taken on at Jennifer's request, to focus on the issue at hand. "Is Angela getting signals she may have been spotted?"

"She hasn't said so, but my experience is, sooner or later, suspicions will be aroused. We're walking a fine line."

"She stands out at Roscoe's. I'd think about getting her out."

"We've decided to give her another week, unless something unusual happens."

"I had called to update you on Nicole Farrell." Dave summarized the exchange they'd had and Nicole's tentative identification of Hoyt, then said, "Maybe you should check Hoyt out. He could be the key to Redfield's murder."

"I'll get someone on it as we have time," Rasmussen said.

"Also, I'd alert Angela about Hoyt. Could be he meets Junior at the bar."

"She's maintaining a log of his visitors—descriptions, times, who's with them—and trying to match the person with the recorded interchanges."

"I asked her about Roscoe, the owner of the bar. Are you guys certain he's not mixed in with Junior and his pals? He must know what's going on."

"We've no hint he is, but he doesn't know Angela's role. She went in and asked if he had a job. We were lucky he happened to be looking for help on the night shift when business is heaviest. It provides her legitimacy."

Dave said, "It seems too convenient." Dave couldn't believe Roscoe didn't know about the recording device. Tables and chairs were moved and cleaned daily by someone, probably not Angela. Even the most dense cleaning person would ask about a strange instrument attached to the underside of the table or in another close location. And checking and replacing tapes on the device daily would be observed by someone unless Angela were the only person present at periods of time, an unlikely event during the time she worked. Customers and other workers came on duty at noon to serve the early afternoon regulars.

Rasmussen said, "Everything seems okay. She's been at this a month without any questions. But, as I said, we're getting anxious."

"Don't push it too long," Dave said, "and place her in jeopardy."

Jennifer met Anita Chandler at The Oases, a mid-scale restaurant a block from the site of the Chester County Bar Association bi-monthly meeting. With ample time before the 7:30 gathering, they had cocktails in the small bar before their reservation time in the dining room. A waitress served them immediately in the sparsely occupied lounge.

Jennifer said, "You probably heard that Judge Young threw out my suit against Black and Redfield."

Anita nodded, sipped her gin and tonic. "I'm not surprised. It's become reasonably certain he has some relation with them."

"My next option will be an appeal to the Circuit Court, but I'd like to confront Young directly."

Anita shook her head. "Submit your appeal. See how that goes. The Court could hear the case, return it to Young, assign it to someone else, or agree with his first ruling. If they do the latter, you've lost, but I suspect they would assign it to another judge. They'd recognize Young's prejudice because of his earlier decision if nothing else."

"I'd like someone with authority to review Young's recent actions, especially those involving Black and Redfield. He may be damaging other clients in addition to my cases."

Anita swirled her drink, now mostly ice. "Talk to Reginald Broom. He's the chair of the ethics committee for the bar association, but the hard truth is they won't touch a sitting judge without compelling evidence of wrongdoing. In spite of the rumors, I'm not sure there's enough about Young to open an investigation."

"I can't lose anything."

"Probably not. Broom would keep your concerns confidential. And he might know of others who've raised questions about Young's ethics. Those rumors are too persistent for Broom not to have heard something."

Jennifer finished her Scotch. "I hate these situations. I thought the law was above petty issues and maintained a purity beyond question."

"Welcome to the world contaminated by greed, political deals, and self-interest," Anita said. "Shall we get our table?"

"Sure," Jennifer said, standing. "By the way, you look great. I'm glad to see more color in your face."

"Thanks, I'm doing well. My last check-up was good and I'm off any treatment now, but it's something hanging over my head for the next five years, maybe the rest of my life."

Jennifer touched Anita's arm. "It'll go okay."

"That's what my husband tells me every day."

Three days later, Jennifer met Reginald Broom in the Marriott lounge after office hours. Broom, an older lawyer who'd practiced in Chester for twenty-five years, was a partner in a large firm focused on corporate mergers, commercial real estate, and bankruptcies. He ordered a club soda. Jennifer asked for her usual Scotch and soda.

Broom said, "My secretary said you wanted to talk about an potential ethical problem."

Jennifer said, "I've had a couple of requests dismissed by Judge Young with no solid rationale for his rulings. In both, he sent a message through his clerk to the effect they were frivolous."

Broom smiled, a father counseling his daughter, "That's all?"

Jennifer sketched out her suit against Black and Redfield, then said, "Some people suspect Young is hooked in with Black and Redfield. Then there's the problem of Young dismissing a case in which his son was the defendant. Mr. Broom, something is wrong."

Broom leaned back for the waitress to place the drinks and waited until she'd turned away. "The committee discussed the basis of the rumors, but tabled the concern for the time being. Young has a reputation for ethical behavior exceeding usual expectations."

"I know," Jennifer said. "That's what most disturbing about my conflicts with him. He's always treated me fairly in the past, but his sense of objectivity is lost on Black and Redfield. He's protecting them."

Broom said, "I don't follow the court docket closely. Was Black and Redfield associated with the son's situation?"

"Their lawyers represented the boy."

Broom leaned closer. "We represented a company contesting a real estate deal by Black and Redfield. My partner thought Young had misread the statute when he ruled in their favor. He met with Young in his chambers but failed to persuade him to reconsider."

"Do you intend to appeal?"

"Yes. Our client has a lot of money involved."

Jennifer said, "Maybe you can advise me about options. I'm leaning toward appealing Young's decision as my best approach."

Broom fingered his glass, his eyes almost closed. "I'd do that. Charging a breach of ethics against Young would be risky, particularly for a young attorney, and would likely fail. It's very difficult to make those charges stick against any judge, but it would be particularly tricky in Young's case. But, I will make the Bar's ethics committee aware unofficially of Young's rulings. Your concerns, the ruling against our client, and the persistent rumors are sufficient cause to reconsider the situation. If the committee agrees, we might challenge Young directly. Let him explain his position without a public hullabaloo."

Jennifer said, "I'd be glad to share my briefs with the committee or discuss my cases with them, if you think it would be useful."

Broom said, "We're meeting next week on another matter. I'll bring back the Young question, see what their desires are, and let you know. In the meantime, file your appeal."

Jennifer shoved aside her glass and reached for her purse. "I appreciate your hearing my concern."

Broom stood, taking the check from Jennifer's hand. "My treat. I hear good things about your practice."

"We've become very busy," Jennifer said, "after a slow start."

"That's the usual evolution." He dropped bills for a tip. "I'll let you know what the committee does."

Dave heard nothing from either Rasmussen or Angela for several days. He resisted an urge to contact them. It was none of his business.

Then on the last day of August, the *Register* carried a headline with two full columns about the arrest of William A. Young, Jr. and three associates in Roscoe's Bar and Grill. They were charged with distributing illegal substances and were being held without bond in the Chester jail. The article detailed the efforts of the undercover police without identifying them. One of Young's associates was Bruce Hoyt, but his relationship to Black and Redfield wasn't mentioned. All of the arrested were being represented by Neil Frawley who called a press conference during which he proclaimed the innocence of his clients and accused the police of using illegal methods and trampling the civil rights of Junior and his cohorts. Frawley predicted they would be found not guilty when all the evidence was presented. The accused were free on bail until the trial.

Reading the paper while at breakfast, Dave wanted to celebrate, but realized the case against Junior might not advance the cause of Jennifer's suit on behalf of the workers. She'd submitted an appeal several days earlier, but had heard nothing yet.

Dave had several small tasks to work on at the office, but his mind looked forward to the long weekend. Gwen was coming tonight and they'd planned to spend the Labor Day weekend and holiday together.

As had become their routine, Dave met her at the terminal after her Friday flight from St. Louis. As soon as they drove away from the building, Dave suspected something was different. Her usual smile and outpouring of news were absent. Rather, she sat quietly, pressed against the door, focusing her attention on passing scenery and other vehicles.

As they sipped drinks on the couch in his living room, Gwen said, "There are a couple of things I need to tell you."

. She twisted to face him. "First and easiest, I have to change my schedule and fly on Sunday morning."

Dave said, "I'm disappointed, but those things can't be avoided."

Gwen sipped her drink. "The second thing is more serious, but I hope it doesn't change things for us. I'm in love with you and believe you love me too. Our times together have been wonderful. But I have a hard decision to make."

She edged closer to him, placed her glass on the table, and took his hand. "The Vice-President of the company called me yesterday while we were changing planes in Kansas City. He offered me the position of Supervisor of Flight Attendants for the airline."

Dave said, "That's great, but shouldn't be a surprise."

Her face somber, she said, "It's a huge promotion and a big salary increase. It's a goal I set for myself when I started. In early May the present supervisor announced she planned to retire at the end of August. An announcement for applications came around about the time we met. I applied and didn't think much more about it until last week. Three of us were brought in for interviews. I didn't tell you because I thought my chances were slim. Both of the others have more experience than I, so I accepted one of them would be more likely chosen. But the group of executives chose me. I have to let the Vice-President know by September 5th."

Dave asked, "What's your reluctance? It's what you've worked for."

"It means I'll be relocated to Kansas City. I won't do routine flights, but will spend my time at a desk in the headquarters other than flights to check on performances. If I say yes to this, I'd like you to come with me to Kansas City."

Dave put his glass on the table. "I'll have to think about this."

Her face close to his, she said, "You could start your own agency in the city. There'd be ample work for you, and we could spend all our free time together."

Dave paced across the room, his mind racing with the implications. "I'll have to discuss this with Jennifer. I couldn't just walk away without giving her time to reconfigure the firm. We've talked about adding another lawyer, but haven't found the right person yet."

She came to stand next to him. "I understand. You don't have to decide tonight."

Dave said, "What happens if you turn it down?"

"I'd go on much as I do now."

"But you'd always know you let the opportunity get away?"

She nodded. "Think about moving with me. We could have a life together. I'd be home almost every night. You could keep working."

Dave pulled her close. "I'll talk to Jennifer on Tuesday. And you're right, I have deep feelings for you and would like to be with you more than we've been able to manage in the few months we've known each other."

In the middle of the night, Dave eased out of bed without disturbing Gwen's sound sleep. He slipped on a robe and slippers and walked outside. In the coolness of the night, he paced across the porch and then to an out-building he'd converted into an exercise space. Images of Jennifer working at her desk wafted into his consciousness. They'd worked hard to build the firm. They'd worried it wouldn't work out when they struggled to pay the lease on the office and at one time, had almost given up. Now he could rip it asunder. From a deep recess of his mind he recalled the momentary desperation he'd experienced when she'd told him George had proposed and his relief when she had voiced reservations. He recalled her somber expression and a couple of tears when he'd told her about a deepening attraction for another woman. That romance had fallen apart for other reasons, but he realized Jennifer had been affected. His usual hard-nosed decisiveness turned to jello. He wasn't prepared to sort out his feelings for a life-change.

NINETEEN

Jennifer had barely entered her office on the Tuesday following Labor Day when she received a call from the Clerk of the Circuit Court, an older woman Jennifer had met briefly at one of the bar association functions.

"I intended to call you last Friday, but things got too hectic. Everybody seemed to have an urgent problem just before the holiday break. Nevertheless, the Judge is referring your appeal back to the Chester courts and is assigning the case to Judge Esther Plunkett. Her clerk will work with you in scheduling a preliminary hearing."

"Did he talk to Judge Young?"

"Yes. He called to tell him why he had given the case to someone else."

Jennifer sank into her chair, relief flooding her for an instant. Her thoughts turned immediately to the suit itself as she went to tell Dave.

"That's good news," Dave said, coming around the desk to shake her hand. "Now you can focus on the issues and quit worrying about Young."

"I assume you saw the paper about Junior's arrest. Have you heard anything more?"

"No, I didn't want to bother Rasmussen over the weekend."

"Did you have a good break?"

Before he could answer, Ellie interrupted to tell Jennifer that Judge Plunkett's clerk was on the phone. Over her shoulder, Jennifer said, "Let's have lunch and get up to date."

After a brisk walk through the noon-day crowd and a brief wait at the restaurant, by 12:15 they'd settled in a vacated booth in Gibbons. All the tables were filled. Single diners occupied most of the bar stools.

Jennifer said, "The preliminary hearing is scheduled for Thursday afternoon. I need to persuade Plunkett there's sufficient cause to go to trial."

"I guess Black and Redfield will contest and ask for dismissal?"

"That's a given. I expect Frawley or one of his buddies to show up, ready for battle, but I'm okay. Plunkett is known for tilting toward the downtrodden and poor. Remember, she's the one who ruled against Jackson Manufacturing in that deal where the custodial workers brought a discrimination suit."

"I recall," Dave said.

The waitress appeared to take their orders, stopping conversation while they requested the lunch special and coffee.

As she left, still scribbling on a pad, Jennifer asked, "You never were able to tell me about your weekend. How'd it go?"

Dave said, "Not very well." His voice rising and falling with emotion, he told her about Gwen's job offer and her wish for him to move with her to Kansas City. As he talked, Jennifer's smile gave way to a sober countenance. She screwed her lips into a tight line. She swiped at her eyes. The implications swarmed around both of them like wasps diving for the kill.

"What are you going to do?" Her voice trembled out a bare whisper.

"I don't know." Dave said. "I had to talk to you before deciding."

Their food was placed, but neither attacked the meal with their usual exuberance. Rather they nibbled and stole glances at each other, not comfortable with revealing their feelings, afraid of saying the wrong thing.

Finally, Jennifer said, "You know I don't want you to go."

"I don't want to wreck our partnership," Dave said. "It's going too well now."

Jennifer said, "It's more than the business." She stirred her soup and took a bite. "Can we have dinner and discuss this more?"

Relieved of an immediate showdown, Dave said, "I'll pick you up at 7:00."

Neither said anything as they walked back to the office, but Dave was surprised when she clasped his hand, something she never did in public. They disappeared into their offices, lost in their respective dilemmas, hoping to discover answers for personal issues somewhere in their work.

Dave parked in the taxi zone in front of Jennifer's apartment building for three minutes before she came through the front door. Her black dress, high heels, sheer nylons, pearls, and subtle makeup combined to scream sophistication. She looked more beautiful than he'd ever seen her.

At their table in Arthur's, they ordered and waited without conversation, each wanting the other to open the agonizing debate.

After the salad plates were removed and the entrees placed, Jennifer said, "I thought about us a lot this afternoon. I can't make a decision for you, but I want to tell you how I think about you—our relationship—personally and professionally."

She laid aside her fork and focused on his face. "I don't want you to go for two reasons. First, our partnership is doing great. We get along well and support each other. We have more clients than we can deal with at times. We're making money and we're enjoying what we do.

The practice has become what I dreamed of doing when I left New York. Professionally, I couldn't ask for better."

When he started to speak, she held up her hand. "Let me finish. From a personal perspective, I'm not very happy. George wants to marry me, but I don't love him and recognize it could be miserable trying to go through the motions of marriage without deep affection for the other person. My mother told me on numerous occasions about the demands of marriage and how you must be deeply committed to make it last."

She paused as though marshalling her thoughts. "This may shock you, but I've been in love with you almost from the time we met. I've kept my emotions in check because of the firm and not having a clue about how you felt. But when I saw your face after I told you George had asked me to marry, I decided I had to tell you how I felt. This thing with Gwen has brought it the forefront before I was prepared to face the issue squarely. But to be blunt, I think you're in love with me, but have held back for the same reasons I have. If I'm reading this correctly, we'd both be sorry if we don't give us a chance. I'd ask only that you put off any decision with Gwen for a few weeks until we sort it out."

After several seconds of shifting in his chair and looking around at other diners, Dave took her hand. "I'm ripped to shreds emotionally. This thing with Gwen and now you telling me how you feel is overwhelming. I don't know how to cope with the conflicts."

Jennifer said, "Confront reality as you do with everything else. Am I correct in believing you have deep feelings for me?"

Dave twisted his wine glass, shuffled his feet under the table. "More than I've ever admitted. I was afraid it would destroy our business relationship."

"We have to chance that," Jennifer said, squeezing his hand.

They focused on their food for a while, occasionally looking at each other. As they finished their entrees and wine, Jennifer said, "Come back to my place for coffee."

In her apartment, Jennifer brewed coffee while he wandered around the living area, examining paintings on the walls and family photographs on a book shelf. He realized he'd not been in her place but once before, a quick stop-by to deliver some document from the office during a time she'd been out with the flu.

She brought coffee in china cups to the table. They sat on the couch and sipped, the silence seeming to increase with each passing moment.

Jennifer put her cup on the table and turned toward him. "Think seriously about what I said before you commit to Gwen and moving." She edged closer to him, their shoulders and hips touching. Her uncovered knees and legs exposed during her movements aroused him.

Excited by her warmth, enticed by her perfume, and wishing to hold her close, Dave put his arm around her shoulders and touched her cheek with his lips. To his surprise she pulled his head to her parted lips. They kissed deeply. He resisted the urge to touch her knees, but caressed her back and neck. They continued to kiss, their mouths exploring, their eyes hooded with mounting passion.

Jennifer stood and unzipped her dress and helped him push it from her shoulders. She slipped it off and dropped it across a chair. She moved against him, searching for his mouth again. His desire increasing, he held her tightly, his hands moving across her hips. She led him toward the bedroom.

Two hours later they came alert and looked at each other. She kissed him and rolled on top of him. They made love again.

Still later, Dave awoke, his head spinning from his emotions and feelings for her. He'd never experienced such desire to meet someone else's needs. Sex had been wonderful, but something unique to his experience had happened. He watched her sleeping, her hair, always neatly arranged, now tangled around her face. He wanted to pull her to him, but didn't wish to wake her. He dropped asleep, his arm around her waist.

Her alarm went off at 6:00. Both came awake.

Dave mumbled through his drowsiness. "I should get home and get ready for work." He rolled off the bed to find his clothes.

Jennifer stood by him. "This is what it could be like every day. We could have a leisurely breakfast and open the office on time."

Showering and dressing at his place, Dave couldn't remember driving home. All his thoughts were about Jennifer and what had happened between them. Memories of Gwen's bright smile and bubbly laugh confused him more.

Still in a daze, he brewed coffee and prepared cereal. Jennifer deserved the opportunity to have them sort through the barriers in their thinking about relationships in and out of the office. He locked the door and got into the Blazer. The right thing to do emerged as he turned out of his drive onto the main road toward the city.

Jennifer had arrived before him and had settled at her desk, a sheaf of papers spread across the surface. She smiled as he entered.

Dave said, "I'm overwhelmed by last night and am still sorting it all out. But, you're right, we need time. We shouldn't rush into something that will change our lives forever."

Jennifer looked into his face. "I know what's right for me. I tried to tell you last night in more ways than one. Our togetherness is the best thing that's ever happened to me."

Dave returned her look. "Let's have dinner on Friday. By then, I will know."

"Don't forget how I feel about you."

"I couldn't," Dave said, "after last night."

Alone in her office Jennifer focused on her presentation before Plunkett, trying to push aside the approaching decision between Dave and herself. She intended to be prepared and aggressive in making the case for Maude Frame and her co-workers. They deserved her best shot. She couldn't be ineffective because of personal issues.

At 1:30 on Thursday, Judge Plunkett called the preliminary hearing to order. "I want each attorney to present the essential facts of their position without attempts to persuade me one way or the other and without attacking each other. If you can do that, I'll arrive at a conclusion by noon tomorrow and we can proceed from that point. After both have made their case, I'll allow time for rebuttals and clarification of positions, if needed."

Jennifer argued Frame and others had been victims of an over-zealous company more interested in profits than in serving long-time clients who depended on insurance coverage for various but vital reasons. Their privacy had been invaded. They had been deceived by the physical exams designed for the sole purpose of discovering potential genetic predispositions to health related problems. She summarized the genetic assays and rationale for the company's dropping selected workers. They had been declared disabled for the purpose of canceling insurance policies. Thus, Black and Redfield had violated the Americans With Disabilities Act.

Ellie, sitting at the table with Jennifer, silently clapped when Jennifer had finished. She'd been organized, forceful, and terse.

Frawley argued Black and Redfield had the obligation to its shareholders to make a profit and had the right to weed out those policyholders who posed the likelihood of costing the company huge amounts of money in the future. It was becoming a common practice among companies who needed to change their operational modes to remain healthy. Black and Redfield was following the lead of others. He maintained the company had the right to cancel policies of anyone predestined to have a debilitating and crippling disease that would cost the organization money for as long as they lived. And if the individual died early, the costs would be greater than if the person lived to the usual life expectancy.

During the rebuttal phase, Jennifer said, 'Black and Redfield broke the law and reneged on its promise to those workers. If every insurance company routinely behaved in that fashion, no one would purchase policies. Clients have the right to believe the company will remain true to its covenant."

S. J. RITCHEY

Frawley stood and said, "Judge, Ms. Watson and her colleagues obtained confidential information on which to base their case. They should be chastised for ignoring the court order by Judge Young and in some other way searching through personnel files. If those data are not admissible, there is no case."

Jennifer had anticipated the charge. "Judge Plunkett, when Black and Redfield refused to tell clients why their insurance had been cancelled, we obtained a court order from a officer of this court to review those files. We acted in good faith in trying to determine the rationale for the cancellations." At one point in her preparation, Jennifer had deliberated about accusing Judge Young of wrongdoing in ruling in favor of Black and Redfield, but decided she could alienate Plunkett.

Frawley said, "The request for punitive damages is ridiculous. These people suffered nothing."

Jennifer smiled as she stood and glanced toward Frawley, "Your Honor, I submit if your insurance policy, one you'd paid premiums for twenty years and on which you depended to care for a misfortunate relative, was suddenly and without explanation dropped, you would agonize and worry over the future. You would worry about whom you could trust if a once-reputable organization abandoned you without recourse because of age or some other factor. Black and Redfield should be held liable for broken promises."

Frawley scowled, but offered nothing more.

Plunkett reminded them she'd provide her ruling by noon tomorrow and asked that the two attorneys meet in her chambers at 11:45.

Jennifer and Ellie returned to the office, but Jennifer couldn't focus on another matter. Her life was in turmoil. The situation with Dave had to be resolved. She was afraid he wouldn't have the courage to say no to Gwen. She should have spoken up sooner rather than waiting for him to make the first move. She'd likely made it worse by seducing him.

Plus, Plunkett had been impossible to read. She'd asked no questions while making copious notes. If Plunkett ruled in favor of Black and Redfield, she would have let all those workers down. She would have treated them the same as Black and Redfield.

TWENTY

Plunkett invited Jennifer and Frawley into her chambers promptly at 11:45 on Friday morning. They each took a worn leather chair in front of the desk after Plunkett sat in a high-back chair behind a desk clean of everything except one open folder.

The Judge started immediately as though she wanted to get an unpleasant task behind her and move on. "I've reviewed the transcript of your presentations and rebuttals, called a couple of out-of-state attorneys familiar with the Americans With Disabilities Act, and read again the background information collected by my clerk. In my opinion, Ms. Watson has made a solid argument for a trial. The workers she represents were singled out based on their genetic profile. Then they were treated unfairly and unlawfully by Black and Redfield who used the power of a large organization to harm the very people they promised to protect and support. It's clear in my judgment the company has broken the laws under the Disabilities Act. But, I would hope you can avoid a lengthy trial and find common ground on which to resolve the issue. If you are willing, I will serve as mediator and save both of you and the courts considerable time and effort required for a trial, particularly if a jury is involved as Ms. Watson has requested. Incidentally, I'd be in favor of recommending a jury hear the case because the outcome may have implications beyond this one incident. As both of you know, the Disabilities Act has received very little attention from the courts and few precedents have been established. From my perspective, a jury of peers should be involved in setting those."

Jennifer spoke up when Plunkett nodded to them for reactions. "Obviously I'm pleased with your decision. I believe we can reach a settlement out of court and I'd certainly be open to trying."

Frawley said, his voice gruff and challenging. "Judge, I don't know how my client will react, but I must confer with them before agreeing to any attempt to settle, especially if the matter of punitive charges remains a part of Watson's plan. Frankly, I am appalled at the ruling and your interpretation of the statute."

Her voice taking on the tenor of a teacher lecturing an elementary school student, Plunkett countered, "Mr. Frawley, I will stand by my interpretations. I suggest you review the Disabilities Act."

She paused, leaning forward on her desk, "How long will you need to consult with your client?"

Frawley examined his briefcase for a moment. "Give me until next Friday."

Jennifer nodded. "That would give me time to discuss options with my clients."

Closing the folder, Plunkett said, "Let's meet again on next Friday at the same time." She came around the desk to shake their hands.

Outside the chambers, Frawley muttered, "What a crock. The bitch ignored Young's earlier ruling."

Jennifer kept walking and entered the ladies restroom near the corner of the hall. She wanted to yell in triumph, but restrained herself. Now she had to consider what would be a fair settlement for individuals like Maude Frame.

Dave and Jennifer had dinner reservations in the restaurant at the top of the Marriott. They were led to a table immediately in the sparsely occupied dining room. The lights of Chester glimmered in every direction, adding to the ambience of the flickering candles, starched linen and polished silver adorning the tables.

Dave said, "I've never been here before. The views are better than I imagined."

She filled him in on the ruling by Plunkett, adding, "Frawley was beside himself. I thought he would croak when Plunkett revealed her findings."

"He assumed she would do the same thing as Young."

She smiled, her eyes lighting with pleasure, "I had to restrain myself by not gloating."

Dave chortled at her facial expression. "You should have suggested he buy out every judge in the system."

He opened the menu and turned pages. "Shall we have champagne to celebrate?"

Her face turned somber. "The question about us is more important."

Dave laid aside the menu. "I called Gwen last night. We agreed it'd be best if I remained here and she went her own way. It was difficult for me because she's filled a void in my life for a while and I have great respect for her. When she asked if our relationship was more than professional, I said yes without revealing details. She surprised me by saying she'd known for some time I was in love with you, but I was too dense—she really meant dumb—to acknowledge my true feelings."

Dave sipped water, than added, "She's the second person to tell me that. Remember Miriam from the television station—she broke up with me because she thought we were involved. She let me know I shouldn't call her again until I'd gotten over my infatuation-that was her word."

Jennifer reached to take his hand. "I told George yesterday. He called about a concert on Sunday evening. I didn't tell him about us, but said I would no longer be available."

"So where do we go next?"

Jennifer said, "We could get a room here and I could seduce you again, but maybe we should start with champagne and dinner." Her toe touched his leg under the table.

Dave signaled for the waiter. "Let's do this up right. There's a lot to celebrate."

As they finished desert, Dave said, "Were you serious about a room here?"

"I'd prefer you come back to my place or we could spend the week-end at your isolated retreat."

Dave grinned. "My place. I'll show you around the land tomorrow with the hope you'll someday be agreeable to moving there."

"Okay, but I'll need to go by my apartment and get different clothes."

He grinned. "You're right. That dress wouldn't quite be appropriate for tramping around, but I could loan you shorts and tee shirts."

"I'm glad you noticed the dress. It's a new one I bought this afternoon after the Plunkett ruling."

"It's sexy and you look beautiful."

"Let's hear what you think after I've spent the week-end with you and you see my out-of-the-office style."

On Wednesday, Reginald Broom called Jennifer. "The ethics committee of the Bar Association met last night. I brought up the matter about Judge Young. We're setting up a meeting with Young and would like you to attend. Bring your briefs and be prepared to review the facts of your case. I don't know if that will be necessary, but we'd like you to be ready. I'm also asking the attorney who handled our case to either attend or bring me up to date on the essential facts."

"I assume," Jennifer said, "the committee believes Young has been compromised?"

"We've learned of three cases in which Young ruled in favor of Black and Redfield when the evidence suggested otherwise. One of our members has reviewed the judgments and believes Young was wrong. That doesn't include your suit because there was never a hearing. Nor does it include the deal with the son. Although the same lawyers represented the son, it doesn't seem to be connected with Black and Redfield."

Jennifer said, "Young, Jr. was arrested last week on another charge of distributing illegal substances. We know one of those brought in with him is an official at Black and Redfield. It could be unrelated, but it's fishy."

Broom said, "We didn't make the connection. You might be prepared to put that on the table if it seems appropriate."

Broom continued, "As you'd guess, we don't know how Young will react. But if he outright refuses to discuss our concerns, we're planning to file a breach of ethics suit and ask that he resign."

"You believe it necessary he resign?"

"Either that or cut all ties to Black and Redfield and agree to recuse himself from their future cases. And revisit those cases in which he ruled in their favor."

Jennifer asked, "May I bring my partner? He knows the details of the son's arrest and charges."

"I'd rather confine our session to the committee and you. And we're all bound to confidentiality. It's too early to go public."

Broom continued, "Tell me when you'll not be available. I'm working with our various calendars to find a convenient time. When I've sorted it out, I'll let you know."

"So you know," Jennifer volunteered, "the Circuit Court referred my case to Judge Plunkett. She is recommending a jury trial if we can't reach a settlement."

"Good luck with the case. I'll call about our meeting."

Judge Plunkett opened her chamber door precisely at 11:45 on Friday. Jennifer and Frawley returned to their usual chairs.

Plunkett asked, "Mr. Frawley, what's your decision about seeking a settlement."

Shifting in his chair to include Jennifer in his range of vision, Frawley said, "We'll agree to the reinstatement of policies, but we're going to resist paying the punitive damages."

Jennifer watched Frawley's expression. His eyes shifted from his notes to her face and to the Judge.

She decided he was bluffing. "Judge Plunkett, my clients are willing to compromise on the damages, but they deserve something for all the worry and frustration caused by the illegal actions of Black and Redfield."

Plunkett said, "I've continued to ponder this situation. If a jury or a judge found Black and Redfield guilty of unlawful actions under the Disabilities Act, there could be significant fines imposed. Mr. Frawley, I suggest you reconsider and we seek a figure less than the one Ms. Watson proposed."

Frawley fumbled through a set of papers on his lap. "My client is not willing to pay a red cent to these people."

When Plunkett looked at her, Jennifer said, "We'd compromise at $7500 per plaintiff and court costs, along with reinstatement of policies without penalty."

Frawley considered for a moment, his eyes shifting from the Judge to Jennifer. "We'll take our chances in court."

Plunkett said, "I'll check the docket and establish a date for a trial And I'll honor Ms. Watson's request for a jury to hear the evidence. An immediate question, how soon can each of you be ready?"

Frawley face's screwed up in distaste, but he muttered, "I'll need a month, Your Honor."

Jennifer replied, "A month will be sufficient for me."

Jennifer left the chamber wondering if she'd made an error in judgment. She'd clearly misread Frawley's intentions about damages. Restoration of policies would have satisfied most of the workers. But they should receive compensation for the dirty tricks played on them by Black and Redfield. Testing the American With Disabilities Act in a court trial might be a liability with essentially no precedent to guide either the judge or the attorneys. Plowing new ground could be filled with unforeseen obstacles and leave her clients holding an empty bag.

Maude Frame answered Jennifer's call on the second ring. "Mrs. Frame, I've been unable to settle your suit out of court. The judge will establish a trial by jury to begin in about a month. You and others will be called as witnesses."

Frame's apprehension was evident by her gasp "I don't know if I'm up to that."

Jennifer said, "Mrs. Frame, you'll just have to tell your story about the physical exams, the notice of cancellation, and the refusal of the company to respond to your questions. I will walk you through your testimony so you'll know what's coming at every step." She'd also prepare Frame for Frawley's bombardment on cross examination, but she didn't want to tell her about that phase yet.

Jennifer and Ellie called the others. Several were non-committal, having decided the whole thing was hopeless. After all, when did an ordinary worker prevail against a large, rich organization with all their high-powered lawyers.

Jennifer began listing the work she had to do. She'd need to get Rose Mitchell from Biological Assays, Inc. geared up to serve as an expert witness. She'd have to select two or three of the workers to testify. Maude Frame almost certainly had to be one. Bannister might be credible. He surely had the guts. Fitzgerald might be too shaky.

She assigned Ellie the task of searching for any recent precedents or rulings involving the Disabilities Act. She called a jury analyst to see if she would be willing to review the pool and help her select the panel most likely to lean in favor of those workers. The potential costs loomed large, enough to put a substantial dent in the firm's reserves if she failed.

By the end of the week both Jennifer and Dave knew they'd made the right decision. At his place on Saturday morning, Dave said, "Have you thought more about marriage, where we live, how much do we tell other people?"

"We could live here," Jennifer said, her eyes bright with pleasure. "I'd like to change several things, but it's doable without a lot of expense."

"Like what?"

"The so-called master bedroom. It should have more light, and I'd want to add more storage space. My clothes won't fit in the closets. And upgrade the bathroom."

Dave said, "I expected you to say that. I've asked a builder to come by this afternoon and look the place over. He can tell us what's possible within the present structure and what could be added. We may want to add an entire wing, including a new bedroom. Convert the old one into a guest room or an office."

Jennifer came to lean against him. "You always surprise me by staying a step ahead."

"Not always," Dave said. "You thought about making this legal?"

"You mean marriage?"

He nodded. "We could live together, but legal issues always seem to favor married couples."

"You having second thoughts about this?"

"No, but jumping into marriage so fast may not be the best idea."

"Dave, we've known each other for three years, have spent most of our working hours together, and we've never had a serious disagreement."

"But you've never seen my habits beyond work."

"I'll take the chance it'll be okay. Let's do it. We can arrange with a Justice of the Peace without a lot of publicity. I should keep my name for professional reasons."

Dave said, "You think through those issues. I'll depend on your judgment. But now, I'd like to go running. You interested?"

"Maybe tomorrow. I need to review those documents Ellie prepared for the Frazier case before this builder comes."

They grilled steaks and opened a bottle of Merlot for dinner. As they finished cheesecake and coffee, Dave turned on the television.

A special bulletin ran across the lower screen, then the news anchor broke into the regular program. "We learned an hour ago an undercover police woman had been killed and her body dumped behind a warehouse on Blount street. A pair of homeless men discovered the body late this afternoon while scavenging through dumpsters behind the building. The deceased has been identified as Angela Johnson. She leaves a husband and two daughters. Anyone having information about the murder is urged to call the Chester police." The telephone number of the station flashed onto the screen for a few seconds.

TWENTY-ONE

Their plans for a Sunday morning hike through the woods were washed out by a downpour derived from a hurricane that had hit the Texas coast two days earlier. Sheets of water cascaded against the windows. Wind gusts whipped across the yard and nearby woods, snapping limbs from trees and sending debris to rest against the buildings.

Having spent the night agonizing about Angela's death, Dave took a chance mid-morning and called Rasmussen, betting the detective would be in his office focused on discovering the cause of the murder of his co-detective.

Dave said, "Sorry to bother you, but I heard the news last night. It's tough about Angela."

Strain evident in his voice, Rasmussen said, "We're all devastated. She had been a great detective for us. Did her job in a professional way. Never asked for favors because of family responsibilities."

"I'm sorry too," Dave said. "Any ideas about what went wrong? Did my meeting her have anything to do with it?"

Rasmussen said, "I doubt it. Roscoe's was overrun with strangers after Junior and his buddies were arrested. Angela reported at least three tough-looking characters she'd never seen before. We suspect they were sniffing around to find out what had gone wrong. Maybe they saw Angela do something suspicious. She and I had talked Friday morning by phone. She didn't express any worries, but went into work as usual. She was there when they closed. Someone attacked her after she'd left the place around midnight."

"I'd bet someone guessed her real role."

"We're bringing Roscoe and two regular workers in for additional questioning. Plus, we're talking with some of the customers who spend a lot of time there. But they're usually under the influence and wouldn't have noticed anything different short of the building collapsing."

"It's worth a try though," Dave said. "If I can do anything, let me know. I'd be willing to spend a few hours hanging around the bar."

"Thanks. I'll let you know."

Jennifer had observed and listened to his side of the interchange. She asked, "You feel responsible?"

"To some degree. People distrust strangers in those places, especially if they do something out of the ordinary. I don't think I did, but you never know how some action will be perceived. Only takes one slip or even a single suspicion by the crooks."

"Are you planning to go back there?"

Going to the window to watch the heavy rain that had started at dawn, Dave said, "Not unless Rasmussen asks. I could get in the way."

Jennifer said, "You okay with the ideas the contractor had about remodeling? You didn't say much." The builder and an architect, partners in a small firm in Chester, had spent three hours Saturday afternoon walking through the house, making measurements, and checking the original plans. Then they presented preliminary ideas and responded to questions and suggestions from Jennifer. They'd promised detailed plans in ten days.

"I wanted it to be what you'd like. I'm not thrilled about vacating while the work goes on. But they're right. It'll be a big mess and we'd get in their way."

"My lease on the apartment runs through December. We could live there. The contractor promised he could do the work in two months."

They stared at the rain for a minute. Dave pulled her close. "Let's do that. I'll get my stuff ready by the time the builder begins here."

Jennifer said, "Since we can't hike, we could go back to bed." She turned to face him and leaned against him.

Dave kissed her. "Good idea."

The ethics committee assembled in a small room off the lobby of the administration building for a quick review before confronting Judge Young. Broom introduced Jennifer to the two other members, both gray-haired white men dressed in expensive dark suits.

Broom said, "I'll take the lead, but encourage each of you to comment or ask questions as you deem necessary. I'll call on Ms. Watson if it seems appropriate, but we know the crux of her case based on our previous discussion. Young understands the function of this committee and no doubt is prepared to refute anything we accuse him of, but let's stick to our guns." They moved toward the Judge's private domain.

Andy Chafin met them in the outer office and escorted them into Young's private space precisely at the appointed time. In the tense atmosphere devoid of the usual greetings, Young pointed them to seats in front of his desk. Chafin closed the door and departed.

Young asked, "What can I discuss with this group?" His brusque tone implied the committee was on a ill-advised mission.

Broom said, "Judge Young, you understand the functions of this committee and know we take no pleasure in our mission today. We've invited Ms. Watson to join us in the event her case becomes an item of discussion."

Broom paused momentarily, then continued, "I'll be straight-forward. Several of your recent rulings have raised deep concerns in the legal community. Two were appealed and your decisions overturned or returned to this court for further consideration. But the underlying basis of our visit is that each of your judgments in those cases resulted in a favorable outcome for Black and Redfield, in spite of evidence running counter to the outcome. The suit brought by Ms. Watson is one example. Also, persistent rumors of payoffs by Black and Redfield have served to deepen our distress. Further, your sitting in judgment when your son was involved is highly irregular, questionable, and unethical. You know, as well as everyone associated with the judiciary, you should have excused yourself when a family member can benefit."

Young broke in. "When my son was brought for a preliminary hearing, no other judge was available. The prosecutor insisted we move forward. As for the other situations, I stand by my decisions. They were based on the evidence presented and the law."

Continuing in an even tone, Broom said, "Judge, we must respectfully disagree. Each member of this committee has reviewed the court records of those disputed cases. Independently, we came to the same conclusion. Black and Redfield benefited from your rulings contrary to the arguments presented by opposing counsels. Every review suggests you ignored the statutes and the evidence to help that organization. This committee is requesting a written explanation with details of your thinking. We acknowledge you may be right, but we wish to understand your rationale."

Young's face darkened as he stared at them. "I'm not going to do that. My reputation for fair dealing is impeccable and I'm not caving in to a bunch of self-appointed vigilantes."

Unfazed, Broom continued, "Judge, we represent the Bar Association. If you fail to comply with our request, we intend to file a breach of ethics suit against you. In our opinion, you have used the power of your office to subvert justice. And we believe the evidence is strong enough to result in censure and a demand for your resignation. You'd be well served to explain your actions rather than stonewall this inquiry. We would like to resolve this without a public revelation involving the press. That serves no useful purpose, but potentially damages both you personally and the court system."

Stone-faced, Young stood. "We're done here. And I don't expect to hear more of this tripe."

They all stood. Broom said, "Judge Young, we expect a response within a week." He handed Young an envelope containing a written request.

The group paused in the foyer of the building. Huddled closely, a member asked, "Now what?"

Broom said, "We'll give him the week. He may come to his senses, but if he doesn't, we'll follow through. Sometimes long-standing judges come to believe they're above the law and can do as they damn well please. They resent being challenged, but often they accept reality after they've had time to consider all the implications."

Jennifer said, "Thanks for inviting me. I learned something today." She'd been impressed by Broom's toughness. He had maintained a stern professionalism during the confrontation. Most attorneys wouldn't challenge a sitting judge. And she'd been surprised at Young's behavior as though he could not be questioned.

Broom said, "We admired your brief against Black and Redfield. I'd like to have you appointed a member of this committee. It's past time we brought in younger and female representatives."

Jennifer said, "I'd be pleased to serve. I need to expand my experience beyond my own practice."

As the group dispersed, Broom said, "I'm pretty sure the chairman will agree with our recommendation. Either he or I will give you a call in a few days."

Driving away, Jennifer realized the committee members had conferred in her absence about both her brief and her potential appointment. She felt good about having three older and experienced attorneys, none of whom she'd known before, support her wider exposure to the legal community.

* * *

With October 15 firmly set for the beginning of the trial, Jennifer focused on preparation, using every free hour to work on the case. She visited with all the workers in an effort to select the ones she'd use as witnesses. She met with Rose Mitchell over lunch and discussed her testimony. She conferred with the nurse at the GM clinic about her role in bringing the workers in for physical exams. She labored through the set of questions she'd ask of every witness and tried to guess who, if anyone, Black and Redfield would use to refute the claims of the workers.

The contractor responded with final plans for the renovation more quickly than they'd anticipated. Dave moved his clothing and personal items to her apartment. Within a day Jennifer realized he missed his house and the freedom of his daily jogs through his property. But he used the exercise equipment on the first floor of the building and ran along the city streets and into the parks. She'd joined him every other day for runs and after the first few exhausting experiences, she'd begun to look forward to the routine.

Three days after their meeting with Young, Broom had called to confirm her appointment to the Ethics Committee of the Chester Bar Association and promised to send her a document spelling out the duties and operating procedure of the committee.

Ten days after the confrontation with Young, Broom called regarding the Judge's failure to respond and to confirm a time for a committee meeting. The next day the committee assembled during lunch in a private room on the second floor of the Marriott.

After a waitress had taken their orders and left the room, Broom said, "I called Judge Young two days ago to remind him of our request for his response. He told me quite vividly he had no intention of explaining his actions. In short, he suggested we go to hell."

Joseph Bell, a partner in a huge firm concentrating on corporate issues, said, "He understands we're serious, doesn't he?"

Broom said, "I thought we'd been clear about our intentions. In my opinion, he expects we'll cave in and let the matter drop. But we should prepare and file a breach of ethics suit. Ignoring him will only nurture his arrogance."

Jennifer asked, "If I understand the process, judges are appointed by the Governor. Should we inform his office of our actions and ask for his intervention?"

Broom nodded. "Good idea. I'll do that this afternoon. The Governor appoints but depends upon recommendations from regional bar associations for nominees. He also solicits opinions of the legislative body, but he holds the final authority."

Bell said, "Young has been in office so long, I doubt this present governor knows who he is, but it's appropriate to touch base with him. There's never a systematic review of these guys. Once you're in, you can stay until age 70. In this state, judges cannot serve after that age, but often they fill in for others during illness or work when the load becomes too much for the others to handle in a timely manner. And given the vacancies, some of these old judges go on almost full time until they die. Effectiveness and even-handedness are forgotten issues."

Broom asked, "Is anyone willing to prepare the brief?"

Bell said, "I'll have a couple of junior guys work on it, then send it around for your review and modification." Jennifer was relieved by Bell's quick response, fearing as the junior member of the committee, she'd be asked to do the scut work. Preparing the brief would have presented a learning experience, but she didn't have the time with the Frame case on her agenda.

Broom said, "I'll call the Governor's office and call Young to let him know we're following through."

After the waitress brought their orders and closed the door, Broom said, "Now let's enjoy lunch. Perhaps Ms. Watson can tell us a bit more about her background and her firm and we can tell her some war stories, but let's not allow those things to deter our eating."

When they all looked at Jennifer, she said, "If you wish, I'll give you a quick overview of Watson and Randle, as well as my own background." She began with her departure from a large New York firm and returning to Chester, the largest city near her home town.

Three days later, Broom called Jennifer. "Ms. Watson, I wanted to tell you before you hear the news in the media that Judge Young has submitted his resignation to the Governor. An assistant in the executive office called me a few minutes ago. Young will use declining health as a reason for resigning."

"I assume we will not follow through now."

"There's no reason to press the issue other than to be vindictive. Young had a long and distinguished career. Something went badly wrong in the past few months, but we'll let him retire without smearing him in his final days. We accomplished our goal of removing a compromised official without making a public ado about it."

Jennifer said, "It seems to have worked out well, although he damaged several people."

"Thanks for your participation, Ms. Watson," Broom said. "And good luck with your suit against Black and Redfield. I'll be interested in how it turns out."

Jennifer replaced the receiver with mixed feelings. Getting Young out of the justice system was a plus, but letting him walk away seemed ill-advised. She wanted him to admit responsibility for those people he'd damaged. Then she worried this confrontational system was making her overly vindictive.

TWENTY-TWO

Promptly at 9:00 on October 15th, the bailiff announced all in the court room should rise as Judge Esther Plunkett took her position to preside over the trial of Black and Redfield versus Frame and others. The court room was half-filled by family members of the workers, several officials from Black and Redfield, a couple of curious observers, and a single reporter from the local paper. In the absence of last-minute motions by either side, they set out to select the panel of jurors.

Jennifer had reviewed the backgrounds of each of the forty-seven individuals from whom the jury of twelve and two alternates would be chosen. She had relied in part on the expertise of a jury analyst, one of a cadre of national experts who made their livelihood advising lawyers about the tendencies of persons from varied backgrounds and how they are likely to respond under given sets of conditions. Jennifer wanted a jury of blue-collar workers who would more likely lean toward protecting the rights of workers rather than supporting a large company that had preyed on those helpless people. She'd prepared a list of general questions for all and specific ones for selected individuals. She would challenge three people immediately because of their affluence and affiliation with other insurance companies. She expected Frawley to seek jurors with exactly opposite leanings, thus the battle could drag on for hours. She'd told Dave the first day would be spent on jury selection, but she was pleased he'd come with her and occupied a back-row seat.

The first prospective juror was an older woman dressed in a poorly-fitted navy suit, no doubt the outfit she wore to church, funerals, and other occasions requiring her to look her best. Her rough hands revealed she was used to manual labor. Her alert face suggested she had considerable common sense based on life's difficult experiences.

Jennifer asked, "Mrs. Pauley, do you understand insurance policies and the commitments companies make when they sell you such coverage."

Nodding her gray head, she said, "I know some things, but it can get confusing."

"Do you have any knowledge of this case?"

Shaking her head, Pauley answered, "No. I seldom read the papers or see the news."

Jennifer passed and Frawley rose.

Frawley asked, "Would you have difficulty voting against a claim for which the person had no right to have all their life? You know insurance policies contain conditions under which the company can withdraw or cancel with appropriate payouts. In those cases, could you vote against the policy holder?"

Pauley squinted at the lawyer. "I try to be fair with everybody."

"Do you have any insurance yourself?"

"No, but my husband has something with his company. He's told me it would help me if he dies before I do."

Frawley paced back to the table and picked up a sheet of paper. After scanning it for a moment, he said, "Judge, I'll accept Mrs. Pauley."

Thus, the first member of the jury was agreed upon. They moved on to the next person, a mid-level executive with a retail chain. Jennifer knew his background included several years as a clerk in a large store in St. Louis. He'd been promoted to a manager position, and later to regional sales director with an office in Chester.

She asked, "Mr. Randolph, do you believe organizations should always make profits?"

Randolph fingered the lapel of his gray suit. "A company's first responsibility is to their owners or stockholders. They should always aim for ways to reward those people who have invested in the organization."

"Even if their actions damage other people?"

"Companies must remember to whom they're responsible."

"In your opinion, are organizations responsible to keep their promises to their clients?"

Randolph said, "They are bound by contracts, but usually those are written with exceptions and waivers. Customers are responsible for understanding the risks."

Jennifer turned to Judge Plunkett. "Your Honor, I'd like to exercise a preemptive challenge and excuse Mr. Randolph."

The third prospect, a dairy farmer living just outside the city limits of Chester, was excused by Frawley after he'd declared his refusal to ever deal with insurance companies after one had failed to reimburse him for fire damage to his barn.

Through the morning, the attorneys jockeyed to fill the jury with those to their liking. By 11:45, five panelists had been approved. Plunkett recessed until 1:30 and reminded the lawyers of the need to move forward more quickly.

Dave waited in the hall as Jennifer arranged her papers in preparation for the afternoon. They walked rapidly to a small diner around the block from the courthouse. Although it was becoming a bit run-down, the Downtown Diner retained its reputation for good food and fast service. Its no-frills atmosphere attracted professionals rushing to meet deadlines and not concerned about impressing a client. Ahead of the noon rush, Jennifer led Dave to a booth along the outside glass wall.

A waitress appeared immediately to take their orders for the daily special.

Jennifer said, "You must be bored with all this wrangling and prodding."

"It's not the most exciting thing I've watched, but I know it's important."

"It is. The decision will eventually rest on those twelve people. I can't afford to empanel one I know will argue against my position. I feel good about the ones we've chosen thus far but I have to remain vigilant."

The chicken soup and grilled cheese sandwiches were placed in front of them and coffee cups were filled. The efficient waitress dropped their check recognizing that most of her noon customers were in a hurry.

Dave said, "I'm going over to the police station and talk to Rasmussen this afternoon, but I'll be back by the time you finish."

"I think it might go faster now that Frawley and I know each other's approach. If there's sufficient time after jury selection, Plunkett will charge the jury and ask for opening statements."

"I'd like to hear your opening," Dave said. "I've never seen you in court before."

"You haven't had many opportunities. As with the majority of cases, most of ours have been settled without trials. I was really nervous at first this morning, but I adjusted."

"Some of the Black and Redfield boys were present. I recognized your old buddy Morton and if my memory of descriptions are on target, Hoyt was there. Another guy seemed attached to them."

"They're supporting Frawley," Jennifer said, shoving the soup bowl aside and blotting her mouth with the napkin.

Dave picked up the check and left a generous tip. They weaved through the crowd at the door, touched hands, and headed in different directions.

Dave stopped in the entry of the Chester police station to read Rasmussen's name and new title—Deputy Director. He found Rasmussen in his office, the usual mug of strong coffee emitting odors and wisps of vapor.

Rasmussen said, "Haven't seen you in a while. Doing okay?"

"Yeah, I got bored watching the trial and decided to check by. Anything about Angela's murder?"

"Nope," Rasmussen said, his face clouding with frustration." We've reached a dead end. Just like with Redfield."

"No one saw anything unusual during her last shift at Roscoe's?"

Shaking his head, Rasmussen said, "If they did, they haven't told our people. It's like she said good night, walked out toward her car in the back lot, and dropped into a dark hole. Her purse was missing, so we're about ready to chalk it up to a robbery gone sour. She resisted and the punk shot her, then carried her body away."

"Probably take two. She was not a small person."

Rasmussen nodded. "It's absolute frustration. We lost a really good cop. I worry about her kids since her husband is not the most reliable citizen I've known."

Dave stood. "Keep at it. I can't accept the robbery motive. I'd bet most night she walks out with other workers. It'd be too risky to grab her with others around and too improbable to luck out on the night she was alone."

"Unless it had been planned to work out that way."

"Could have happened," Dave said.

Rasmussen said, "I've talked to the Chief about your involvement. If you're still willing, we'd like you to nose around Roscoe's. Go in for a drink, talk to the bartender, maybe get to know Roscoe himself. We'll pay your normal rate for a few hours."

"That's unusual, isn't it?"

Rasmussen said, "It's been done before and you have the moxie to find out things our own people haven't. They're too constrained by the rules and regulations to be very aggressive."

Dave nodded, thinking he could work a few visits into the bar around his other cases and the trial. Jennifer thought the trial would be over in three days, but after observing this morning, he thought they might still be debating about jurors. "I'll do that for you guys. I respected Angela, although I talked to her only once."

"Just keep up with your time and let me know. I may kick in a bonus of free coffee once in a while."

"That may be enough to convince me to become a permanent member of your force."

At the door, Dave paused. "Jennifer and I are getting married. We haven't set a date yet, but it'll be a quiet deal—her family and a few friends."

Rasmussen came around the desk to shake his hand. "I'm pleased for both of you. I knew it'd happen. You two are meant for each other."

"It took us a while to figure it out and we hurt a couple of nice people."

"That's not unusual. Just so you finally got it right."

After Dave left Rasmussen, he went by a local hardware store still functioning in a downtown location to check on possible plumbing hardware replacements for the bathroom in the house. The wide range of options made deciding longer than he'd expected. He returned to the court room as the final jury member was agreed upon. Now almost 4:30, Plunkett suggested they recess until the morning at which point she would instruct the jury with opening statements to follow. Neither attorney objected, not wishing to irritate the Judge. Plus, they were ready for a break.

Dave waved to Jennifer when she turned to find him, then walked into the hall while she stuffed papers into her briefcase.

He was gazing out the window at the traffic along the street, aware the audience had dissipated and Frawley had walked past. He heard Jennifer's heels clicking on the tile floor. He turned to see her disappear into the women's restroom. Bruce Hoyt and another man followed her in.

Dave raced to the door. A woman, arguing and resisting, was being shoved out by a large arm.

Dave barked to her. "Get security—now."

He pushed through the door, partially barred by the man who yelled, "You can't come in here."

Dave slammed him against a panel around one of the private stalls. The man struggled to keep his balance, clawing for a gun in his arm holster. Dave hit him solidly in the throat, sending him crashing to the floor, gasping to get air. Dave took his gun and clipped him across the head. The man collapsed in a heap. Dave dropped the gun in the waste-basket.

Hoyt had Jennifer pinned against the outside wall, one hand at her throat. She screamed and clawed at his face. Her purse and briefcase were on the floor.

Her resistance had surprised and frustrated Hoyt. When he raised his fist to hit her, Dave grabbed his arm and twisted hard, backward and upward, using both surprise and leverage. Hoyt screamed as his elbow wrenched out of place.

Jennifer regained her balance and moved toward them as Hoyt struggled with Dave.

Dave yelled, "Go find security."

Dave rammed Hoyt against the wall. "Now, you fucking bully, I'm going to hurt you real bad." He punched Hoyt in the nose, smashing the cartilage, sending blood streaming down his shirt and coat.

Hoyt tried to throw a punch with his good arm. Dave kicked him in the gut, then under the chin when he doubled over. Hoyt's knees wobbled, but Dave slashed him across the throat with the side of his hand.

Hoyt dropped to his knees, gasping for air through his damaged trachea. Dave kicked him in the ribs. Hoyt sprawled onto the floor, moaning and clutching his side.

Dave walked out, passing two security guards on the way in with Jennifer close behind.

One guard asked, "What happened?"

Pointing to Hoyt and his crony, Jennifer said, "These two attacked me. Arrest them. Charge them with assault with intent to commit murder."

The second security guard muttered, "Looks like we need an ambulance. Go call 911."

Five minutes later, a uniformed cop and Rasmussen appeared along with an ambulance and paramedics.

Rasmussen took charge. "What happened?"

Jennifer explained she'd been followed into the rest room and attacked. The woman who'd been ejected by the thugs pitched in, "They threw me out. I'll charge them with assault myself."

Rasmussen waved a cop over. "Get this lady's name and address and hold her until either I or someone can talk to her. Don't let her walk away and lose track of her."

Rasmussen turned to Dave. "And you intervened?"

"I convinced them it was a bad idea to assault my partner. They got the message."

He told about seeing Hoyt and his buddy follow Jennifer into the restroom. "I knew they meant to hurt her, try to intimidate her to drop the suit against Black and Redfield or cripple her so she couldn't continue. I couldn't let that happen."

Hoyt was loaded onto a stretcher and rolled into the ambulance. As they wheeled the apparatus along, a paramedic fixed a breathing apparatus over Hoyt's nostrils and mouth. His buddy, disoriented and stumbling, was led to a patrol car by a cop.

Rasmussen asked, "Ms. Watson, you intend to file charges?"

"Yes. They intended to kill me or harm me so I couldn't continue with the trial. If Dave hadn't been here, they would have succeeded."

The ambulance pulled away, its siren screaming.

Dave said, "There's a weapon in the trash can. You may want to recover it. My fingerprints will be on the barrel."

Jennifer said, "If it's okay, I'd like to retrieve my purse and briefcase."

Rasmussen said, "Someone will bring them out to you. I'd like both of you to come by the station and make a formal statement."

Jennifer looked at her watch. "Let's do it now. I'm too busy with court in the morning."

An hour later, they drove away from the station.

Dave said, "You want to grab a pizza to take back to the apartment? Neither of us wants to prepare food tonight."

"The Pizza Inn on 25ᵗʰ is fast." She slumped against the seat, then placed her hand on Dave's leg.

TWENTY-THREE

The front page headline in the morning *Register,* **Attorney Assaulted In Court House,** jumped out at Jennifer as she picked up the paper outside her apartment door. Two columns chronicled the details of the episode, featuring the intervention by Dave Randle, the lawyer's partner in a downtown firm.

Bruce Hoyt, an official at Black and Redfield Insurance Company, had been hospitalized with a dislocated elbow, damaged trachea, broken nose and two cracked ribs. An emergency tracheotomy had been necessary to aid his breathing, but his prognosis for survival was good. His accomplice, Luke Denver, had been treated for a possible skull fracture, and released to the custody of the Chester police. Hoyt was being guarded by the police. Both men had been charged with assault. Neither Jennifer Watson, the target of the accused, nor Dave Randle responded to calls.

Jennifer handed the paper to Dave. "If this account is correct, you damaged Hoyt pretty badly."

"I intended to." He sipped his coffee and scanned the article. "Jennifer, you have to understand these guys. They play for keeps. They will kill or maim anyone who shows the slightest weakness."

She sat next to him and spooned cereal into her mouth for a bit. "You know you can be scary, don't you? And dangerous?"

Dave shoved the paper aside. "I'll never hurt you, if that's a concern."

"It's not," she said. "I always feel safe with you. I know you'll protect me regardless of the circumstances. Yesterday was an example."

Judge Plunkett called the session to order and immediately asked for a conference with the attorneys in her chambers. She disappeared to the rear of the dais. The bailiff led Jennifer and Frawley down a short hallway and opened the door for them.

Still standing and robed, Plunkett said, "I saw the morning paper. I'm concerned the jury has been tainted by the news of the attempted assault on Ms. Watson. Having an official of Black and Redfield involved only makes the situation worse. I'm certain they've seen reports on the news."

Frawley said, "Ms. Watson will come across as a heroine and have their sympathy. I'd like a mistrial declared and start over after the publicity had subsided."

Jennifer said, "Judge Plunkett, that was the purpose of the attack. They intended to render me unable to continue or worse. Black and Redfield should be held responsible and at the very least be in contempt of court."

His face reddening, Frawley bellowed. "You can't hold my client responsible for this situation."

Staring at Frawley, Jennifer said, "Both Hoyt and Denver are employed by your client. I'd bet the truth is that they were ordered to attack me for the very purpose Judge Plunkett has stated. It's called trial by manipulation and intimidation. But I'd suggest Judge Plunkett canvass the jury in private and determine the appropriate course of action. She can decide if they've been rendered partial."

Plunkett said, "That's a reasonable suggestion. If the majority seem to have been influenced, I will dismiss this group and we'll go back to the pool."

Frawley said, "I'd like a change of venue. Publicity has made it impossible to find people who've not heard about this thing. I insist you talk to the presiding judge."

Plunkett smiled. "Mr. Frawley, as of yesterday morning, I am the presiding judge. This is what I'm going to do. I'll talk with the jurors and evaluate their positions. Let's plan to convene court at 1:00 this afternoon. And neither of you may discuss this with the media. Clear?"

As they turned to leave, Plunkett said, "One more thing. Mr. Frawley, communicate with your client organization. One more incident like yesterday's will result in serious consequences for Black and Redfield. The justice system will not be intimidated by strong-arm tactics. Understood?"

Frawley mumbled, "Yes, Your Honor."

Jennifer allowed Frawley to leave ahead of her. She didn't relish another confrontation in the hallway.

At 1:00 p.m. Judge Plunkett called the court to order and asked the attorneys to approach the bench. Leaning forward, Plunkett said, "I met with the jurors individually and decided they have retained their objectivity. Two of them had not even heard the news. And none of them know the two men who assaulted Ms. Watson are connected to Black and Redfield. Let's move ahead and start with opening statements."

Frawley started to object, but Plunkett held up her hand. "There's no reason to drag this out, Mr. Frawley. We can reach a fair judgment here."

Standing in front of the jury with a notepad in his hand, Frawley opened with his statement. He argued any company had the obligation to make a profit and in this instance Black and Redfield had done nothing more than put themselves in a better position for the future. "It's like dropping a line of merchandise when it's obvious you're going to lose money. You cannot continue to push those goods when the public won't buy them. All Black and Redfield did was drop a group of policy holders who were too risky for the organization's future financial health. The organization cannot be held liable for doing what any good business would do. In addition, each of these people would have received a substantial payback from the premiums."

Without notes in her hand and looking the consummate professional, dressed in a navy suit, lavender blouse, and navy pumps, Jennifer walked near the jury box.

She smiled at the group, holding their attention. "I intend to present evidence that a group of workers was mistreated by Black and Redfield. They were chosen based on their genetic makeup, something none of us can control. They depended on their policies for retirement, for health benefits, and for support of relatives. Most had paid premiums for years. Then, without notice or explanation, their privacy was invaded and their policies were cancelled. Furthermore, I will demonstrate how Black and Redfield has broken the law under the Americans With Disabilities Act. I ask each of you to give attention to the witnesses and place yourself in their shoes as you consider the merits of this case. Thank you."

She smiled again and returned to her seat.

Frawley called Nicholas DeRosa, the President and Chief Executive Officer of Black and Redfield. Dressed in an Armani suit, the tall, gray-haired, black-eyed DeRosa exuded a mix of supplication and confidence as he took the witness chair. He immediately made eye contact with the jury, suggesting he'd had experience at this game. Jennifer had seen his name on the list of witnesses, but had no idea of Frawley's approach, even after brain-storming possibilities with Ellie and Dave.

Frawley led DeRosa through a set of questions to establish his background and credibility. DeRosa had started as an insurance salesman immediately after graduation from Boston University. He'd progressed through the ranks with a major underwriter. He'd been Vice-President for Corporate Insurance before being chosen to head Black and Redfield.

Frawley asked, "What attracted you to assume the leadership of Black and Redfield?"

DeRosa said, "I was approached by a service that recruits individuals to executive type positions. I checked on the company and liked its potential. It had a solid record in the region, and I believed it had the possibility to expand its reach and become a national player."

"Did the company require significant restructuring and reorganization?"

His eyes surveying the jurors, DeRosa said, "Certain modifications were essential if we were to attain the goals I had in mind and which the Board of Directors supported my recommendations."

"May I assume the company would not reach those goals without changes in personnel and operating policies?"

"Correct. We needed to eliminate any departments that were losing money or were failing to generate profits. We needed to bring in a couple of experienced managers, particularly as we moved into the corporate business. Those rearrangements meant we had to terminate a few people who wouldn't be able to adjust to the new structure and increased or altered performance demands."

"Have you been pleased with the changes?"

DeRosa smiled. "Yes, there's been excellent progress in the nine months I've been here."

Frawley paused as though shifting gears. "In the case of the workers at GM, what prompted the company to cancel their policies?"

Obviously prepared for the question, DeRosa looked at the jury, then said, "Over time, we intend to drop most individual policies and concentrate on corporate work. We dropped those few because the possible liability outweighed the gains. As other policies come due or run their typical course, we will honor those, but will no longer service individuals. We'll let others do that."

Frawley said, "That's all I have for Mr. DeRosa, Judge Plunkett."

Jennifer walked close to the jury box, putting her in position to see both the witness and the reactions of the jurors. She asked, "Mr. DeRosa, when Black and Redfield decided to terminate the policies of certain workers, were you concerned about their welfare?"

Nodding his head and frowning, DeRosa said, "We always think about the consequences of our actions, but we had the legal right to cancel. We tried to focus on the ones who could cause us the most damage financially."

"Or the ones most likely to cash in early because of illness?"

DeRosa's frown deepened. "Those are the ones who will lose money for us."

"And you felt no obligation to honor those policies, although those clients had faithfully paid their premiums for years?"

"Our first responsibility, Ms. Watson, is to the company. Each policy contains conditions which allow the company to cancel at any time."

"How did you choose the ones to be dropped?"

DeRosa looked at Frawley before saying, "I must admit I don't know the details. I left the decision to others. But I do know that we focused on policy holders with the greatest risk to the company."

Jennifer eyed the jury. Their blank faces revealed nothing. She trusted they remembered her request to put themselves in the shoes of the dropped workers. She said, "Thank you, Mr. DeRosa. Nothing more, Your Honor."

Frawley called Rogers Morton and asked about his affiliation with Black and Redfield.

Morton said, "I'm the Vice-President for Account Maintenance." He fingered his maroon tie to make sure it had remained in place.

"How long have you been with the organization?"

"Fifteen years."

"So you've experienced the changes and seen the improvements in the business under the new management?"

"Yes." Morton shook his head and smiled, almost a smirk. " Black and Redfield is destined to become a leader in the business."

"Were your responsibilities increased during the reorganization?"

Nodding his head again, Morton said, "Dramatically. I was moved from sales to have more oversight of accounts and client relationships." Morton's pleased expression became more evident as he talked, a wisp of a smile breaking through his usual dour countenance.

Frawley asked, "And you were responsible for initiating changes in policy holders?"

"Yes. It was an important phase of making the company more profitable and in shifting more toward the corporate side. We felt we couldn't delay until policies ran their typical course."

"Did the approach result in cancellations other than those of the plaintiffs in this case?"

Morton nodded, his shoulders shifted to assume a take-charge posture. "We dropped coverage of several small companies who refused to modify their current policies to meet our expectations. We continue to review each segment of our business."

"And that was part of the strategy to make the company more profitable?"

"Correct."

Frawley said, "That's all, Your Honor, for Mr. Morton."

Jennifer moved to her usual position enabling her to see both Morton and the jury. She asked, "Mr. Morton, can you describe the process by which you selected those workers to be dropped?"

Morton shifted in the chair as though to ease a pain. "We knew we had to get rid of policy holders who might cost us enormous amounts in the near future. It was basically an exercise to delete high risk clients."

"I fail to understand, Mr. Morton, how the dropping of fourteen clients would alter the profit for Black and Redfield in a significant way. Would you explain to the court?"

Morton smiled. "Of course. As I said, the number represented those at highest risk. They could potentially cost the organization millions."

199

"And you personally supervised the process to identify those individuals?

"Yes."

"Do you understand the American With Disabilities Act?"

"I've read it."

"Were you aware Black and Redfield acted against that law?"

"Ms. Watson, I don't believe we did. We were absolutely legal in our actions."

Jennifer stepped closer to Morton. "Weren't your actions essentially declaring an individual disabled prior to their actually becoming disabled and unable to function?"

"We didn't see it that way," Morton said, his face frowning.

"Why was Black and Redfield unwilling to communicate the process and the rationale with those policy-holders?"

Caught off-guard, Morton squirmed in the chair, his face becoming a bit paler. "We knew they wouldn't understand and it would be a waste of our time and effort."

"You knew they would object and result in a publicity problem for the company. Isn't that correct?"

Morton squirmed in the chair, muttered under his breath, and looked at the jurors who were frowning and shaking their heads. Jennifer said, "Thank you, Mr. Morton. That's all I have, your Honor."

Frawley rested his case, although his witness list contained other names, one a prominent medical researcher.

Plunkett declared a recess until the following morning at 9:00.

Jennifer left the courtroom optimistic about how the day had gone. Frawley had not surprised her, although she'd expected additional witnesses. The jury appeared unimpressed by the executives who'd defended profits over client welfare. Now she had to be on her toes tomorrow and not let her advantage slip away. Her witnesses were prepared if they didn't succumb to the pressures Frawley could mount.

Two reporters met Jennifer at the outside door of the courthouse. A woman from the *Register* asked, "After yesterday's attack, did you consider asking for a change of venue or a delay in the trial?"

Shifting her briefcase to the other arm, Jennifer said, "There was no reason to delay."

She moved around the reporters. For a moment she thought they were following and quickened her pace, but they'd given up.

Dave left the apartment near 7:00 p.m. to initiate his assignment for Rasmussen. He parked three blocks away from Roscoe's, trusting his vehicle would still be mobile after being left vulnerable in a neighborhood of homeless guys and small-time hoodlums who would steal from their mother.

Outfitted in jeans, a wrinkled tee shirt, sneakers, and a Cardinal baseball cap, he strolled into the bar and took a stool at the counter. Two bartenders worked rapidly to keep up with the demands of the fully-occupied place. A big-screen TV blared forth. The Cardinals were leading the Giants in the bottom of the fourth.

Dave ordered a Killian draft and focused on the game for a while, sipping from the stein to make it last. After a while he twisted to survey the crowd. Most were workers killing an evening until time to return to a rooming home or a motel for a few hours, sleeping for a few hours before another day on a dead-end job. The table previously reserved for Junior and his cohorts now had five guys crowded closely together, talking loudly and watching the game. They were betting on each batter and exchanging coins as they won or lost.

After an hour Dave paid his tab and left the bar. He walked a block, stepped quickly into the doorway of an empty building and waited. After an uneventful five minutes, he went to his Blazer. It had survived undamaged.

Returning to the apartment, he found Jennifer hovered over her notes for tomorrow's session. She put down her pen and turned, "Catch any felons?"

"Not tonight. Everything's quiet."

TWENTY-FOUR

The second day of the trial started with Jennifer calling Maude Frame to testify. Frame's hands shook and her voice, feeble under normal circumstances, trembled as she vowed to tell the truth and nothing but the truth.

Jennifer led her through a set of questions they'd rehearsed three times, revealing her reason for having an insurance policy, her promptness in paying every premium, and her dismay when the coverage had been cancelled without warning.

From her usual spot on the floor, Jennifer took a step closer to the witness box. "What did you think when you realized the consequences of the cancellation?"

Frame brushed her face with a gnarled hand. "I thought I'd missed a payment. I called to be certain. The woman who answered just told me several policies had been dropped, but she refused to tell me why."

"And you called a second time?"

Frame nodded, loosening a few gray hairs from pins. "I hoped I'd get someone else, which I did, but the response was the same. I'd been dropped and had no way to be reinstated. Two days later, I decided to contact you."

Jennifer asked, "Do you worry about your son?'

"That's why we took out the policy. Now I don't know what will happen to him. The government is so unpredictable, I can't depend on them." Her voice faded to almost a whisper.

Jennifer passed and Frawley walked quickly to stand against the witness box, almost touching Maude.

His voice harsher than usual, Frawley asked, "You understand business, don't you?"

Jennifer realized Frawley meant to intimidate the older woman, but she knew Maude was tougher than she appeared. Frame responded. "I won't ever trust insurance companies again. They don't keep their promises."

"Mrs. Frame, did you understand the stipulations in your policy? Black and Redfield had the right to cancel."

Her voice stronger, Frame said, "I know what the salesman said when we signed up. He told my husband and me the policy would never be changed and would support our boy after we had died. Either he lied or the company big-shots did."

Three of the jurors nodded and smiled.

"Did you or your husband ever read the policy?"

"We did, but the wording in all that fine print is too hard to understand. We trusted the salesman."

Frawley asked, "Mrs. Frame, do you understand business has to make a profit?"

Frame nodded. "They took our money for a lot of years. Then when they found some way out, they cancelled. They've made a profit on our backs."

Frustrated and intelligent enough to realize he was losing the battle with this woman, Frawley passed.

Jennifer led Bannister through a similar set of questions. He worried his wife would need money when he died. His entire testimony challenged the insurance industry. At one point he called them crooks.

Frawley passed without a cross examination of Bannister.

Jennifer called Rose Mitchell. Her face could have been set in concrete, no emotions showing. Jennifer knew Mitchell disdained this activity and wanted it to be over as quickly as possible.

Jennifer asked, "Ms. Mitchell, was your company, Biological Assays, asked to conduct genetic assays on a group of workers from the GM plant and by whom?"

"Black and Redfield Insurance contracted with us to analyze blood samples from forty-two individuals."

"Did you know the reason for their request?"

Shaking her head, her first departure from a rigid posture, Mitchell said, "No. We completed the assays and forwarded the results to Mr. Rogers Morton as our contract specified."

"Were the assays unusual?"

"We do genetic testing routinely, but we've never done so many on a single contract."

"Why would you typically run those tests?"

"Most of the time, a physician has requested an assay to support the diagnosis of a medical condition in a patient."

"Were the persons from the GM plant you tested aware of the process?"

"I had no way of knowing. We sent a technician to the GM clinic to collect the samples at the request of Black and Redfield."

"Did those persons sign a consent form?"

"Not to my knowledge. We assumed those matters had been taken care of by the nurse or by the insurance company."

"When did you learn those individuals had their insurance policies cancelled?"

"When your partner, Mr. Randle, visited our facility."

"Can you tell briefly what happened after his visit?"

"I discussed the possible implications of genetic testing with you. Later we received a court order to release the results to you. At your request we evaluated the data from the persons who'd been cancelled and compared those with the others."

"How many were found to have some genetic characteristic which would predict a disease at some point in their lives?"

"We did assays for forty-two. Fourteen of those have a genetic pre-disposition for a medical disorder."

"Tell the court," Jennifer prompted, "about the implications related to the presence of such genes."

Mitchell hesitated, organizing her thoughts, then said, "The conse-quences of having such a gene increases the probability the person will have a disease. For example, if your genetic code contains a certain gene, you may be more likely to come down with diabetes than the population in general. It is not an absolute certainty, but it raises the chance."

"Thus," Jennifer said, "Black and Redfield set out to determine which of those workers were likely to cost them money for treatment .or who might die earlier than predicted by actuarial data?"

Mitchell said, "I can't speak about the motives of the organization, but that would be one possibility."

Jennifer shifted her position slightly, signaling Mitchell the line of questioning would change, then asked, "How does the Americans With Disabilities Act come into play when individuals are denied employ-ment based on their genetic makeup?"

"The law states that genetic testing is prohibited for purposes of deciding on job applicants. Declaring an individual disabled based on genetic testing is illegal."

"Would this apply to insurance policies?"

Mitchell said, "I've not searched for precedents, but I'd guess it does. It'd be the same principle. Declaring a person uninsurable based on their genes is the same as denying a handicapped person the right to a hold a job for which he is qualified."

Jennifer said, "Thank you. I have no further question, Your Honor."

Frawley followed his routine of leaning against the witness box to be as near the witness as possible. He asked, "Did your organization release the results of those assays to Ms. Watson in spite of the assay's ownership by Black and Redfield?"

Mitchell said, "We gave her the results on the basis of a court order, not before."

"Were you aware Judge Young had denied such a request earlier?"

Mitchell shook her head, "No, we weren't, but the order we received was legitimate, thus we responded."

Frawley asked, "Do you have a solid basis for saying the Disabilities Act can be applied to insurance policies as well as work place issues?"

Mitchell considered her response for a moment. "Ms. Watson asked for my opinion. I based my answer on the principle that you can't treat an individual as disabled until they are actually declared disabled through a reputable medical assessment of their condition. How they are treated after that may depend on the limitations imposed by their condition."

"So you really don't know, do you?"

"Mr. Frawley, no one knows until the issue has been tested in the courts. I believe this case is one of the early tests."

Frawley decided he'd run out of challenges for Mitchell. He passed.

Jennifer stood at the table to say, "I have no additional witnesses, Your Honor. I rest my case."

Judge Plunkett said, "It's now 11:30. I'm going to recess the court until 1:30 at which time we will hear closing arguments." She banged her gavel and collected the papers she'd referred to during the session.

Jennifer and Dave walked to the diner. Once seated in a booth, she said, "Well, this afternoon will be critical. I can never read a jury and have some feeling about how they're viewing the evidence. I have to impress them with the damage done to those workers or they may find in favor of Black and Redfield."

Dave touched her hand. "They haven't been swayed by Frawley. He comes across as an arrogant jackass, revisiting the same point over and over about how companies exist to make money."

Jennifer waited until the waitress took their orders, then said, "We'll see. Have you heard anything about Hoyt? Has he been released from the hospital?"

"He's still there. He's hooked to a respirator."

"You almost killed him."

"I should have. Rid the world of one more hoodlum masquerading as a business tycoon."

They watched the noon traffic until their food arrived.

Jennifer asked, "Will you be in court this afternoon?"

"Until the end. Tonight I'm going back to Roscoe's. I'm making progress, talked to a couple of regulars, but I've not learned anything useful."

"How long?"

Dave shrugged. "Hard to tell. I'll give it a few more nights, then talk to Rasmussen."

Frawley began his closing by moving directly in front of the jury. "I've demonstrated through the testimony of two outstanding business executives the reason for Black and Redfield's actions regarding these insurance policies. They were losers. They were making the company a loser. The company had no choice if it were to remain in business. If the company failed, hundreds of people would be hurt when the organization could no longer provide services. And Black and Redfield had the legal right, under conditions spelled out in each policy, to cancel those policies. While I can sympathize with those who claim they could not understand the fine print, those people had a responsibility to read the policies, find help if necessary in order to know what the various stipulations meant, and take actions needed to meet their particular needs.

They failed to do that and now want Black and Redfield to rescue them from their own short coming."

Frawley stepped back, removing his hands from the railing surrounding the jury box. "I don't need to take much of your time to make the point. You are intelligent people who understand the nature of business. Now, about the matter of wrong-doing under the Disabilities Act. My opponent wants to saddle Black and Redfield with a crime when no law has been broken. There are no precedents for this charge relative to insurance. And there are precious few precedents for work-place incidents. It's a shell game based on an ill-conceived and foolish piece of legislation enacted by politicians looking for votes. You have the opportunity to cripple this inane act before more damage is done. I ask you to deny my opponent's search for fame by establishing a precedent."

Frawley looked for a time at the jurors, then said, "Thank you. I know you will do the right thing." He returned to his chair.

Jennifer stood in front of the jury, making eye contact along the two rows of the panel. "This case represents the classic confrontation between day-by-day workers struggling to make ends meet against a large, rich corporation led by greedy and unscrupulous executives. Companies hire expensive attorneys to construct contracts with loopholes filled with gobbledygook so the average person cannot decipher and understand the potential consequences. Talk about a shell game. It's played out every day and workers pay for those games while company executives get rich."

Jennifer moved a step closer to place her hands on the railing. "This case is simple. Twelve workers had their privacy invaded, then based on genetic assays they were not privy to, had their insurance policies cancelled so Black and Redfield could make a few more dollars. They were not told about the tests being conducted and could not find out why they were no longer covered by policies they'd owned for years.

"Further, it's clear Black and Redfield declared these individuals disabled and no longer fit for coverage long before a single one of them was truly disabled. They were still working full-time. That is against the law. Mr. Frawley is correct in that precedents for this illegal act under this law are non-existent, but that doesn't mean you cannot interpret this statute and decide Black and Redfield broke the law. That is an important role juries play in our democratic society. You have an opportunity, truly an obligation, to judge the merits of this legislation and decide how your fellow citizens should be treated. Put yourself in the position of the defendants. Recognize a genetic test could declare you disabled, cause you to lose your job, or have long-term contracts broken by companies who take advantage of the situation.

"I ask you to find in favor of these workers and find Black and Redfield guilty of breaking the law under the Americans With Disabilities Act. Thank you."

Jennifer smiled at the jury and returned to her seat. She wanted to dry the moisture from her palms on her skirt, but ignored the impulse until the judge began to charge the jury and attention turned to Plunkett. Then she pulled a tissue from her jacket pocket and dabbed the wetness.

Plunkett reminded the jury of their responsibility to make their decision based on the evidence presented. She added, "You have two judgments to make. First, did Black and Redfield wrongfully cancel the policies of the workers and if so, should they be held liable for both reinstatement and punitive damages. Secondly, did Black and Redfield break a law under the Disabilities Act. If so, you should recommend a fine to be imposed by the court.

"If you require anything to assist you in reaching your decisions, please tell the bailiff and we will provide you the information."

When the jury filed from the room, Judge Plunkett announced, "The bailiff will contact the attorneys when the jury is prepared to render its verdict."

Dave decided he should go back to the office rather than wait around the court house. Jennifer settled into a vacant conference room after telling the clerk where she would be. She spread out papers for a suit she was preparing for a woman against a contractor for allegedly failing to properly frame her house. One corner of the structure had sagged four months after she'd moved in. The builder argued shifting ground had caused the problem. Jennifer's client charged him with shoddy workmanship and demanded he fix the problem.

For a time she had difficulty concentrating, her thoughts lingering with the Frame situation and worrying how the jury would find. She'd made the best argument she could. Now the decision rested with twelve souls with no vested interest in the deal.

At 3:30 the clerk came in to tell her the jury had asked to confer with Judge Plunkett. The clerk didn't know why, but guessed it'd be some time before they would conclude.

At 4:45 the clerk returned to tell her the jury had been granted an overnight absence and would reconvene at 9:00 the following morning.

She returned to the office.

TWENTY-FIVE

Dave slipped onto the only vacant stool at the bar and ordered a draft beer when the bartender got to him. Roscoe's was filled again with faces he recognized from his previous visit, but there were several he'd not seen.

He sipped his beer, turned on the stool to survey the crowd for a few minutes, then watched a rerun of a sit-com. The guy next to him was complaining to his buddy about the washout of the Cardinals' game.

Roscoe came by Dave's spot twenty minutes later. He stopped and said, "You're becoming a regular. You live close?"

Dave said, "I'm in a rooming house over on Blount. Working on a construction job for a few weeks, then we'll move on. You own this place?"

Roscoe wiped at the bar with a towel. "Me and the bank. I'm buying it from an insurance company, but they insisted I get a loan through a bank rather than with them."

"Business looks good," Dave said. "You're full every night."

Roscoe nodded. "Yeah, but the profit margin is low. Have to pay too much for help these days."

Dave asked, "I was here a couple weeks ago when we'd come to bid on the job. What happened to the woman bartender? She quit?"

Roscoe scanned the nearby customers, all engaged in conversation or staring into space. "She got killed. Some punk shot her behind the building. Hauled her body away."

"That's awful. She was a good-looking woman."

"Good worker too. I've missed her."

"Cops figure out who did it?"

"They never do. I told them what I suspected, but they didn't give it much attention."

Dave sipped beer, deciding how hard to push the opening. "You suspect someone?"

"A group of guys got arrested for dealing while they were in here. Two days later, some guy in a suit came around mid-afternoon, asking about Angela. Next night, she got killed."

"Sounds suspicious to me," Dave said.

"I'd never seen the guy before, but I'm not out front all the time. Big man, hands like a construction worker, but wearing an expensive suit."

Roscoe shuffled away, then picked up an empty mug and placed it in the sink.

The stocky guy next to Dave twisted on his stool, wiped a pudgy hand on the sleeve of his khaki shirt, and said, "I overheard you and Roscoe talking about Angela. I seen that guy in here once. He was sitting with those guys who got arrested. Never knew any of their names until I read about them in the paper."

Dave asked, "You live near?"

"Yeah. In an apartment in the next block. Come in here every night, pretty much."

Dave said, "Too bad about the woman. Maybe she heard those dealers talking and they decided not to risk her blabbing to the cops."

"My guess is some guy tried to make out with her and she said no. He got pissed and conked her."

"Maybe. She was good looking. I wanted to meet her and try my luck."

"Yeah, so would most of the guys here, but she was too snooty. No flirting around. I asked her out once, but she just walked away."

"Maybe Roscoe will find another like her."

"Hope the next one is more friendly." He shoved off the stool. "Time for me to turn in. Tough day tomorrow."

"See you around," Dave said, draining his mug.

He eased out through the crowd. His Blazer, parked in a different location than before, had survived again.

At 8:30 the next morning Jennifer called the clerk in Plunkett's court to ask that she be notified at her office when the jury had reached a decision. She'd intended to wrap up the construction suit and move on to other matters, but she couldn't concentrate. The prolonged jury session baffled her. She couldn't believe they'd take so long, but maybe one person was holding out for an opinion different from the majority. Maybe the Disabilities Act had complicated the issues.

She'd reached the point of total ineffectiveness when at 10:30 the clerk called. "The jury will report at 11:00. Judge Plunkett wants to finish this by noon."

Jennifer had settled into her chair in the court room as Plunkett entered and the bailiff announced court in session. The jury filed in, their faces haggard and drawn, in Jennifer's mind evidence of an intense debate that had frayed nerves and rattled composures.

Plunkett asked for the report of the foreman. The usual passing of their decision back and forth proceeded, then Plunkett said, "What say you?"

The older man, dressed in a frayed brown suit, his tie askew, stood. "On the matter of cancelled policies, we find in favor of the plaintiffs and recommend their policies be reinstated without penalty.

"On the matter of punitive damages, we find in favor of the plaintiffs and recommend Black and Redfield pay $50,000 to each of the individuals affected."

The gasp from the audience, primarily families of the workers, caused the foreman to stop and glance to Judge Plunkett until the whispering diminished.

Then he continued, "On the charge of breaking the law under the Americans With Disabilities Act, we find Black and Redfield guilty and recommend a fine of $50,000." He handed the paper to the bailiff and dropped into his seat, relieved to be out of the spotlight.

Frawley scrambled to his feet. "Your Honor, I move the punitive damages and the fine be set aside."

Plunkett considered a moment, then said, "I'll take your motion under advisement and I'd like to meet with the attorneys in my chambers as soon as we adjourn."

She thanked the jury for their work and banged the gavel, closing the session.

By the time Frawley and Jennifer entered Plunkett's private chamber, she had removed her robe and draped it across a chair.

Clearly frustrated and mad, Frawley said, "Judge, the damages awarded by this jury are outrageous. I demand you ignore that recommendation, along with the unnecessary fine. The whole thing is ridiculous."

Jennifer started to speak, but Plunkett raised her hand to stop her. Plunkett looked at Frawley. "Both of you need to understand the reason for the lengthy time of deliberations by this jury. Reaching a decision against Black and Redfield was easy for the jury. But they struggled for hours over the amount of damages. When they conferred with me, they wanted to know if an amount had been put on the table at any time. Although reluctant, I did reveal the amount you had dickered over during the pre-trial hearing. Mr. Frawley, I'm not going to overturn their recommendation because I know the amount was not arrived at without significant debate and deliberation. This may sound petty, but you could have settled the entire matter by accepting the figure proposed by Ms. Watson.

"You obviously have the option to appeal, but I'm going to let stand the recommendations on both the damages and the fine. You have thirty days to file with the Circuit Court of Appeals, but I'd like you to think seriously about not taking that step. It would likely be a wasted effort and could very well result in an increased fine."

His voice almost whining, Frawley said, "I'll confer with my client."

"Let me know what you intend to do. Now I'd like to meet alone with Ms. Watson."

After Frawley had closed the door, Plunkett said, "I think the damages are a bit too high, but I dislike second-guessing a jury that struggled so hard to reach a decision they believed was fair. But what I wanted to say privately is about the Disabilities Act. You have been a key instrument in establishing an important precedent. Other courts and attorneys will refer back to this case as guidance for future actions."

Jennifer smiled and leaned forward in her chair. "If it's not overturned on appeal."

"It won't be. You made a solid case. The fine may be tinkered with if Frawley appeals, but the decision on the Act itself will stand. I'm sure of that. And you should realize, it's rare to bring about a breakthrough. I commend you for having the foresight to open the way on behalf of disabled people."

"Thank you, Judge Plunkett. I appreciate your saying those things."

When Jennifer reached for her briefcase, Plunkett said, "May I ask you a question about obtaining those assay results. Did you know Judge Young intended to resign and waited for that to happen before approaching another judge?"

Jennifer stood, thinking about the implications of her response for both herself and her friend, Anita. "To be honest, I went around Judge Young. He'd come down in favor of Black and Redfield because of some unethical connection. He'd refused to tell me why he ruled as he did. I conferred with another judge who risked Young's ire and issued the court order to release the data. I know this was not completely kosher, but my clients and I had been treated unfairly. Events following proved me correct."

"It was sad to see him leave under a dark cloud, but one which he created. Most of his colleagues never understood."

Jennifer said, "My partner and I are working on another phase of this case. Judge Young's role may become clearer soon."

Plunkett said, "I trust it will not damage him further."

Back in the suite, she found Dave in his office. "You had lunch yet? Let's walk over to Gibbons if you haven't."

"How'd it go?" He shoved his chair away from the desk.

"I'll tell you as we walk. Let me drop this briefcase and check my messages."

Five minutes later they emerged onto the sidewalk. Jennifer told him about the verdict as they moved through other pedestrians on their noon-hour break.

Dave stopped and pulled her close. "Great. We'll celebrate—go to the most expensive place in town." Still holding her near, he kissed her. "All that worrying for naught."

"That's the way I am," she said, holding his hand as they started walking. "But now I have a decision to make about the money. We usually charge one-third of the settlement, but I'm inclined to retain just twenty percent in this case. Those workers need the money more than we do and the lower amount would cover our costs yet give us a nice fee."

"I'd go along with that. We're doing okay now, even have a good reserve in case we hit a downturn."

"The only unknown is the possible appeal by Frawley. The amount could be lower, but Plunkett seems confident it wouldn't be altered by the courts."

"Let's check on the house after work today."

"No bar gig tonight?"

"I'm checking with Rasmussen this afternoon. I may have something for him to follow through on. I called earlier but he was out."

At the door of Gibbons they waited for five minutes until a booth became vacant. Antonio waved to them from behind his usual station behind the cash register.

Rasmussen was waiting when Dave knocked on his door. "So you discovered something?"

"Maybe. This regular in Roscoe's described a man who sounds like Hoyt asking about Angela the day before her death. He'd also seen the same man with Junior and his boys. I think you should squeeze Hoyt until he talks."

"You think he killed Angela?"

"More likely he hired some goon for a few bucks to do the job. Maybe two since the body had been moved."

"I'll check it out. The hospital took him off the breathing apparatus yesterday."

"I'm skipping my bar duty tonight unless you tell me differently."

Rasmussen swiveled his chair and stood. "Rather than my talking with Hoyt, why don't you? You have his attention."

"If you like. Same rate as usual?"

"Sure. Just don't get carried away and knock Hoyt around any more."

Dave looked at his watch. "I'll do it now, but I need to check on something at the office first."

He started for the door then turned back. "If I do this, I've probably blown my cover at the bar."

"Tell you what. Go back and question Roscoe about Hoyt's conversation with him. Hoyt's not going anywhere for a while and chances are he won't talk without his lawyer being present."

"I'll get it done tomorrow afternoon," Dave said, thinking about checking out progress on the house renovation tonight. "It might be better if I meet Roscoe when there's not a big crowd at his place."

"Call me after you've seen Roscoe. That may give us a clue about tackling Hoyt."

At 3:30 p.m., Dave pushed through the door at Roscoe's. The place was empty except for a janitor arranging chairs around tables and emptying ash trays into a trash cart. One of the soaps showed on the television.

Dave asked, "Roscoe around?"

"Yeah, go through the door behind the bar. He's in an office in back."

Roscoe was adding numbers on an outdated calculator, its gears whirring and grating as though one more figure would be its last. Dave waited until the machine stopped, then rapped on the door jamb.

"You got a minute?" Dave asked, when Roscoe looked up, his face frowning at the interruption.

"I suppose." He pointed to an empty hard-backed chair. "You're off work early today."

Dave said, "We took a break this afternoon to get ready for a big job tomorrow. But I'm interested in the thing you told me about the guy asking around about Angela. I'd like to know what he was asking."

Roscoe eyed Dave's face, trying to read his mind. "Don't recall much. It was a busy night, lots of noise. Basically he wanted to know if I thought she was a cop working undercover. I hadn't a clue if she was or wasn't. She did her job, was dependable, never caused trouble like a couple of other women I've hired in the past."

"Had she done anything to suggest to the guys running drugs she might be watching them?"

"Nothing obvious to me, but I don't catch on to things right off."

"What'd you tell him?"

"Like I said, I had no idea. She hadn't done nothing to make me think she was."

"Had you ever seen him before?"

"Not in the bar, but I got to thinking about it later. I'm pretty certain I passed him in the front of the Black and Redfield building one day when I'd gone there to sign an amendment to my lease."

"Did you tell the cops about that?"

"No, but they never asked directly. And I hadn't remembered at the time."

"I'd like to bring a photograph of this man by tomorrow. Maybe you can be sure."

"I'll give it a try. Angela was a good worker. She didn't deserve to get whacked."

Dave stood. "Any of that drug crowd around anymore?"

"Not since the ones got arrested. Still in jail, I guess, or moved their operation to another place."

TWENTY-SIX

Dave returned to Roscoe's the following afternoon with five photos, including one of Hoyt, he'd gotten from Rasmussen. Roscoe huddled over the ancient calculator with a stack of bills near. In the dim light, the place seemed more like a dungeon than an office. An aroma of pipe tobacco permeated the space.

When Dave showed him the pictures, the bar owner squinted through his bifocals for several seconds, picked up one, then nodded, "That's the guy." He gave attention to his pipe, then knocked the ash into a tray on the desk.

"And that's the only time you saw him? What about the night Angela was killed?"

Shaking his head, Roscoe said, "Didn't notice him. We had a big business that night, lots of people because of some reunion event at the high school. A lot of old timers from the school dropped in. Stayed busy until closing."

Exceeding his specific mission, Dave asked, "When did you last see Angela that night?"

Roscoe scratched a hand through his thinning black hair, "Right after closing time. Four of us worked together to straighten things up a bit after the last customer left. It's always a mess. We leave most things for the janitor who comes in around ten every morning, but we pick up empty mugs and glasses, look for any personal items left by customers, retrieve the tips. Like every other night I took the cash drawer back to the office and stuck it in the safe. By the time I went back front, she had gone. The two men were fixing a light fixture some idiot had busted."

"And you didn't hear anything unusual outside?"

"No and none of the others did either. The cops asked us about gunshots, yelling, cars revving, things like that."

"Is it possible one of her co-workers killed her?"

Shaking his head, Roscoe said, "No. We walked out together. Must have been twenty minutes after she'd left."

Dave put the photo back in his jacket pocket. "Thanks for your help. I'll come in again soon."

Roscoe asked, "You working for the cops?"

Dave grinned. "I help them out at times but I'd like you to keep that to yourself." He left Roscoe staring at his back as he went through the door into a sunny late afternoon. He passed two of the regulars he'd seen each time he'd patronized the bar. They nodded and grunted.

Dave caught up with Rasmussen as he came out the front door of the station. "Desk jobs let you leave early."

Rasmussen chortled. "I wish. Any luck with Roscoe?"

"He identified Hoyt as the one asking about Angela. I'm sure he'd testify in court if you get that far."

"I'm on my way to the hospital now. Hoyt is being released into our custody, but he'll have bail within a few hours. That lawyer from Black and Redfield has been in already."

They ambled toward Rasmussen's car, passing several cops reporting in at the end of their shifts.

Standing next to the car, Rasmussen said, "We discovered something very interesting this afternoon. The gun you took from Hoyt's accomplice during the assault on Jennifer was the one used to kill Angela. Ballistics are a match."

"It's all coming together," Dave said. "I bet you can pressure that goon into implicating Hoyt."

"Probably, but we can't use the same tactics you do," Rasmussen said, opening the door to his vehicle.

"Will he be released on bail along with Hoyt?"

"Nope. As soon as we made the ballistic match, the prosecutor changed the charge to murder. He won't get out."

"Take care," Dave said. "Let me know about Hoyt and if I need to do anything else."

Through the open window of his cruiser, Rasmussen said, "This should finish it. Call me about your hours."

As Dave and Jennifer returned from their early morning jog, the phone was ringing as they opened the door to the apartment. Dave grabbed the instrument. Jennifer stopped to listen, expecting news about Frawley's appeal.

Rasmussen said, "Glad I caught you. As expected, Hoyt was released on bail late last night. One of our civilian clerks overheard him telling his attorney that the first thing on his agenda was to get revenge for what you did to him."

Images of an irate Hoyt racing through his mind, Dave said, "I'll stay alert."

"Make Jennifer aware, also. He may do something to her to get back at you."

"I should have killed the bastard."

Rasmussen said, "I won't comment on that, but I wanted to let you know. It may be nothing except release of anger and trying to impress people around him, but who knows."

"I appreciate you letting me know," Dave said, replacing the receiver.

Her hand on his arm, Jennifer asked, "What was that about?"

As he told her, her eyes widened. Dave suspected memories of Hoyt shoving her around and looming over her were haunting her.

Her fingers tightened on his arm. "Dave, this is scary. Hoyt is a madman."

"I agree, but we should continue our routine. Keep alert to any thing unusual."

Dave headed for the shower, scenarios of past conflicts running through his thinking. He hated to be the prey. But he worried more about Jennifer. Maybe he'd find Hoyt today and confront him. But he wouldn't tell Jennifer. He couldn't leave her unprotected if she left the office. But with several other people on the same floor she would be safe in the office. Hoyt wouldn't come into a crowded building to attack her, although he couldn't be sure. He'd assaulted her in a public restroom at the courthouse. But more likely, he'd sneak around or hire some goon to take a shot at one or both of them when their guard was down.

At 9:15 Dave called Black and Redfield and asked the receptionist if Hoyt would be in today.

After a moment, she said, "Mr. Hoyt plans to be in his office this afternoon. Would you like to make an appointment?"

"I need to check something first. I'll get back to you."

At 4:00 Dave walked into the suite where Hoyt and Morton had offices. Ignoring the receptionist who smiled in greeting, he pushed into Hoyt's office. Hoyt had his back to the door, gazing out the window.

When the door clicked closed, he turned, recognized Dave, then yelped, "What the hell you here for?"

Dave approached within an arm's length of Hoyt. "I heard you wanted revenge. I came by to give you the chance."

"Who told you anything?"

"The cops overheard you blabbing to your attorney and called me. What's important is I know and I want you to understand something." He moved even closer to Hoyt. "If you or some thug you hire ever gets close to Jennifer Watson or me, I'll kill both of you."

Gaining his bravado, Hoyt said, "I don't like to be threatened."

"I don't give a damn what you like. You've been put on notice. I'd suggest you take it seriously. You won't get a second chance."

Hoyt moved toward his desk and reached for the telephone. Dave clamped his wrist, causing Hoyt to wince. "Don't try calling for help. They can't get here fast enough to save your sorry ass. And don't think about sending some idiot to jump me in the parking lot."

Dave released Hoyt's wrist and moved to the door. "Remember my advice. See you in court." He walked out and went down the stairs, avoiding the elevator. He exited through the service door near his car parked along the delivery drive. As he drove past the front of the building, two security types were outside.

After dinner, Jennifer said, "Let's drive out to the house, I'd like to see how things are progressing."

Dave flipped off the news program on PBS. He believed he'd seen a car tailing them from work today, but he hadn't been certain. A blue Pontiac had followed them from the office, but sped past them as they turned into the parking garage. He decided the thugs would have given up for the night, if in fact they were trailing them. He wanted to dismiss the incident as incidental, but his instincts suggested otherwise.

"Okay, let's do it and hope the builders haven't disconnected the power."

Everything seemed normal as they pulled from the garage into the light traffic of early evening, the street lights cutting through the twilight. Dave observed nothing out of the ordinary as they progressed along the avenue.

But a mile out on the less-traveled route to the house, Dave saw in the rear-view mirror a car, its headlights on high beam, closing fast on them. For an instant, he ignored the warning flashing through his brain, thinking it was more likely a bunch of teenagers testing their skills on an isolated road. But his years of training screamed out to take no chances.

He commanded, "Jen, we're being followed. Hold on tight."

She twisted around to look, asking, "What's happening?"

Dave jammed on the brakes and whipped onto a forest road, one he'd jogged numerous times. The trailing car sped past, but the squeal of brakes told Dave what he wanted to know.

Two hundred yards along the one-lane dirt road lined with trees on both sides, he turned right onto a side trail and killed the lights and motor. The silence was broken only by the roar of the chase car as it reversed and came back toward the point Dave had turned off.

Jennifer said, "What are you doing?"

"Hoyt's goons are after us. Stay put. Lock the doors and get down. Don't move until I come back." He reached across her to take his .38 from the car pocket, touched her hand, and eased out the door, closing it gently.

Lights swept along the main road, hesitated for a brief moment, then turned onto the forest trail. The hired guns intended to track them down and earn their reward.

Dave trotted to the site where he'd left the dirt road and crouched behind a large rhododendron, its full leaves shadowing him from anyone except the most experienced woodsman. The dim moonlight could be a problem if he moved, but he was in position to react to the guy in the passenger side, more likely the shooter.

The Pontiac, its lights on high beam, eased along the rutted lane, its chassis dragging on the surface at intervals. The driver skirted around a deep pothole as he neared Dave's spot. The head and shoulders of a man wearing a baseball cap leaned out the window, holding a rifle at the ready.

Dave shot him in the shoulder. The man screamed, the rifle bounced onto the dirt, partially under the moving vehicle. The rear wheel crunched the stock. The goon yelled, "Holy shit. Get out of here."

Dave shot through the windshield, shattering the glass. The driver, unnerved by the shots out of the darkness, accelerated to back out, but jammed the car over the stump of a large oak. The rear chassis became wedged.

Dave shot out headlights, and raced toward the rear of the stalled car, the engine roaring as the driver tried to escape the trap of the stump. Dave jerked open the driver's side door and hit the man across the face with the butt of his gun. Blood spurted from his forehead as he sagged onto the dusty trail.

When Dave got back to the Blazer, Jennifer was outside, standing behind the front of the vehicle. He said, "Let's go."

"What happened? I was afraid you'd been shot."

"Jump in. I'll tell you on the way." He wanted to admonish her for leaving the Blazer, but let it pass. He hoped they weren't in more of these situations.

From the house, Dave called Rasmussen's home phone. On the fourth ring, Rasmussen's familiar voice answered.

Dave said, "I want to offer a unique opportunity. Bring Hoyt and a second patrol car. Meet me at the corner of Route 639 and Farris Avenue."

"Is this some kind of game?"

"In a way. I've captured Hoyt's thugs and I'd like to get the three together. You will want to hear their confessions and observe Hoyt's reactions."

After a few seconds of consideration of the strange request and recalling other exploits of Dave's, Rasmussen said, "May take me an hour. We'll have to find Hoyt."

"If you can't find him, come anyway. Let's plan on meeting at the junction in an hour with or without Hoyt. There's a little store there. See you in the parking lot."

Dave and Jennifer were parked by the quick-stop grocery when Rasmussen pulled in and parked by them. A patrol car followed. Hoyt peered out the rear window.

Dave yelled to Rasmussen, "Follow me."

The three-car cavalcade drove to the forest road. The Pontiac remained as Dave had left it. With everyone closing around the stranded vehicle, Dave opened the trunk. Two guys popped their heads up, relieved at the inrush of fresh air.

Dave said, "Hoyt, these are your goons. They've told me how you promised them $3000 each if they killed me, plus a matching amount if Jennifer was killed. I didn't follow through on my promise to kill them and then you. I'll let the police and the courts decide your fate. And by the way, one of your clowns needs medical attention. He's been shot through the shoulder, but he'll live."

The patrol officers helped the gunmen out of the trunk, handcuffed them and led them to the sedan, its flashers sending eerie signals through the woods.

Rasmussen said, "Hoyt, you're headed back to jail with another charge to confront. I doubt the judge will agree to bail this round."

Dave said, "Probably need to move this car in daylight. The headlights are gone."

Rasmussen said, "I'll need both you and Ms. Watson to come to the station and make a formal statement about what happened here. Sometime tomorrow will be okay."

As Rasmussen followed the patrol car out of the forest, Jennifer leaned against Dave. He circled her shoulders and held her close.

He said, "Let's get home. We'll visit the house again tomorrow night."

Back in the Blazer, Jennifer said, "God, what a night," laying her head against the seat rest. "I'm glad I don't have to be in court tomorrow. I'd never function."

"This should end our worries about Hoyt."

"I should hope so, but I'm still thinking about pressing forward on the assault charge."

TWENTY-SEVEN

The Chester County prosecutor, Randall Johns, called Dave two days after the Hoyt confrontation and subsequent arrest. Rasmussen had been right. Hoyt would not be granted bail again.

Johns said, "We're working on the Hoyt case. As you would know, there are multiple charges and scads of loose ends. One of those pieces not settled yet is the murder of James Redfield. Bill Rasmussen suspects Nicole Farrell knows more of the details and suggested I call you about getting her to testify. He indicated you know how to contact her."

"I can call her," Dave said, "but getting her back here may take an extradition process. She left because she feared for her life. I don't know if that has changed."

Johns continued, "We have some evidence to suggest Hoyt and his cronies murdered Redfield. Plus, we think Nicole overheard Hoyt threatening to carry out such act to Gerald Dewberry. Dewberry either objected fairly strenuously to the deed or threatened to alert the police. That's why he got knocked over. Or he knew who had done in Redfield and that led to his own murder."

Dave said, "I'm not certain she knows those details."

"Rasmussen has considerable faith in your being able to find out." The tone of Johns' statement made Dave think that confidence wasn't shared by the prosecutor. After a bit of hesitation, Johns continued, "We're willing to reimburse your firm for travel to Nicole's location and your interrogating her about what she knows. Then if her testimony appears to be valuable, convince her to return for the trial. We'd guarantee protection if that remains a worry to her."

"I'll call her tonight, "Dave said, not convinced Nicole's contribution to the prosecutor's case could be very important. Maybe they knew something he didn't know. Or they could be using the ploy of getting her back here to charge her with conspiracy in Dewberry's death. After all, as the only beneficiary, she had the most to gain.

Trying to allay his concerns about any games being played by the prosecutor, Dave called Rasmussen as soon as he disconnected from Johns.

Rasmussen said, "I assume this is about Johns contacting you about Nicole Farrell."

"You read my mind," Dave said. "I'm willing to assist, but I don't want to become the instrument that gets her back here only to have her charged with some crime. I know you'll be candid with me."

Rasmussen was quick to respond. "As far as I know, it's not some ruse. Johns wants to tie everything up tight and thinks her testimony about the argument between Hoyt and Dewberry might be valuable."

"I'll contact her," Dave said, "but if she gets charged with something as a way to make her testify, I'll be more than disappointed."

After dinner Dave called the number he had for Nicole. She answered on the second ring.

He said, "Nicole, Dave Randle. I'm calling about a tricky issue." He related the scheme outlined by Johns and updated her about Hoyt and the trial.

"I don't know very much. I've told you everything I overheard the night Hoyt came to our house."

"Would you be open to reviewing the events if I came there? Often people remember things if the right question is asked."

Nicole pondered for a few seconds. "I'm willing, but make certain no one trails you here. I'm still concerned about my safety. Things are going well for me here and I don't want to foul it up."

"I'll let you know my schedule and will call this number. You decide where you want to meet."

"How's my sister, Heather? Have you seen her?"

"I saw her and a companion at lunch a few weeks ago. I've not talked with her for some time. You want me to call and ask?"

"That'd be nice, but don't tell her you're coming here. She'll do something silly like try to follow you."

Three days later Dave flew into Minneapolis. He'd told no one, except Jennifer, his destination and had chanced purchasing a ticket just before departure of the early evening flight.

He rented a car at Avis and drove to a motel on the edge of downtown. He picked the place at random along a strip of fast-food restaurants and other motels, not knowing the area at all.

When he phoned Nicole, she suggested they meet for breakfast at a restaurant within walking distance of the motel. He called Jennifer to see how her day went, but primarily to hear her voice.

Under a gray sky promising rain later in the day, Dave walked the two blocks to the restaurant. Nicole showed at the appointed time. Her facial features were less strained than the last time he'd seen her. Dressed in a gray pant suit and low heels, she looked to be a professional woman in charge of her life. They settled into a booth against the windows. Several customers, apparently regulars by the tone of their conversation with the two waitresses, occupied other booths and a table.

Nicole, seemingly at ease, ordered scrambled eggs and coffee. Dave replicated her request, then as the waitress walked away, said, "Thanks for meeting. I don't know how much time you have, so I'll get right to the point. As I told you over the phone, I promised the Chester prosecutor to review the events of the Hoyt visit and determine if it's worth your testifying."

Nicole leaned aside as the waitress poured coffee. "I've told you everything I know, but if he thinks that would be useful, I'd take a chance on coming to Chester. From what you've told me, I'd be safe. And I'd like to know those murderers end up serving time."

"With Hoyt in jail and his buddies worried about being caught up with him, I think you'd be okay. But the Chester police would provide protection if you wish."

She sipped coffee, vapor rising around the rim of the mug. "After you called, I thought more about a return. I need to settle the estate and sell the house. I've decided to locate permanently here. I've made friends, found a church I like, and my business is booming."

"The prosecutor will want to review your potential testimony before the trial. As far as I know, the date hasn't been set yet, but I'd think they'd want to wrap it up before Christmas."

Their eggs and toast appeared. They ate for a few minutes. The other customers left, gunning their pickup trucks in the gravel lot, sending small stones flying against the outside wall. One of the waitresses muttered, "One day one of those idiots is going to bust the glass."

Nicole smiled at the comment. "If I were to come around Thanksgiving, would you be available to escort me to the house and make sure everything is okay? I'd feel more secure with you than with some cop I've never seen."

Jennifer had planned on their moving to the house during the Thanksgiving holiday period when their business was typically slow. She'd be disappointed if he wasn't around to help. Dave said, "I'm committed to another task at the time. Could you come the week before? I'd be sure you were safe at your house or you could stay at a hotel if you're concerned."

She pulled a calendar from her purse and scanned it. "I could work that. I'll call you with my flight schedule if you will meet me at the airport."

Nicole drained the last of her coffee. "I'll set up meetings with my bank, but I need a lawyer." She stopped for a moment, then added, "Maybe your partner could work with me. It shouldn't be complicated. It's the probate of Gerald's will and selling the property. All of our bank accounts were joint so that should be straight-forward."

"I'll have her call and tell you what she might need."

She slipped out of the booth to stand. "I apologize for causing you to come here. I should have decided sooner about returning to Chester."

"It's okay. The city will pay my expenses." But he experienced some frustration for wasting the time. His other cases were lagging while he chased this witness who could add very little to Johns' case.

Jennifer and Dave visited the house often now as the contractor neared completion. The work had been delayed for ten days because of a late delivery of the windows for the new bedroom. But a move at Thanksgiving was still in the cards. On the weekend after his return from Minneapolis, they began the process of rearranging and uncovering some of Dave's furniture. They shopped for a king-size bed and matching furnishings. Dave accepted the fact that his rustic, Spartan existence would change dramatically.

Back in the apartment, they prepared dinner and watched the news while they ate.

Dave said, "We should make this relationship legitimate by Christmas. If you haven't changed your mind after living together after the past weeks."

Jennifer put aside her plate and sat on his lap. "I want to marry you more than ever. It's been great for me. I've thought about dates because I'd like to have my parents come." They lived in a small town thirty miles from Chester. Dave had never met them, but Jennifer called them every week and visited as often as possible. She'd mentioned moving them into a retirement community on the outskirts of Chester, but they were resisting, not ready to give up their home and friends.

"That'd be nice," Dave said, kissing her neck. "But don't you think we should visit them before."

"We'll go next Friday night and come back on Sunday. Then you'll be ready to meet our elusive client. By the way, she called me yesterday about closing her affairs in Chester."

Jennifer snuggled closer and kissed him.

Jennifer's parents, Jim and Doris Watson, appeared on the porch of their small frame house as soon as Dave and Jennifer drove into the driveway at dusk on Friday.

As she opened the car door, Jennifer said, "They're eager to inspect this person I'm marrying. They'd given up on my finding anyone."

"I'll try to behave."

"Remember, there's no cohabitation and hanky-panky while we're here."

"That will be difficult," Dave said, as they pulled overnight bags from the trunk of her Accord.

Through the evening, Dave watched the interactions between parents and daughter, one they obviously loved and were proud of. Jim had been a mail carrier on rural routes for forty years. Doris had taught in the local elementary school. Both were frail, moving with caution around their worn furnishings, but they were alert, asking questions, and telling Jennifer about local events.

He accepted they were reserving judgment about him until later, wondering if this muscular, short-haired person was the right choice for their daughter. Over the course of the evening and the next morning, Dave understood they respected their daughter's opinion and trusted her to have made a good decision. At one point Jim had teased Jennifer about jumping fast after delaying for years with the other fellow she brought home once.

Nicole Farrell returned to Chester on a late-night flight. Dave met her at the airport, helped her retrieve her luggage, and followed her Hertz rental car to the Dewberry house. At her insistence, he entered with her and walked through every space. In the quiet, nothing appeared amiss. The telephone worked. Spiders and other bugs had taken over the corners and areas of the ceiling. Dust covered the wooden tables.

"Nothing has been touched," Nicole said, as they returned from the basement. "I should be okay here for a couple of days."

"No one knows you're back, not even your sister. You can maintain a low profile. Put the car in the garage. Don't turn on all the lights. Keep the drapes drawn. Keep out of the neighbors sight as much as possible."

Nicole said, "Thanks for your help with my paranoia. I'm meeting with Ms. Watson in the morning. After that, I'm seeing a real estate agent."

"What about the furniture and personal items?"

"I plan to give Gerald's clothing to Goodwill. Probably scrap a lot of stuff and move some of the furniture to the house I purchased in Minneapolis."

Dave edged toward the door. "You know my numbers. Give me a call if there's anything I can do."

At 4:30 the next afternoon, Nicole phoned Dave at the office. "I've discovered something you may wish to have. I was packing Gerald's clothes into boxes for pickup by Goodwill. In one of his suit coats I found a computer disk. It has information about Gerald's concerns about Black and Redfield and about Hoyt. I haven't taken the time to scan all the files, but it may contain clues important to the prosecution of Hoyt."

"Have you met with Johns yet?"

"Tomorrow morning, but I'm reluctant to give him the disk until I have your opinion about its importance."

Dave said, "I'll pick it up in a few minutes and review it tonight."

"Someone took Gerald's home computer and never returned it. Can you find out about it?"

"I'll inquire. I expect the cops took it when they were investigating his death and it's stored away in the evidence vaults. Probably forgot about it."

"I'm surprised they didn't find the disk during their search."

"It's easy to miss things," Dave said, knowing some investigators were sloppy or they never thought anything vital might be on a disk and not on the hard-drive.

TWENTY-EIGHT

Back in the office with the computer disk, Dave began the search process of Gerald Dewberry's files. Fortunately, the files had been saved in the system they used routinely in their office. Several were irrelevant to his goal, but one contained a set of rambling thoughts and Gerald's summations about events taking place at Black and Redfield. At the end of the file, a couple of pages were devoted to three different sessions with Hoyt and Morton.

Dewberry had detailed the conflict with James Redfield. In a meeting with most of the staff the old man had argued against the termination of insurance policies held by the GM workers. He'd been particularly vocal about the refusal of payment to a small company who'd had a fire in a storage area, destroying a large inventory of products and threatening the future of the business. Redfield reminded Hoyt and Morton the small company had been one of the first clients of Black and Redfield, had always paid premiums, had never filed a claim before, and deserved reliable treatment from the insurer. Hoyt and Morton insisted in applying a disclaimer related to arson and save the money.

According to Dewberry the debate had spilled over into the hall after the formal session. When Redfield persisted and threatened to go to the regulatory agency, Hoyt grabbed his arm and warned him the result could be drastic if he did. There had been no direct threat on Redfield's person, but the implication seemed obvious to bystanders.

Dewberry sketched the meeting between Hoyt and himself at the Dewberry residence. Gerald told Hoyt if anything happened to Redfield, he would go to the cops. That's when Hoyt suggested Nicole would be in danger if Gerald continued his resistance to the changing of policies.

Gerald's date on the last note had been five days before his death and two days before Nicole had skipped town. Gerald had completed the file the same night Hoyt had barged into his residence.

Dave printed the file and made a copy. He also copied the entire disk onto a blank he retrieved from their office supplies.

Then he called Nicole, told her what he'd discovered, and suggested he accompany her to the meeting with Johns.

Johns invited them into his office, a large space on the third floor of the administration building. Smiling and thanking them for coming, he led them to a set of four chairs arranged around a coffee table.

Johns began, "Ms. Farrell, I appreciate your coming and hope you can shed some light on the activities of Bruce Hoyt leading up to the death of both your husband and James Redfield."

Twisting her fingers together, Nicole murmured, "I've told Dave everything I know which isn't much. He suggested I should testify if it's important. I'm willing to do that."

Dave said, "Nicole found something in Gerald's personal things that will be useful." He handed Johns the copy of the documents he'd printed from Gerald's disk. "This summarizes Gerald's version of events near the time of his death and the arguments between Hoyt, Rogers Morton and Redfield."

Johns read the two pages while they waited. He scanned the pages again. "This is helpful, but I doubt it is admissible."

"But," Dave said, "it gives you a basis on which to question Hoyt about both Redfield and Dewberry. Gerald worried Hoyt would do something to prevent Redfield from going to the authorities. When Redfield was killed, Gerald became a risk because he'd warned Hoyt about harming the old man. Then Gerald was murdered."

Johns laid the papers on the table. "You're correct, of course. This information is a big break. Hoyt has stonewalled our efforts to tie him to Redfield."

Dave handed Johns a copy of Gerald's disk. "Both of us have screened the files on this disk and believe the printout is the only part relevant to the case. But you may wish to reexamine the entire disk and decide for yourself."

"You've been thorough," Johns said. "What we'll do is question Hoyt again based on this information and push him to admit his involvement. He'll want to make some deal. This will give us another bargaining chip."

"Dave said, "If he deals, there won't be a trial. And bring in Morton. I suspect he knows what went on, but has stayed out of the light, so to speak."

"Good suggestion. We'll likely know how it's going to go within the next week to ten days. But, while Nicole is in town, I'd like to prepare a deposition of her knowledge about the conflicts. Just in case."

"When may I do that?" Nicole asked.

"We'd be able to do it after this meeting," Johns said, "or we can set up another time."

"I'd like to do it and get this behind me."

"Would you like your attorney present?"

Nicole hesitated until Dave said, "It'd be a good idea. Sometimes these questions take strange angles you may feel uncomfortable answering. Jennifer would be able to guide you around the rough spots." He still harbored doubts about Johns' real motivation in bringing Nicole back and didn't want her to stumble into some admission that would get her charged for withholding information or some other minor violation.

Johns said, "Why don't you call your attorney and then we can set a time."

Two week later Jennifer, Dave and Rasmussen were at Gibbons for lunch, seated at a table in the rear of the restaurant. Rasmussen had invited them to celebrate the outcome of the case against the Black and Redfield employees.

As the waitress departed, still writing orders on a pad, Jennifer said, "Nicole Farrell couldn't add much to the conflict between Gerald and Hoyt, but the computer disk revealed a lot."

Rasmussen added, "You're right. We were able to pressure Hoyt into admitting he'd hired a thug to get rid of James Redfield. They arranged to drive Redfield to the airport on his last day as a final courtesy to the founder. But instead, they took him into a wooded area, killed him, and tossed his luggage into a dumpster behind the big Wal-Mart store. We never found it. The time lapse had been too long."

"Did Hoyt identify the henchman?"

"No, but my suspicion is it was the pair you chased away the first time he'd put them on your tail. The bottom line is Hoyt is the guilty party. After he realized the whole ploy was coming apart, he revealed a lot."

"What about Morton?"

"We've pushed him hard. He's good at wiggling around the questions, but he's going to be charged as an accessory in connection with Redfield. He made the contact with the guys who carried out the crime. Maybe he didn't know what Hoyt was asking them to do, but I'm guessing he did."

Dave asked, "Then DeRosa was never implicated?"

Rasmussen shook his head. "Somehow he stayed away from all the internal bickering and left the dirty work to Hoyt. Morton took care of the policy cancellations and that side of the game. But I remain suspicious of DeRosa. He must have known what was going on and at the least didn't stop the dirty tricks and criminal activity."

"Black and Redfield will survive," Jennifer said, "but they'll be struggling for a while. Payments to those workers and the fine related to the Disabilities Act will put a dent in their reserves. The publicity has damaged their reputation. That will require some effort and passage of time before they are out from under those clouds. But DeRosa seems to know where the company is going and is taking the right steps to change the culture."

Dave asked, "What about the drug-running operation?"

"Somehow Hoyt became acquainted with Junior Young after he'd been released by his father. Hoyt saw the connection as a way to make a lot of money on the side and keep the Judge under his control. Junior will testify that Hoyt met with the Judge and Junior and threatened to expose Junior unless Young continued to lean in favor of any Black and Redfield issue. I'm still surprised Judge Young went along."

"His entire career became tainted," Jennifer said, "protecting his jackass son."

"Happens often. Public officials become immune to any accountability, particularly those with long appointments." Rasmussen sipped water, his eyes surveying the restaurant, a place where he never felt completely comfortable. Then he added, "The D.A. is not completely in agreement with letting Young walk away. He's asked us to investigate his relationship with Black and Redfield a bit more thoroughly. I wouldn't be surprised if Young is charged with criminal conspiracy before this is all over."

Following a brief lapse in the conversation, Dave said, "We got involved because of a simple request from Heather Farrell to find her sister and Maude Frame's cry for help with reinstatement of her insurance policy. But I never understood why Black and Redfield picked on those workers. It couldn't have saved much money."

Jennifer said, "They thought the workers would cave in and not fight back. And in the minds of Morton and Hoyt, every dollar mattered. Cost them big bucks in the end."

"By the way," Dave said, "Heather is moving to Minneapolis to be near her sister."

The waitress brought their orders and a bottle of Merlot. She went through the ritual of having Dave okay the wine, then poured glasses for each.

Rasmussen raised his glass. "Here's to the future." They sipped and then tackled their soup.

Rasmussen asked, "When's the big date?"

Jennifer laid aside her soup spoon. "We've decided on 2:00 in the afternoon of Sunday, December 15th. My parents will come for the occasion. My friend, Judge Anita Chandler, will do the honors at our house."

Dave said, "We'd like you and your wife to join us. We're inviting Ellie from the office and Anita's husband."

"So a small affair," Rasmussen said. "Sounds nice. We'd like to come."

Jennifer touched Rasmussen's arm. "Dave wanted to invite Antonio Gibbons and his wife, but I vetoed the idea. Anita would be leery of any association."

Rasmussen grinned. "So would I. He hasn't been the target of our department for quite some time, but the rumors linger about his activities."

Dave said, "I won't defend Gibbons other than to tell you he's been a great help to me and indirectly to the police department. But while we're updating the record, there's one other thing we should tell you. We've invited Andy Chafin, Young's former clerk, to join our firm. He'll start January 1st. He seems to be a good match for us and will take some of the load off Jennifer. It will mean we're moving to a larger suite on the second floor."

"Will you change the name?"

"Not soon," Jennifer said. "We'll stay Watson and Randle."

A mischievous gleam in his eyes, Rasmussen said, "You've done well. I hope this marriage step doesn't put a crimp in your style."

"Not much danger," Jennifer said. "Now I'll be able to supervise Dave day and night." Under the table she tapped his leg with her foot.

ABOUT THE AUTHOR

S. J. Ritchey served as a faculty member in Nutrition and as an Academic Dean at Virginia Tech earning an international reputation for research in human nutrition. He published a textbook, numerous chapters in books and over a hundred scientific papers. Following retirement he began writing fiction. He has short stories in magazines and in two collections published by Blue River Writers. His series on the Watson/Randle partnership began with the publishing of Scams and Murders. Runaway Witness is the second in the series.

The author lives with his wife, Elizabeth, in Blacksburg, Virginia, and since his retirement, they spend summers at her family cottage on Lake Couchiching near Washago, Canada

ACKNOWLEDGEMENTS

My sincere gratitude is expressed to members of Blue River Writers – Judy Beale, Carter Elliott, Lesley Howard, Susan Huckle, Joe Maxwell, Bill Mashburn, and Paul Poff for their honest critiques, helpful suggestions, and unwavering support. Special thanks are extended to Joe Maxwell for help with the cover and his efforts to discover errors in the manuscript.

As always, I acknowledge the support of my wife, Elizabeth, who helped with the cover, and for her tolerating my hours of staring at a computer screen.

ISBN 141207523-8